KISS OF THE GOBLIN PRINCE

SHONA HUSK

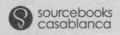

sourcebooks
casablanca

Published by Sourcebooks Casablanca, an imprint of Sourcebooks, Inc.
P.O. Box 4410, Naperville, Illinois 60567-4410
(630) 961-3900
Fax: (630) 961-2168
www.sourcebooks.com

Printed and bound in Canada.
WC 10 9 8 7 6 5 4 3 2 1

Chapter 1

THERE WERE NO DECORATIONS IN THE CHURCH, NO family or friends filling the pews. Amanda paused and glanced at the altar where Eliza's groom waited with his brother. She took a breath and forced a smile. Eliza wanted this, and even though Amanda thought her sister-in-law was rushing to marry a man she hardly knew, she had to be happy for her. Eliza certainly seemed happy, happier than she'd been for years.

"She's on her way," Amanda called to the men as she walked down the aisle with her daughter, Brigit, at her side. The black-and-white bridesmaid dress restricted each step—well, that and the heels. She couldn't remember the last time she'd gotten dressed up. When she'd gotten married it had been in a registry office. That seemed so long ago now she could've been another person. She had been another person back then. Young and carefree. Her life had changed so fast. Widowed three months later. She glanced at Brigit, the only part of her husband she had left.

At least Brigit wasn't hampered by her dress. She walked very carefully clutching the ring Eliza was going to give Roan as if it was going to jump out of her fist. From her other hand hung the white and black little bag, made especially to match the dress. But it wasn't for show. Inside was Brigit's inhaler. She couldn't go out without it. Anything could set off a fatal asthma attack.

Please not today.

Roan turned and nodded. All Eliza had told her about him was he was from Wales and he had money and a brother. Her gaze flicked to the other man in a black suit and lingered for longer than was polite. Dai stood to one side. His long hair was loose but not scruffy. The hair and suit were at odds with how she'd thought he'd look. She'd been told he was a scholar. When she'd been at college none of the professors had looked like him. He was too…too something she didn't want to label.

Dai turned his head and caught her gaze. His eyes were dark and mesmerizing. Her heart gave a solid thump as if beating for the first time in years. Her smile widened before she could stop her lips from moving, and then a slow, creeping heat colored her cheeks. It had been a long time since she'd had such an instant reaction to anyone. The last man who'd done that had been her husband and he'd been dead seven years. Dai gave her a small nod and a smile that made her feel like she was the one walking down the aisle.

Get a grip. It was a wedding and she was just in a happy, romantic mood because of Eliza. She was living vicariously through her. Being in love was exciting…even if Eliza was rushing to the altar with a man she'd known for only a heartbeat.

Wonder what Dai thinks of the quick wedding. She'd have to ask him later. And also take the opportunity to find out a bit more about the King brothers—for Eliza's sake.

She and Brigit took their places on the other side of the altar with the scowling priest looking on. Brigit opened her hand for the third time to check on the ring.

"You'll do great," Amanda tried to reassure her.

Brigit nodded and then looked at the men on the other side. She frowned and whispered, "Why does Roan's brother have long hair?"

Her little voice echoed in the empty church. Amanda wilted on the inside; there was no way he could've missed the comment.

"I don't know," Amanda whispered with an awkward smile stuck on her lips.

He didn't need to cut his hair; it suited him, softened what otherwise might have been a fierce expression, with dark blue eyes someone could drown in.

Dai's gaze landed on Brigit, his face neutral as he spoke to his brother in another language, Welsh maybe, from the soft lilts. Amanda held her breath, ready to leap to Brigit's defense, waiting for him to either laugh or scowl at her daughter. He did neither.

"I like it long," he said in English with an unidentifiable accent.

Amanda sighed. At least he wasn't a children-shouldn't-be-heard type of academic.

"If he wouldn't cut it for my wedding, I don't think he'll ever find a reason to." Roan glanced at the church door as if he thought Eliza had changed her mind.

Amanda knew that wouldn't happen. Eliza had gushed about Roan. And he was an improvement on ex-fiancé shifty-Steve, now awaiting trial for fraud. But it was still too fast, not even long enough to give the thirty days' notice to put in the paperwork. This was a wedding in a church that wouldn't be valid, but neither Roan nor Eliza cared. At least if it didn't work there'd be no divorce paperwork either.

She shook her head and glanced at the stone floor. It had been so long since she was in love she'd forgotten what it was like. Her gaze landed on Dai again, as if drawn there of its own accord. When she realized she was checking out how nicely the suit fit his body, she looked away and studied the stained glass window before he could notice she was looking, again.

It was one thing to look at a man, and it was very easy to look at Dai and wonder what he looked like beneath his clothes, but it was another thing to act on it. She glanced at Brigit. Unlike Eliza, Amanda couldn't take risks and leaps of faith.

As she watched her sister-in-law walk down the aisle, Amanda realized she was jealous. Not pea-green, but enough that she knew what she didn't have, and what she'd lost. Matt should've been here watching his sister marry, watching his daughter grow up. Part of her had died with him and the rest had forgotten how to live as she'd poured her attention into Brigit and her battle for survival.

She didn't hear the words of the vows, only the echo of the words she'd promised years ago. Her finger touched the wedding band Matt had given her. His was at home, barely scratched after only three months of use.

A tiny bell chimed through the church. She gasped as she realized Brigit had dropped the ring and was scrambling to retrieve it as it spun on the stone floor.

Eliza let out a small laugh.

A peal of thunder rolled over the roof. Dai glanced up as if he could see something no one else could. He spoke in Welsh and his brother nodded.

"And so it is. The vows are accepted," Roan said in English.

Accepted by whom? A trickle of ice traced down her spine, the church suddenly cold. Who were these men?

She turned away when Roan and Eliza kissed, unable to fight the rising disquiet, her gaze caught and lingered on Dai. She couldn't even remember what it felt like to be kissed by a man. Dai was watching her. The moment they realized it, they both looked aside as if they'd found something else suddenly absorbing.

"It's like in *Cinderella*." Brigit was grinning at the idea that her favorite fairy tale could come true.

Amanda stroked her daughter's hair and hoped that Brigit would be saved the heartache she'd experienced. It was a relief to step outside. The sky was clear, and while the winter sun was bright, it lacked the heat to take away the chill. She shivered as gooseflesh rose on her arms.

"Here." Dai offered her his jacket, leaving him only a shirt and waistcoat against the cool weather.

She hesitated, not sure she wanted to take anything from him when she knew nothing about him. But that would be churlish and today wasn't about her.

"Thank you. Are you sure you won't be cold?"

He shook his head, his dark hair spilling over his shoulders. "This is practically summer."

"Of course." He was used to freezing Welsh winters and snow.

She draped the jacket around her shoulders, the lining still warm from his body. For a heartbeat she let herself be enveloped in his warmth and scent. Her body responded, craving a touch or something. It had been so long since she'd been close to any man. She pushed down the feelings. She was too old to fall over the first handsome man to offer her his jacket. Too old at twenty-seven. That little bit of envy grew a little more.

If she could, would she? If Brigit never knew, did it matter? She twisted the ring on her finger, then stopped, horrified at what she'd been thinking. Could she really betray the man she loved for a moment of pleasure?

Brigit counted out jumps and hops on the pavement, entertaining herself while they waited for the cars. Her handbag swung from her wrist. Amanda wanted to ask Brigit to stop, but she bit her tongue. She couldn't wrap her daughter up in cotton wool and force her to sit still in case she had an asthma attack—no matter how tempting the idea.

Her gaze slid sideways, but Dai had his back turned to her and was studying the church. He probably wasn't interested in her anyway. What man wanted an instant family? And if they did, it made her suspicious. On her other side, Roan and Eliza were talking softly. Their hands linked as if nothing could separate them.

That was what she missed the most. Having someone there. Someone she could count on. Someone to hold her. She closed her eyes and took a deep breath. For just a moment she let her imagination wander. What would it be like to be held by someone other than Matt? To have more than Dai's jacket around her? She shivered as if cold fingers traced the nape of her neck.

"The cars are here." Brigit grabbed her hand.

Complicated. She opened her eyes. Dating was complicated even without a fragile child that required constant attention.

Two black Jags parked in front of the church. Eliza had told them to be back in half an hour, but the wedding had taken less time than that. On the way here the guys had been in one and the girls in the other. Now Roan and Eliza would take one, which left her and Dai and Brigit with the other.

Dai held open the car door and Brigit slid into the backseat. Amanda followed, carefully swinging her legs in, knees together. *Stupid slim-fitting dress.* Then he closed the door and got in the front. Out of the cool air, she took off his jacket and laid it on the seat, even though she wanted to keep it wrapped around her and hold on to his warmth a little longer.

She licked her lips, ready to try to get some answers. She had a hundred questions she wanted to ask, but quizzing him in the car probably wasn't the best idea. Brigit listened to everything. With a small sigh, she leaned back and gazed out the window. Later.

Or maybe she was just making excuses to spend more time with him.

The chauffeur drove back through the city and stopped at the gourmet pizza shop not far from Eliza's house. Dai went in and picked up the order. There was no fancy reception, just pizza and champagne. She watched as he walked back to the car, her fingers brushing his jacket. He didn't move like someone who'd spent his life behind a desk. There was a grace that athletes and people who understood their body acquired. There was more to his life than study.

But it was much easier to label her attraction as curiosity and ignore the tightening in her belly. She touched the ring on her finger; she'd never taken it off.

Couldn't. Yet something about Dai made her want to explore the possibility.

Dai got back into the car and gave her a small smile as if he knew exactly what she was thinking. She forced herself to focus out the window. She didn't have time to indulge or even dabble in lust, and Eliza's new brother-in-law was definitely the wrong person.

With the pizza almost gone and an empty bottle of champagne sitting in the middle of the dining table, everyone eased back in their chairs. Pizza tasted better when it hadn't been stolen and brought back to the Shadowlands. Dai's lips curved. Everything tasted better when not eaten in the Shadowlands. He finished his champagne and flexed his fingers against the glass. He'd never expected to be eating in the Fixed Realm again, as a man. But then he'd never expected to live again as a man. For too many centuries he'd thought either the curse or a blade would claim him. Despite his years of magical study he'd never have guessed the cure to release him and his brother from two millennia of entrapment would've been as simple as love.

Then again, loving a goblin was never simple.

After everything they'd lived through, Roan deserved to be happy. He glanced at Amanda, who was pointedly studying her champagne. The gold band on her finger glinted in the light. She wore it even though her husband was dead—Eliza had been most helpful in filling in the details. Roan had made him and Eliza swear that neither of them would speak about the curse, goblins, and the Shadowlands to anyone, as if he were still king and could order the past away if no one ever spoke of it again.

Even if Dai lived for another two thousand years, he'd still wear the scars of his past. Unlike Roan, he couldn't wash off the Shadowlands' dust and move on. In the Fixed Realm the magic he'd studied became real and usable. If he let his vision slide, he could see the threads of magic that made everything...or that everything made, depending on the school of magical theory.

Roan and Eliza walked into the living room and put on some music. Amanda's daughter slid off her chair and followed them, fascinated by the wedding— more than her mother had been. Amanda had smiled and nodded throughout the ceremony, but he'd seen the reservation in her eyes...and that wasn't all he'd noticed. Even when he wasn't looking at her, he'd felt her gaze on him. It was an odd sensation to be looked at and not have the viewer recoil in horror; he had to remind himself he no longer looked like a goblin. It was odder still to feel the fragile magic of attraction spin out from her and reach for him, seeking a connection he doubted she even knew she was making and he wasn't sure he wanted.

For half a second he considered pushing the threads away, but he was curious. And he liked her smile—the unguarded one that lit her eyes and let him believe for a moment that he could live the lie Roan wanted him to and be a normal, modern man. For his brother he would do that today. Tomorrow...he'd see.

He put his elbows on the table and rested his chin on his hands. Amanda looked up and their gazes met. For half a heartbeat he saw more than he expected in her green eyes. More than a passing interest. Hunger, desire, longing—then she blinked and it was gone.

Maybe he imagined it, or saw his own emotions reflected there. After two thousand years as a cursed man, maybe he didn't know what he was seeing or what he wanted. It had been so long since he'd had a choice. Even before the curse, his life had been in the hands of the Roman general Claudius. A hostage to guarantee Roan's good behavior. All it had done was fuel their need for rebellion. Without the druid's curse, they would have died Celtic warriors.

Amanda ran her tongue over her lower lip and leaned forward. He smiled, encouraging her attention even though he knew it was a bad idea. Yet he couldn't bring himself to brush her off. He was too tempted to see how close he could get to the fire before getting burned.

"Was that Welsh you were speaking in the church?"

He opened his mouth to answer, but realized he couldn't lie directly to her. "A dialect." An ancient dialect no one else spoke. The language of the Decangli was as dead as the tribe.

"What did Roan mean when he said the vows were accepted? You're not part of a cult?"

Dai laughed. "No cult." He thought rapidly through the service to find an explanation. He couldn't say the gods they'd been raised to believe had witnessed the vows. She wouldn't accept that. Magic and gods didn't go hand in hand anymore, people no longer believed in magic. "The ring bouncing thrice on the floor was sign of good luck. An old sign of good luck."

More half-truths. If he wasn't careful, he'd trip on his lies and be caught in a net of his own making. Music filtered into the dining room. A slow song. He knew he'd be escaping the house for a long walk when Amanda and Brigit left. He didn't want to be in Roan and Eliza's space. He needed to find his own place. Nineteen centuries of living with his brother in the Shadowlands was long enough.

Amanda nodded, as if accepting what he said as truth. "He loves her?"

"He does, with all his soul." Or whatever was left of it after the curse. But that at least wasn't a lie.

She stood and smoothed her dress over her hips in a gesture that drew his gaze without him realizing. He looked up before he was caught lingering over the curve of her waist.

"Do you dance?" Her voice was soft and uncertain.

"Pardon?"

She glanced at the table then back at him, this time speaking with more confidence. "It's a wedding; will you dance with me?"

Amanda walked around the table, her steps short because of the narrow skirt of the dress. But it clung to her legs in a way he'd noticed as she walked down the aisle, and in a way he couldn't avoid noticing now. He learned to control the physical response to attraction long before; the self-loathing that usually followed wasn't as easy to contain.

He got up. "I'm not very good." There'd been no call for dancing either as a Roman slave or as a goblin.

"You don't have to be. It's a slow song," she said, like it explained everything.

Dai inclined his head. This wasn't a battle he was going to win, and losing should be more enjoyable. Any other man would've leapt at the chance to dance with her, but instead he was wrestling with memories from his old life that threatened to poison his future.

He took her hand and her fingers curved around his. Her hands were cool and her touch light, as if she wasn't sure about what she was doing. Her other hand skimmed over his chest to rest on his shoulder like a feather. He faltered for a moment, not sure what to do. He'd spent his life fighting both Romans and goblins, and too long at the mercy of Claudius. Was he even capable of the gentle touch Amanda deserved?

"On my waist," she murmured, her lips curving in a small smile, as if she was just as hesitant as him.

"We could go into the living room." His hand settled on her waist, the dress silky beneath his palm.

Amanda tilted her chin and looked up at him. "No, here is fine."

She moved a little closer, her perfume not masking the warm scent of her skin. She moved slowly, her body lithe in his hands. They were close, yet he wanted to pull her closer and feel her against the length of his body.

But if he did, he knew what would follow and he could only resist so much before he would succumb to the sensation. He focused on the woman in his arms and the light touch of her hands on his skin. He couldn't remember the last time someone touched him without the intent to injure. Or the last time his hands hadn't damaged all they touched.

He glanced down, but her eyes were closed. Her expression wasn't one of contentment, but one of sadness. The gold wedding band on her finger shone in the light. He was standing in for the man she still loved. For a moment he wanted to be the one to remind her what a living one felt like—after all, she shouldn't be wasting the life she had pining over what she'd lost. Life went on, whether you wanted it to or not. He'd learned that the hard way. In his next heartbeat, he knew he could never be what she needed. He knew his reactions weren't right, and he would never be normal. He was too broken.

The song ended, but neither of them pulled away. Her hand remained on his shoulder, their fingers still linked. Those little, magical threads were already strung between them, creating a bond.

She opened her eyes and glanced up at him, then leaned a little closer. He wanted to kiss her to see how she'd react. But he took a breath and pushed down the sharp-edged desire. For a moment he'd let himself be lost and he didn't want to spoil what had happened by taking something that wasn't offered.

"Mom…"

Amanda pulled back and released his hand as if she'd been stung. The magic between them snapped. The loss was as sharp as a whip, then gone almost before he could recognize the sting.

Brigit glanced between her mother and him, and he knew he'd crossed a line that had never been drawn before. She'd never seen her mother with a man.

"Will you dance with me, Mommy?"

"Yes, of course, sweetie." She took her daughter's hand, but as she reached the archway leading to the living room, she glanced over her shoulder at him. Her lips were parted a fraction as if she wanted to say something, but she just smiled and turned away.

Dai blinked slowly and let his vision shift so he could see the weave of magic. She might be walking away, but those tentative golden threads reached for him. This time he let his own meet hers halfway, even though he knew if she took them back it would hurt.

But it was his choice to make. After so many years his life was his own to command. No king. No Claudius. No curse.

He was free, and he was beginning to understand what that meant...even if he wasn't sure what to do next.

Chapter 2

AFTER AMANDA AND BRIGIT HAD LEFT, DAI HAD GONE for a walk, not wanting to linger in the house, but also needing his own company. He wanted to unravel what was happening between him and Amanda in private, and examine the delicate bond between them without having to answer to Eliza's raised eyebrows—she hadn't been so wrapped in the wedding not to notice something was going on.

The sun was starting to drop away, and the temperature was falling with it, so he began to loop back to Eliza's street. He strolled past the big houses overlooking the river, as if each owner was a king of his own small tribe. The gardens were carefully trimmed and trained in the Roman way, as if even nature could be bent to human will.

Instead of going straight back, he delayed a little longer and went to the park where he'd seen a dying tree. Over the past couple of days as he walked he'd tried to look beyond what everyone else saw and into the way everything was constructed. If he used the magical sight for too long, it made his head ache. But he was willing to risk it today.

He needed to know if he could heal the tree…and then maybe himself.

Dai took a seat on a bench covered in symbols he was unfamiliar with, then took a breath and let his vision slip. He tried to focus on the threads that wove tightly together to make up the tree, but his mind wasn't truly on the magic. It kept drifting back to the few moments he'd held Amanda.

He glanced at his hand, seeing more than just skin lined with faint scars. He saw the magical construct of his body and the golden strands that linked him to Amanda. He wasn't imagining her interest. This was the proof—not that he'd be able to explain it to anyone.

If he had his books on magic, healing the tree would've been easy. He ignored the doubts that rose about fixing his own scars; healing was a fine art for even in the simplest case, and his damage was far from simple. He rolled his shoulders, but the tightness remained.

Tree first. If he killed it, it didn't matter as it was dying anyway. If he healed it…well, he'd be one step closer. He was tired of waiting for Birch Trustees to finish examining his library. He and his brother had stashed much of their hoard there over the centuries. The secret bank was known for handling unusual requests with discretion. For the most part, Birch had been nothing but helpful since he and his brother had broken free and become human. The bank had transferred their gold and silver and gems into regular human bank accounts, then supplied fake IDs all round. They had eased what could've been an impossible transition.

At first glance there was nothing to distinguish him from any other man in the Fixed Realm…except he'd outlived Rome and knew magic was real. With the sight he looked at the web of lines that made up his hand as he flexed his fingers. Oh yeah, he was a regular twenty-first century man.

And he was finally able to put into practice the things he'd studied but had been unable to do as a goblin. He didn't need to touch the tree. He could see how the fibers of the trunk were snagged and twisted, cutting off the life that pumped through the earth and eddied around its roots. From his training, he knew it was possible to heal the damage; whether he could do it was another question.

The risk of failing held him motionless. He'd spent too much time studying instead of acting. He'd waited so long to be rid of the curse, and before that he'd been fighting to be free of the bloody Romans. He wanted a life, now.

He forced himself to act. His fingers twitched against his leg as he imagined smoothing the strands of magic that made up the tree. He forced his will into thought. The tangles unraveled and the tree gave a shiver as the life force of the earth was again able to flow freely. If it had been that easy to break the curse and pull the gray of the Shadowlands out of Roan, they would've been free centuries ago.

He paused to watch the tree and see if the magical changes would hold. The tree sighed as if touched by a breeze, but the changes did more than hold. Buds began to form, and new leaves unfurled as if it was spring and not mid-winter.

"Too much," Dai muttered and tried to pull back some of what he'd done, but the tree pushed him away. The throbbing in his temples began as he tried to do too much with the magic he could barely control. Then the pain spread, tightening around his skull like hands seeking to crush the bone. With a gasp he released all hold on the magic and let the tree win the fight for survival. He lacked the heart to kill anymore.

He blinked to clear the sight, but the headache remained—a warning he was pushing too hard. Everything was easier on paper and in theory. Cautiously he looked around, his heart rate rising as if he expected his tampering to be discovered. But no one noticed that nature had gone wild. Humans didn't see the magic happening right in front of them anymore. In his time, they would've. Next time he would be more careful.

And much more practice was needed before he tried to remove even some of the small scars that marked his body. Then he could try the big one. He closed his eyes and felt the hot pulsing of the fibrous talons lodged in his chest and locked around his heart. With the sight he'd be able to see them, but not one wise man or mage had been willing to risk removing them out of fear of killing him and having to face the wrath of the Goblin King.

Paths you have to walk alone, they'd say as they shook their heads.

That magical grip around his heart would kill him, it was feeding off him, now he no longer had the magic of the Shadowlands and the curse to keep him alive.

Dai opened his eyes and saw the world as any other person. There were smaller magics he could practice with—ones that didn't involve life and death. He glanced at the tree but couldn't contain the smile. The tree was alive.

His stomach grumbled, but he sat a moment longer enjoying the last of the sunlight and the feeling of being hungry. It had been a long time since he'd wanted food—or needed it. In the Shadowlands they had existed more like goblins than men, fed by the dark magic that corrupted souls. Living there left a stain. He took a final look at the tree as he left. Someone might look twice and think they'd remembered wrong, but no one would suspect the truth.

<center>~~~</center>

Eliza's grand two-story house was silent when he got back. No doubt Roan and Eliza were still upstairs. He didn't resent what Roan had; he'd once wanted the same, now he wasn't sure if he was still capable. He'd lived with violence for so long, as victim and perpetrator, that he didn't trust himself. And then there was the magic. He flexed his back as if he could dislodge the persistent weight lodged between his shoulders.

From his temporary downstairs bedroom—he had no desire to be closer to Roan and Eliza than he had to be—he gathered clean clothes and ripped out the sales tags as he walked to the bathroom. What had once been a guest room and en suite at the back of the house had been turned into an office by Eliza's father. He liked it, a room full of books. It was like a small version of his library in the Shadowlands but specialized in law instead of magic. Eliza's father would've been an interesting man.

Once he got his books back from Birch, he'd need a whole house to put them in. Texts in every language ever written and lore on more systems of magic than people knew about from cultures that had passed without recognition. He hadn't been able to stomach the thought of all that knowledge being lost in the Shadowlands forever,

so he'd deposited his life's work in the vaults of Birch
Trustees. Now they were taking their sweet time returning his books.

He shivered, as if just the thought of the Shadowlands
could chill him to the core, and turned on the heater even
though it wasn't that cold. Not like when he'd been
forced to break the ice before washing when he was
younger. The shower water warmed while he stripped.
All his shirts had long sleeves to hide the marks on his
body. The mirror kept his secrets.

Across his skin inked in black were sigils, symbols, and texts in a hundred different languages. All
of them now dead. They were the marks of holy men
and voodoo priests, witches and wise women that had
marked his progression through the various studies of
lore. They didn't just mark his skin; they marked his
very being, pulsing with power, and couldn't be removed. Not that he would. It had taken too much to
earn them.

Cuneiform wedges fell from his hip down his leg, a
protection against evil. Sanskrit wrapped his wrist and
forearm in a proverb he'd failed to live by. A mark of
initiation burned into his thigh; on the surface it was
nothing more than a crescent moon. On his chest, over
his heart, lay a spider at the center of her web. Today she
was upright. She'd never moved in the Shadowlands,
but in the Fixed Realm she did. And it was unnerving.
He touched the spider but felt only his skin. A spider
weaves the web, makes it suit her purpose, but never
spins without reason. Pity he didn't know what the
movement meant.

Beneath the magic that had failed to break the druid's

curse were the scars that rippled across him like he was a badly woven cloth riddled with uneven weft and knobbled threads. There were knots and thickenings where he knew his skin showed the thin white lines of wounds healed long ago.

He huffed out a breath and looked at his skin as Amanda would. In that moment he knew he could never let her see. He'd never shown anyone, not even Roan. He would erase the scars, if not the memories. He ran his fingers over the bumps in a rib that had been broken too many times. The urge to use magic burned his fingers, but he hesitated. The tree had grown out of control. What if his bone did something unexpected? He didn't know how to stop it without his books to refer to. It had been easier to experiment on himself when searching for a cure to the curse when he hadn't been expecting to live—or wanting to live. Now he didn't want to get killed while trying to fix himself.

His fingers traced up his chest to the growths that weren't part of his body but were inside his body. Wrapped around his heart and through his ribs were the talons like malformed hands. He didn't know when they'd grown, but by the time he could see the magical web of the world, they'd been there. And Dai didn't need magic to know they weren't healthy.

After all this time he was still cradled in Rome's brutal hands. The old hate of all things Roman bubbled to the surface, no less bitter than it had been nearly two thousand years before. Four years at the general's beck and call had done more than mark his skin. He was willing to risk whatever it took to remove those bloodred and black claws sucking the life out of him. With magic he plucked and pulled, but the talons dug deeper, thrusting through bone and invading his heart.

He gasped, struggling for breath against the stabbing pain, tearing at the muscle. He caught himself on the edge of the vanity. "Damn it."

The mirror shattered as if he'd punched the center. The claws eased their vicious grip. No amount of magic could pry the poisonous grip from his body without killing him. After 1,951 years, his body was still enslaved.

Dai shook his head. He didn't need the sight to know why the damage hadn't healed. He'd been denied vengeance on the man who'd stolen his life long before the curse had laid claim to his soul. No matter what the mystics and monks had advised, forgiveness was a pill too large and too jagged for him to swallow. He'd rather live with the talons than let General Claudius off the hook.

Some lessons he'd failed and continued to fail. The tattoo around his wrist burned as if punishing him for his hate or reminding him to let go. His face was reflected back at him in broken pieces. He wasn't whole—and never would be. A broken mirror couldn't be fixed, and its shards would cut everything they touched. He was a hazard, a wound waiting to happen.

The golden threads that linked him to Amanda pulsed with life. He should sever them. Who knew what danger she would be in by being connected to him? But he couldn't do it. She'd feel the same sting, and even though it would last only a moment, he couldn't hurt her. She deserved better.

Dai placed his hand over the center of the broken mirror. The glass flexed and reformed with a slight tremble. Only a small dent in the middle gave away the damage. Not perfect, but close enough. A smile crept up the corners of his lips, maybe some things could be fixed. He touched the uneven surface. Not all magic was beyond his control. But his scars ran deep, and he didn't have enough magic to fix himself. No one did.

———*m*———

Amanda shook out the bridesmaid dress and placed it on a coat hanger. It was a beautiful dress, even if it was impractical. Her fingers skimmed over the black fabric, but her skin remembered Dai's light touch. She was sure she'd seen something in his eyes when he'd looked at her, and yet it was as if he was afraid to touch her. Like she was made of glass and would break.

She shook her head and placed the dress in the closet. At least she'd be able to wear it again since it was black. For the first time, she was glad Eliza's ex-fiancé had gone for a black-and-white themed wedding. But the dress was out of place in her wardrobe. It wasn't the only dress, but it was the only evening dress. When was she ever going to wear it? To a school assembly? To work? How about the park?

Who was she kidding? It was never going to be worn again.

Tears burned her eyes, but she wasn't upset about the dress. She didn't know when she'd get to dance with a man again. Being in Dai's arms made her realize how alone she was. She swiped at the stray tear. She was tired. It had been a long day, and an emotional one. Watching Matt's sister marry was always going to wake his memory. But that's all it was. She couldn't dance with a ghost.

—∿—

Their dog's barking woke Amanda. But it was the following low growl that really scared her. Her stomach contracted and the hair on her arms spiked. She eased out of bed and took the heavy flashlight out of her nightstand drawer. Without turning on a light she slipped out of the bedroom and padded down the hallway. The sound of her footsteps was drowned out by the tumble of blood through her now wide awake body.

"Mom?" Brigit asked.

Amanda gasped and spun, her pulse erratic, muscles tense. Brigit had taken ten years off her life. "Shhh. Go back to bed."

"Why's Sheriff barking?"

"I'm going to find out," Amanda said as forcefully as she could without raising her voice above a whisper.

"Can I sleep in your bed?" Brigit rubbed her eyes as if she wasn't fully awake.

"Yes." She shooed her with one hand.

Brigit wandered, half asleep, into the bedroom.

Sheriff was still growling at something out front of the house. The dog's lips were pulled back in a snarl she'd never seen. Amanda swallowed, crept up to the window, and peeked out the vertical blinds, expecting to see nothing, hoping the dog was barking at a stray or the neighbor's cat.

He wasn't.

Her stomach fell to the floor and bounced. Sitting under the streetlight out front of her house was a man. She squinted. No not a man, a lanky boy with gleaming white skin.

One of the kids she counseled found her house. She held her breath as if he'd noticed the disturbance of the blinds and seen her there watching. Maybe it wasn't Flynn. It could be any teen loitering.

The skin down her back prickled. How many albino teens were running around Perth? What were the odds that it would be one of them and not the one she saw on a weekly basis?

Her grip on the flashlight tightened. Why was he there? How did he get her address?

Amanda remained rooted to the floor, her body refusing to move. She was alone with only the dog for backup. They were in a pretty safe neighborhood, and she'd never had a reason to be afraid before in her own house—but she'd never had a patient stalk her either. She eased the blind back into place, then counted to ten and peeked again. He was still there, unmoving in the bluish light as if he had all night to wait. What was he waiting for?

For her to come out?

Never. She wasn't stupid.

She should call the police. Except he'd done nothing wrong…and if she did, he'd know she called them. Sheriff whined and Amanda risked another glance outside. As long as Flynn didn't do anything but watch her house, she wouldn't do anything either. Yet she still went around the house checking the locks on all the doors. The front, back, and laundry. Then she checked again, the windows too. As a woman and child living alone, she was very security conscious. It was why she bought Sheriff, who was lying in the front hallway, whining to be let out.

She gave the dog a pat. "Good dog."

Sheriff's tail thumped on the tiles.

Maybe she was overreacting; if Flynn wanted to break in, he would've done it by now. And she couldn't spend the rest of the night watching him. She shivered as the adrenaline left her system and the cold seeped up her legs from the floor tiles.

On the way back to her bedroom, she picked up her cell phone. Brigit was already asleep in the middle of the bed. Amanda eased in, careful not to wake her daughter, but knowing she wouldn't be able to find rest so easily. Brigit coughed and wheezed. Amanda waited with fingers crossed, hoping that nothing else would happen, but Brigit settled.

Maybe she should stay with Eliza for a few days—no, Dai was there. Besides, that wasn't a solution. She didn't run away from her problems. She faced them head on and tackled them to the ground, yet it would be nice to have someone to do the tackling with. She didn't like feeling vulnerable. She wished there was a man in the house, someone to make her feel safe. But it wasn't Matt who was first in her thoughts.

It was Dai. And that was just as unsettling as the troubled teen outside.

Chapter 3

AMANDA'S LAST APPOINTMENT OF THE DAY DIDN'T SHOW up. Flynn couldn't afford to skip a visit; if he did, she had to report it. Attending counseling was part of the court order that had kept him out of juvenile detention after he was caught stealing. She gave him a few more minutes, hoping he would come in with a good explanation after waiting outside her house the other night.

A knock at the door broke her thoughts, but it wasn't the white-skinned, white-haired Flynn. It was two cops. She swallowed and tried to suppress the rising sense of dread. This wasn't going to be good news. What had Flynn done this time?

"Mrs. Coulter?"

"Yes, how can I help?" She stood up and offered her hand.

The cop shook her hand and sat down with a nervous glance around her office. Some adults never got over the fear of being in high school. His partner hovered near the door as if expecting trouble.

"Have you see Flynn Lloyd today?"

Amanda shook her head. "He was due to come in."

"Had any problems with him?"

"No, never. He's polite and happy to talk most days." Which was more than she got from half the kids. Mostly he talked about being bullied. Kids were cruel, and he looked very different. He also acted different, like he wasn't part of the world and held himself separate.

"Saturday night he attacked a man and took his watch."

That didn't sound like Flynn; he'd never been aggressive. Flynn wasn't a bad kid, but he had kleptomania, and it had brought him before a judge one too many times. Unlike most kleptomania sufferers, his stealing was limited—he only ever took golden-colored things. Pens, paper, coins, foil-wrapped chocolates, and lately actual gold. But he could never explain why he took it and added it to his collection. If he gathered paperclips he might have been okay, but people valued gold and as a result the police weren't too happy with Flynn.

"Are you sure you have the right kid?"

"How many albinos go to this school?"

Amanda's heart sank. *Only one*. Had he come to her for help and she'd ignored him? Or had he come to her house after he'd attacked the man? The thought made her ill.

She forced herself to speak, even though she already knew the answer. "Was the watch gold?"

The cop frowned. "How'd you know?"

"Flynn has kleptomania. When he sees gold he can't help himself." Yet he'd always been happy to pay for the things he'd stolen. It had never been about what the items were worth, only what they were made of.

"He beat a man unconscious. He knew what he was doing. Consider him dangerous."

Amanda kept her face neutral thanks to years of practice. No matter what kids told her she always looked calm and caring. Flynn wasn't violent. What had changed?

"What'll happen to him?"

Flynn's parents had bailed him out of trouble before and they'd all sat down to discuss treatment. The antidepressants were working...had he stopped taking his meds?

"His father wants him to be taught a lesson this time. Hopes to scare him straight."

Amanda shook her head. "That won't work. He needs help, not jail."

All the work she'd put into him would be unraveled because his father was embarrassed by his son's looks and behavior. Going to jail wasn't what Flynn needed. But he might be beyond her help now. She'd try his cell phone and see if she could convince him to turn himself in. Lawyers could make a psychiatric case that would keep him out of jail.

"Sorry, ma'am. Assault is a police matter. If you see him, ring." The cop got up.

He'd see her calling the police as a betrayal of trust, and at the moment that was all she had. He wouldn't hurt her; she was the only person who he confided in, and the only one who didn't see him as freak. A word he used to describe himself. But she couldn't let the invasion of privacy go. She had Brigit to look after.

"He came to my house Saturday night."

The cop paused. "Did you speak to him?"

Amanda shook her head. "He was just watching the house."

"If you see him again, ring emergency. Don't approach him." With the warning the two cops left.

The door to her office was wide open, but she didn't care who saw as she let her body sag. This was the worst part of her job. Flynn wouldn't be the first student to be arrested, but she thought they were making progress. Somehow she failed him when he needed her, and it was a bitter reminder she couldn't save everyone.

His lungs burned as he struggled for breath. Blood pounded in is ears. The only sound in the barren, gray landscape was coming from his exhausted body as he ran. Dai stumbled and fell. The gray dust of the Shadowlands clung to his skin and stained like it was trying to reclaim him. He couldn't go on. Beneath him, the ground shook with the footsteps of the goblin army as they chased him. Hunted him. A human in the Shadowlands was a delicious target. The goblins would strip his flesh and use his bones to make weapons.

Dai forced himself up. He had to keep running. Running where?

There was nowhere to hide in the Shadowlands. This barren land was the birthplace of nightmares. They would burst free of his mind and become killing flesh. Every horror brought back for endless torment, a permanent reminder of what he'd done. He spun, searching for the rock spire that had been home for too many centuries. Created by Roan, it had been the fortress that had kept the goblins out and the gold in. There he'd be safe if only for a moment. He'd spent all his life on the edge of being safe, and cutting himself most times in failure.

The gray dust plains stretched on forever, broken only by stunted twisted trees and the oily river that slithered like a snake over the ground confusing anyone who used it for guidance. In the distance, the castle rose like a needle and pierced the sky. He'd never make it. The goblins would be upon him. He'd spent two thousand years surviving—part human, part goblin—banished and cursed.

But that was over.

He ran on, kicking up puffs of dust. He didn't belong back here. He was human and back where he belonged in the Fixed Realm. How did he get back to the Shadowlands? What happened? Why was he back in the hell he'd escaped?

His leaden legs buckled. He put his hands out as he fell. Cold seeped from the ground into his skin, into his bones. The dust on his skin made it gray as if he was goblin again. He couldn't go back. He was never going back. He was free.

As he stared, the joints on his hands swelled and his flesh lost all pink and faded to gray. He touched his face, but it wasn't his. It was the goblin's face he'd worn for two millennia.

The curse wasn't broken.

A rasping cry left his fleshy lips.

He was goblin.

———— ∾ ————

Dai jerked awake and sat up in bed. His body rigid. His heart racing like he'd been running for his life. The darkness closed in around him. He slowed his breathing and blinked, calling on the magical sight. Even in the dark, the web of strings that made up reality appeared. With a tug, the lights in the study came on—all of them, desk and ceiling. He squinted against the brightness, but his hands were pink, not goblin gray.

And he wasn't in the Shadowlands. He was in the

room filled with unused law books. The best room in the house was always filled with books, and in Eliza's house, that room was unused for years until he took it over. He lay back down on the makeshift bed that was squeezed in between shelves and the desk and chairs, and scrubbed his hands over his face. It was his face. Not the disfigured, bulging eyes, wide mouth, and hooked nose he had been cursed to bear. A man in the Shadowlands, a goblin in the Fixed Realm and belonging nowhere.

Slowly, his pulse settled, but he kept the lights on. The nightmare that visited him every night for the week he'd been back in the world of men was still too fresh and too close to the reality he only just escaped. What a goblin would do to a human in the Shadowlands was enough to give him nightmares for the rest of his life…even without the ones that haunted his sleep. He pushed aside the old memories. He had too many and had lived for too long. Longer than any man should.

He stared at the ceiling. He couldn't sleep with the lights on, and he couldn't turn them off in case the shadows crept back in and tore apart his sleep. There were too many horrors waiting to wake him, and all were of his own creation. A litany of mistakes and misdeeds. He closed his eyes and hoped he'd be proven wrong and that sleep would come, and it would be peaceful. He counted the beats of his heart. Nothing. He was still awake.

Another night wasted.

Dai tossed back the covers and got off the air mattress. Borrowed furniture, borrowed room, borrowed life. He raked his fingers through his hair. Staying here in the hope that Amanda would come around and see Eliza was foolish. One dance and a tiny bit of magic and she was in every thought, if not dream. He doubted she was having a similar problem.

He picked up the newspaper he'd bought the day before while out walking and flicked to the real estate section—the bit he'd skipped reading while trying to learn more about the world. He wasn't sure what kind of house he was looking for, only that he needed something. He couldn't roam Eliza's house all night. But if he had his own place, there would be no one to disturb.

He sat in the leather chair behind the large desk and spread out the paper. It almost felt like he was researching ways to break the curse again. It wasn't homesickness that caught him unaware, as the Shadowlands had never been home, but he missed his library and his desk with the outdated map of the world inlaid on its surface. Maybe he should've stored that with Birch too—he doubted the goblins would value the antique.

Hindsight was always perfect, but in the moment he did what he thought best, not expecting to ever have need for his books again. He'd never planned on being part of the world of men again. He'd expected to die or fade to goblin like his cousin Meryn.

Meryn still linked Dai to the Shadowlands. Unlike his tentative, golden connection with Amanda, blood ties couldn't be broken. He was bound to Meryn by a sickly, gray thread, a constant reminder of everything his cousin lost. A reminder of what Dai could have easily become. Goblin. A heartless, soulless beast blind to anything but gold and battle. Maybe Meryn didn't even know what he was missing. No goblin he'd ever caught or killed seemed to be aware of anything being amiss. They were perfect in their own hideous ways. Like a dog after a bone, they lacked a mind to reason with. And yet they survived in the Shadowlands, a place more desolate than any desert or ice-coated land.

Dai checked his hands again. He was still getting used to seeing himself as human in the Fixed Realm. He'd been goblin on the outside and human on the inside since being cursed. Although toward the end he was dangerously close to losing his soul and becoming totally goblin. He was sure the shock of being human would pass…he hoped the nightmares would as well. He vowed to catch up on the missed sleep during the day when his nightmares had less power.

He glanced at the clock. Hours until daylight. Perhaps a beer would help him nod off, and he'd manage another hour or two of sleep.

With a small effort of will and a slight tweak of the threads, a bottle of beer floated into his palm. Creating a beer out of nothing would've been true skill but would require a source of energy—there was a reason real magic users tended to be thin. Magic burned energy. He blinked and cleared the magical sight.

The icy bottle chilled his palm. He shouldn't be using magic for such petty purposes; he shouldn't be playing with it at all. He had to fit in with modern society. His fingers made patterns in the dew on the glass. But he couldn't give up magic any more than he could quit breathing. It was part of him…and for the first time in his life he had real power.

Not a slave.

Not a cursed man.

He didn't know what he was.

Dai twisted the top off the beer and flicked it at the

bin under the oversized desk. The lid rattled around the bottom before stilling. He propped his bare feet up on the edge of the table. The long-sleeved T-shirt and flannel pajama pants kept the chill off the rest of his skin. If he couldn't sleep, he might as well do something useful like find a place to live. Come morning he'd ring Birch and start asking questions. A week should be long enough to examine his books. And as much as he liked experimenting with the magic, having his texts would make things easier. He began searching the newspaper for a place big enough to store his whole library.

The sound of birds jerked Dai awake and his feet slid off the desk. His hand reached for the knives he no longer carried as if he were readying for battle. In that second he realized where he was. He took a breath and relaxed. He'd grown so used to the silence of the Shadowlands that the usual sounds of the world had the power to startle him. He glanced out the window. Daylight stained the sky pink.

He flexed his fingers. The weave of reality was all around him, begging to be played with. The threads, split and joined, wove around each other and tangled. So beautiful, so easy to manipulate. The window unlocked and opened at his thought. He sucked in the cold morning air. His lungs cramped and shivered like they had in the Welsh winters when mist lay heavy on the ground, and ice had lined any still water. Outside, the sun crested the roofs and moved higher just like it always had. He watched, mesmerized by its movement. There was no sun in the Shadowlands, no night, no day. No life. Only eternal gray and the knowledge that he would never be able to make the bastard Claudius pay. The muscle in his jaw tightened. Some crimes were unforgivable. He understood that too well. In his darkest nightmares, the blood was still on his hands.

There was a knock on the door a half-second before it swung open.

Dai pulled down his sleeves so they covered the marks on his arms. He wasn't ready for the world to see his past. "And if I'd been naked?"

"I would have closed my eyes." His brother stood in the doorway. He was hardly recognizable. A man, not a goblin. A husband, not a king.

"You're up early." Since the wedding a few days before, Roan and Eliza took their time getting up in the morning.

"I saw the lights on."

Through the open door Dai saw the house was too well lit for early in the morning. Crap. Had he been turning on all the lights in the house every night?

"You also left the fridge open." Roan nodded at the two empty beers on the desk.

"Sorry."

He'd never thought to close the fridge, simply willed the beer to his hand and didn't consider the process. He frowned as he thought about the way he was using magic. Could he get a beer without opening the fridge?

It would mean altering the material of the fridge for just a moment so the beer could pass through. The practice of magic was proving different to the theory. His fingers curled as he was tempted to try, but he would have to wait for Roan to leave. His brother knew nothing of the magic he could use and that was probably for the best. The magic Roan used in the Shadowlands had almost taken his soul. He'd only worry if he knew.

"You didn't sleep again." Roan leaned against the door frame.

"Too much noise in this realm." Dai tried on a crooked smile.

Roan pressed his lips together but let the lie pass. "You will get used to it."

How could he tell Roan that surviving the curse was never a plan he'd made?

They'd vowed to die before fading to goblin. But every thread of the Shadowlands that ran through Roan and tied him to the curse was replaced by Eliza's love for him, and his for her. She did everything he'd tried to do for centuries in a few short days. The death he expected had been exchanged for a second chance.

"I'm sure I will." Dai flipped the newspaper closed.

Roan paused with his hand on the door frame. "You'd tell me if it was something serious."

"I'm fine." Dai forced a smile and relaxed. "It's just goblins keeping me up." That at least was the truth. Erasing the memories of the Shadowlands was harder than searching for a cure to the curse.

"The curse is broken." Roan's fingers whitened against the wood like he could force Dai to believe it.

He already did. He was in the Fixed Realm, and there was no going back.

Being on hold was like existing in the Shadowlands—meaningless. It was the third time Dai was transferred to

a different department within the Birch Trustees. He'd
never gotten the runaround as a goblin.

Chatter filtered in through the open study door. Dai
lifted his head. He recognized the voice and laughter
as clear as sunlight. Amanda. His lips twitched as he
remembered the way she'd looked at him at the wedding. The last woman who'd smiled at him that way
had ended up whipped and sold, with Claudius making
sure Dai watched from screaming start to bloody end.
Seiran's only crime was that she was caught kissing
him. Claudius was a sadistic son-of-a-bitch.

"Mr. King, how may I help you?" The voice was oily,
as if used to smoothing over all manner of problems.

Dai stood, immediately on guard. "When can I collect
my books?"

Not that he had anywhere to put them yet, but he
needed them. It made him anxious that the bank had
already kept them so long.

"They are being catalogued and the contents examined, sir." The words were slick, as if read from a script.

"Why does Birch need to examine them?" When he'd
packed them all up and deposited them in the Birch vault
with the rest of his ill-gotten goblin wealth, it was so
the world wouldn't lose the knowledge contained in the
books and scrolls if he died. Goblins had no respect for
anything that wasn't either a weapon or gold; if it was
both, it was a highly valued item indeed.

If he'd known he was going to live and Birch was
going to take their time returning his treasure, he
would've put it somewhere else where he could've
retrieved it at his leisure. He knew plenty of secluded
caves, lost tombs, and the like where they would've

been safe from weather and archeologists who'd lock up the books and spend the rest of their lives wondering what they meant. He knew what they all meant. It was his life's work and a distraction from the ever-present weight of the curse slowly stealing his humanity. That thirst for knowledge—and love for his brother—kept him from turning fully goblin.

"Just a moment, sir."

Amanda's laughter echoed down the hall, but he pushed down the warm thoughts that sound brought, because he knew they would be followed by memories he'd rather forget. It wasn't her fault; the damage had been done hundreds of years before. Yet she called to him in a way he couldn't describe. He wanted to know what it would be like to kiss her and break down the boundaries he'd built for himself.

The phone clicked, and once again hold music filtered down the line.

Dai clenched his fist and the lamp on the desk blew, followed by the light overhead. Glass hit his hands like brittle rain, but Dai remained silent. He knew when to play mute. It was a useful skill for a slave to have and had saved many fights with his brother.

Aggravating whoever was on the phone wouldn't help his case. Instead he focused on a melodic chant monks had taught him to gain control of the anger. He gritted his teeth and forced the words to flow through his mind. Learning to control the fury that could never be spent by shedding Roman blood had been the first step to learning how to master himself and then magic.

Wielding magic was like holding any weapon—it required training or the user was more likely to injure himself. It was one thing to know which end of the sword to hold, but another to be able to handle the blade in battle. He'd never had the opportunity to use magic while goblin, and now that he needed help there was no one left alive to ask for guidance. All he had left were his books.

And Birch had them.

He glanced out the window. Roan was digging in the yard. Since breaking the curse, he'd busied himself around Eliza's house as if he'd been there all his life. If Dai dug into the magic of the world in the same way, he'd do irreversible harm. Who knew what the shock waves would do, or what threads would loosen? It would only take a few cut threads to unravel the world as everyone knew it and make it into something else. He swept the broken glass to the side with the edge of his hand, then changed his mind and used magic to push the shards back into place as if the bulbs were never broken. The familiar pressure in his temples returned. He didn't remember being told magic would hurt. But then what didn't?

"I'm sorry for keeping you on hold. The processing is taking much longer than I first thought." The man paused. "Is there any reason you require *all* of those magical texts?"

Dai narrowed his eyes. There was something beneath the question, like the slither of scales over skin. A shiver ran down his spine. The real issue wasn't the texts; it was the magical secrets they held. The lore he'd paid little attention to when his sole aim was breaking the curse, information he could really use. Dabbling in magic without proper safeguards was dangerous.

While searching for a way to break the curse, he'd studied under masters of the art in the Fixed Realm, but everything had been theoretical. As a goblin, he'd been unable to practice human magic—but he'd understood it the same way he'd understood the Shadowlands magic, even though he couldn't use that either. His knowledge had given him standing despite his goblin appearance and his inability to perform even the simplest trick. The theory and practice were different and he'd forgotten too much, or remembered the wrong bits. Either way the answers he sought were in his books.

He projected a calm he didn't feel into his words, as if he didn't truly care about the delay. "No, just interested in curses." He forced out a dark laugh. "They've fascinated me for too long." He wished he'd paid closer attention to the other studies of magic.

"Mmm." The Birch employee didn't believe him. "So you aren't using magic?"

His heart gave a heavy thump. Did they know? He turned the question around and answered before the pause could become suspicious.

"Don't you think if I could actually use magic, I would've broken the curse that bound Roan and me to the Shadowlands a little sooner?" Not a total lie. He would have broken the curse a lot sooner if he'd been able to use magic while in the Shadowlands. No one in their right mind wanted to live in the Shadowlands— he'd spent as much time as he could in the Fixed Realm, but looking like a goblin had its own problems.

Why was Birch Trustees so interested in books about magic?

"Yes. I'm sorry, Mr. King."

He winced at the use of his name; he was never going to get used to hearing it.

"Birch will be in contact in a few days regarding your library." The line went dead.

Dai placed the phone down carefully instead of slamming it into the table the way he wanted. They wouldn't call. If he wanted his books back, he would have to fight for them. The same way he always had to fight for everything.

He closed his eyes as the talons pressed closer to his heart and the pain radiated through his back. There had to be another way—yeah, don't use magic—but he knew he couldn't just stop. The world tempted him to play with every breath. It was around him, part of him, the way the magic of the Shadowlands had been part of Roan. Fixed Realm magic was different though; it didn't require the payment of soul. Well, most Fixed Realm magic didn't. The kind he wanted to use didn't. The other kind, well, he'd survived one curse and had no intention of being part of another. Some magic was best left well alone.

The room became too small. He didn't want to hide from the world, but he wasn't sure how to be part of it. Roan had easily thrown off his past. From Goblin King to husband in days.

For a moment when he held Amanda he'd thought he could be like Roan and put aside the past and be someone else. A clean slate. But as desire awoke in his veins, it stirred the ancient demons from their sleep and his flesh crawled at the thought of being touched by anyone. There was a reason he'd been celibate in the Shadowlands, even when women came to entertain and fill their pockets with silver.

He opened his eyes, knowing he couldn't avoid her, but not knowing what to say. What did she expect from him? It would be much simpler to tell her the truth and walk away before he could see the expression on her face. But that was never going to happen. He was going to have to struggle on and pretend to be normal—whatever the hell that meant.

If he wasn't living here, he could avoid her. He wouldn't have to deal with anyone. Being on his own was becoming more attractive by the moment. He picked up the phone again and rang the real estate agent.

Chapter 4

"COFFEE?" ELIZA HELD UP A WHITE MUG AS IF SHE KNEW Amanda wouldn't be able to resist the offer.

After a couple of nights of broken sleep, Amanda would've drank anything that vaguely resembled coffee. "Only if the machine is on."

She needed it. Between checking on Brigit and peeping out the front window to see if Flynn was watching her house, she'd hardly slept. And when she had, Dai invaded her dreams.

"It's always on for you." Eliza smiled as she got out milk. She was almost glowing. Whatever Roan was doing could only be good. It was about time Eliza had some luck and love in her life after that scumbag Steve destroyed her family's legal firm. Amanda looked away with a small shake of her head.

Who was she to judge? She'd married Matt two months after discovering she was pregnant. Hopefully Eliza would have better luck.

Brigit crossed her arms and stood sullenly with her head turned pointedly away from Amanda. It was her latest phase, the suffering seven-year-old who doled out the silent treatment when she wasn't getting her way. It could've been worse. The fearsome fives had involved many, many tantrums.

"Can I watch TV, Eliza?" Brigit asked.

Amanda faked a cough. Brigit had also grown out of her manners.

She rolled her eyes as only a disgruntled child could. "Please." The word was loaded for Amanda's benefit.

"If you can't ask politely, you can stay here in the kitchen." If this was her daughter at seven, what would she be like at seventeen?

She saw many teenage girls walk through her door with imagined issues, but she also saw the teenagers with real problems on whom everyone else had given up. Even their parents. Some days she wanted to chuck it in and get a job that didn't suck her dry. But it was part time and during school hours, and she liked to think she was making a difference. That lie was becoming harder to believe after Flynn's violent robbery.

"Well, you could've sent me to school."

"You had a bad night." Like every other night when she was sick, Brigit struggled to breathe with the asthma squeezing her lungs.

"I have a cold." Brigit glared, her lips pressed into a tiny pout. "So what?"

"Better you stay home instead of spreading your germs." Amanda gave her daughter a firm glance that Brigit ignored.

"If I'm well enough to come out—"

"We can always go home and you can go back to bed." She'd let Brigit go to school the day before. But after last night, she needed a quiet day. If not at home, then there with Eliza.

Brigit opened her mouth. She liked having the last word on everything. Maybe Amanda had been too soft and had left reining Brigit in until too late. But it was hard being the only parent and harder to watch her daughter suffer.

"You can watch TV," Eliza said, breaking the stand-off. In the background, the coffee machine gurgled. At least with Brigit watching TV, Amanda would get five minutes to sit and relax.

"Thank you, Auntie Eliza." Brigit suck her tongue out at Amanda as she strolled to the living room with her little handbag full of medication over her shoulder. It didn't matter what she did or what therapies they tried; nothing lessened the effect of the asthma.

Amanda pretended not to notice and let her go. She wasn't the best parent after four broken hours of sleep. Just once it would've been nice to be able to share the load.

Eliza placed a steaming cup of coffee in front of her. "Asthma playing up again?"

Amanda took a sip and regretted it as it burned the tip of her tongue; the coffee was far too hot.

"She doesn't get it. A cold could be fatal." Brigit had been hospitalized many times because of a cold, or spring pollen, or anything that triggered a severe attack. The asthma wasn't improving. If anything, the doctors thought Brigit was getting worse. Her lungs were becoming more sensitized and prone to attacks. Six months before, they had warned her there was a strong chance Brigit could die.

Amanda refused to believe the doctors. So they had started experimenting with new age treatments. Things science couldn't prove would work. Halotherapy helped for a week, maybe two at a time. The turquoise necklace she'd bought her for her birthday didn't seem to have made any difference. Nightly oil rubs of cardamom and cedar wood helped her breathe a little easier, but it wouldn't save her. Brigit needed something stronger, something that would cure her. One of the women in the halotherapy salt room recommended a healer who thought disease was caused by damage to one's aura. It was a worth a try.

Eliza bit her lip.

"Don't you start," Amanda warned. Eliza would side with Brigit. It was easy for Eliza to say she was over-protective because she didn't have kids. She didn't have a sickly child and no backup for when things went down-hill in a couple of trapped breaths.

"I said nothing." Eliza filled her own cup. "One day you'll have to let her grow up."

Amanda listened to the banter of the cartoons in the background. She was still so little; she deserved the op-portunity to grow up. But if her asthma didn't improve, or they didn't find the right medication or a new age cure, even that small dream was under threat.

"Not yet." Brigit was all she had.

She wrapped her hands around the cup, but the heat from the coffee didn't warm her. Every birthday was a reminder of how many years Matt had been gone. She couldn't lose Brigit too. Amanda forced a smile and changed the topic. "So when are you going on your honeymoon?"

"We're waiting until Steve's trial is over."

"At least the media has cleared off." They'd been camped on the front lawn for several days after Eliza's ex-fiancé had been arrested for embezzling funds from the law firm.

"A footballer's divorce is much more interesting."

"Especially when the wife is caught with the assistant coach." The scandal was front page news. Football players couldn't stay out of the headlines for long. Six months before it was drug use and before that drunken, debauched parties.

"Allegedly." Eliza waved her finger.

"You're still a lawyer at heart."

Gunn and Coulter closing was still a sensitive issue. But it was the subject of her new man and marriage that Eliza dodged the most, as if talk of love would upset Amanda, or point out her own lack of romance. Eliza pulled out a box of chocolate chip cookies and offered them to Amanda. Silence spread between them as they drank their coffee.

She sighed into her coffee cup. Unlike Eliza, she couldn't drop everything and take a risk on a man she barely knew; she had to think of Brigit too. Amanda wasn't jealous. She had a lovely daughter—well, she was lovely most of the time—a house, and a job. Everything she needed. She swallowed the coffee without tasting it. But not everything she wanted.

That one dance with Dai stayed with her. Those few minutes reminded her what was missing in her life, and she couldn't blame the sudden realization on being caught up in the moment, not when she caught herself wondering what would've happened if Brigit hadn't walked in. Would he have kissed her? In her mind he did, and she enjoyed it. And she wasn't sure she liked what that meant. How could she wear her wedding ring and think of Dai?

"So, how is married life going?" she asked, hoping

for a distraction from the unsettling line of thought. But she was aware Dai was in the house and when she saw him she didn't know what she'd do. Maybe whatever had happened existed only in that stolen moment and he'd be just another man who would fail to spark any lust.

It had been a long time since any man had been able to arouse any interest. Yet he slipped under her skin with a smile, and she hadn't felt a thing until her blood began to heat. Once she looked into his eyes, she had trouble looking away. There was something about him…like he was a mystery to unravel.

"Good," Eliza said with a small smile and a nod. "Really good." She raised her eyebrows a fraction for emphasis.

"I don't need those details." Although ever since the wedding, Dai creeped into her thoughts, and one imagined kiss led to other things. She cut off the thought before it had time to grow. She wasn't a teenager full of unrestrained hormones that needed to be released. No, hers had packed up sometime before Brigit's birth. Their return was poorly timed.

Even though questions rested at the end of her tongue, she couldn't ask about Dai without Eliza getting the wrong idea. The last thing she needed was Eliza playing matchmaker, so she asked about Roan, hoping Eliza would reveal something about Dai in the process. Something that would quell the attraction she'd forgotten could exist when looking at a man. Too often looks didn't match the reality.

"How does Roan like Australia?"

"He likes it. It's very different from where he grew up."

Eliza focused on her cookie as if it was the last one in the world. She wasn't lying, but she was hiding something.

"He's not going to drag you back to Wales, is he?"

"No. He has no plans to go back."

Amanda took a sip of her coffee while she thought. She only flew back to Sydney once a year so her mother could see Brigit, but she still went back because family was important—even if she was more than ready to leave after a few weeks. Her father didn't recognize her, and hadn't for years, and her mother acted happy, but more than a decade of playing caregiver was sapping her strength. Last time she'd visited she'd found a pair of men's running shoes that weren't her father's. Her mother was having an affair. She should hate her for betraying her father like that, but he wouldn't care. He didn't even know who he was anymore.

"What about his family?"

"Except for Dai, all dead."

"Really?" No one could lose all their family. There were always aunts and uncles and cousins.

"Mother died in childbirth, father of natural causes…"

"And?" Amanda prompted, sure she was about to get a piece of important information about the King men.

Eliza lowered her voice. "His sister died when he was young."

So that was the family secret, one that must have torn them apart. "That's awful. How old was she?"

"Eleven."

Amanda shivered; she'd been only a few years older than Brigit. Losing Brigit would kill her. "How did she die?"

"Dai mentioned her in passing but then wouldn't say

anything more. They never talk about her," Eliza said with a look that meant Amanda shouldn't talk about her either.

People reacted differently to grief. She talked about Matt. She wanted Brigit to grow up knowing who her father was, even though she'd never met him. Matt had swept her off her feet. They'd been madly in love and when she'd accidentally become pregnant they'd eloped. Eliza and Matt's father had been furious. He'd thought she'd trapped him to get to the Coulter wealth.

How long until Eliza was having babies and moving on?

Amanda swallowed the last of her cooling coffee. She was only two years older than Eliza, but it seemed like decades. She felt middle-aged and stuck in a rut of her own making with no idea how to climb out.

She checked her watch. She needed to get to school or she would be late for her first appointment, and while she hated leaving Brigit, she needed to work. Matt's portion of the Coulter Trust was for Brigit when she got older. The small monthly stipend she drew only covered the mortgage because she refused to use up her daughter's inheritance.

"Are you sure about looking after Brigit?" She trusted Eliza, but she wasn't sure about the new men in Eliza's life.

"Yes. If there's a problem, I'll call." Eliza liked spending time with her niece. Did she look at Brigit and see a piece of the brother she'd lost? Eliza gave her a hug and then released her. "Go on. We'll be fine."

Amanda picked up her handbag. "Thanks."

She went into the living room and gave Brigit a kiss, then rummaged through her bag for her car keys. As she glanced up she saw Dai. For a heartbeat, neither of them moved.

He looked just as she remembered, attractive with an edge that was almost hidden behind the very neat, not quite relaxed way he dressed. He made jeans and an untucked shirt look too sexy, as if he should be wearing…what should he be wearing? She frowned, and he looked away as if the painting on the wall had suddenly caught his attention.

"Are you going out?" she asked, noticing the jacket he had slung over one arm.

"Yeah." His almost black hair swept past his shoulders as he gave her a single nod. Academics didn't look like Dai. Or they weren't supposed too. They were meant to be older, mustier, and less attractive. And definitely less male.

Her heart gave a patter of excitement she tried hard to ignore.

"Do you need a lift?" The words were out so fast her brain didn't have time to register or approve them. What would spending more time with him achieve?

Maybe he'd answer some more of her questions. The long hair and hard, dark blue eyes were at odds. Then there was the travel. He'd studied languages where they were spoken, not from textbooks. Lived life on the edge in places sensible people steered clear of. She could only imagine the freedom of packing everything into one bag and taking off for somewhere on a whim.

"I'm only going into the city. I can catch the train."

"The train? Eliza won't let you drive her car?"

"Can't drive a manual," he said with a hint of a curve on his lips.

She bit back the grin that wanted to form and returned a polite smile instead. He could translate obscure languages, yet he couldn't handle a stick shift. Since she'd already put out the offer she might as well go the whole way even though she knew better. But curiosity won over common sense. Giving him a lift would hardly bring down civilization, and yet it felt like she was stepping into uncharted territory. Maybe that was all she needed. To get out and talk to interesting people. And Dai had her interest.

"How about I drop you off in Subiaco and save you the walk to the train station?" That would give her some time with the man who looked like he'd be more at home on a battlefield than in a library.

He glanced at the floor as if he was ready to admit defeat, but when he looked up he was smiling. "I'd like that."

———◦◦◦———

Dai closed his eyes and rested his head against the headrest of the car seat. He hadn't found a polite way to refuse her offer, so he'd accepted the ride. The motion of Amanda's car rolled his stomach and made him regret eating breakfast, and closing his eyes to the oncoming traffic didn't help. There was too much color and movement in the world and it was zipping by far too quickly.

The visits he'd made at night to the Fixed Realm to obscure, isolated wilds and hidden tombs had only hinted at how the world had changed. Seen with eyes untainted by the lust for gold or the quest for magic, the world was fascinating. Everything was different. From the trees that didn't shed in winter to the buses that stopped every hundred meters or so to let people on or off. Then there were the cars. Everybody drove; their cars hurtled along the roads at speeds that the horse-pulled wagons of his day could never have reached.

It was unnatural to travel at that speed. If he let his vision slide into his magical sight, he could see how the vehicles cut through the fabric that made up the world, sliding through the ever-changing mesh. He couldn't work magic fast enough to keep up. Not yet anyway. Nor could he drive. At the moment he had no intention of learning.

The gut-wrenching pull of crossing between the Fixed Realm and the Shadowlands had never caused him so much trouble. He'd grown so used to the calm gray of the Shadowlands, he actually missed it. He never thought he'd miss the endless plains of gray dust that passed for landscape. But he didn't miss the slow, seeping cold that sucked at the marrow of his bones, or the hungry ache that couldn't be filled with knowledge…or eventually gold. A goblin's hunger knew no bounds.

As a distraction, he fiddled with the stereo. Music, like language, could identify a culture. The melodies grew and changed as outside influences permeated. That didn't make all of the music on the radio pleasant, and Amanda's choice banged around the car like a battle cry for the dead. The rapid drums echoed in his pulse. He'd missed the beating of his heart for centuries and now he wanted it gone. He couldn't control the involuntary beating or the direction of the blood it pumped through his system. Sitting so close to Amanda, all he could think of was her, and the subtle scent of her hair and skin. His body responded as if she'd run her fingers over his skin.

He was being controlled by an animal instinct he thought he'd caged long before.

He closed his eyes and fisted the hand she couldn't see. His nails dug into his palm as the monk's chant began running through his head. It was his body and he was going to control it—in sickness and in lust. Lust got people into trouble, and then people got hurt. The pain in his hand made the chant pause. All he knew was violence…and yet he was only hurting himself now. He forced his fingers to relax.

Amanda dialed the music down to a murmur. He was aware of every move she made as clearly as if he had his eyes open and was watching her. He opened one eye and glanced over. She was looking at him, not the road. His gut tightened as cars swept past, but she was unconcerned. He forced his eyes to open, but she noticed his discomfort at being in the car. So much for acting normal.

"You get motion sick?"

If that's what the nausea in his belly was, then apparently he did. He almost found it funny. He'd fought battles against Romans and goblins, been coated in gore, spent centuries barely existing in the Shadowlands, crossed between realms, and raided tombs filled with all manner of creepy-crawlies, including magical entities that were created to guard the dead, but traveling in a car made him ill.

"I'm not a good passenger." Not totally untrue. He didn't think he'd be a good driver either, despite the license in his wallet.

"I'll distract you." She flicked him a smile that did

nothing to settle his stomach or pulse. "Eliza said you taught English overseas."

"Among other things." He couldn't just say yes and lie like Roan expected him to.

"Is it true you speak several dead languages?"

What had Eliza been telling her? Obviously enough to make her curious and leave him to dodge her questions. "If I speak them, they aren't dead."

"Touché." She grinned, her eyes off the road for longer than was safe.

His lips curved immediately in response, and the monk's elaborate, and supposedly soothing, chant evaporated like water in the desert. The words he'd been taught that calmed the anger and suppressed unwanted desire had no effect when confronted with Amanda. He was defenseless. What use was magic when it didn't work when he needed it?

"What are you doing today?"

"Looking at apartments."

"Oh, I thought you'd stay with Eliza and Roan longer."

Dai shook his head and looked out the window. A shadow flickered across the glass; he turned to see what it was but only saw Amanda, with her sun-kissed golden hair, expecting him to make conversation. He wasn't very good at that either. Slaves spoke only when spoken to, and living in the Shadowlands wasn't exactly conducive to chatting. But if he was trying to find things to talk about, he wasn't concentrating on the speed of the car.

"You're off to work?" The crisp white shirt and dark pants didn't look like the clothes Amanda would choose to wear every day. But what did he know? The only other clothes he'd seen her in was a bridesmaid's dress.

His palm warmed as if remembering the touch of the satin against his skin.

"Teen angst doesn't stop because Brigit is sick."

Brigit, brown-haired and brown-eyed. The first time he saw her he was struck by the similarities between her and his sister. But where his sister was bold and ready to fight with anyone who dared to argue with a Decangli princess, Brigit wouldn't even meet his gaze. She seemed to look through him, as if there was something more interesting just behind him. It was unsettling.

"What's wrong with her?" She looked healthy enough to his eye, but then he'd never studied medicine. That had been Anfri's job before he'd faded to goblin—to stitch and patch when they got cut up in battle.

"Chronic asthma." There was a tightness to her words, as if by saying them, she was giving them power.

He nodded like he understood and made a mental note to look up the condition. Next time he saw Brigit he would look a little closer and see if the illness showed up in the threads that made up her body. If his scars did, then maybe other illness did. He wished he'd paid more attention to healing than curse breaking and making.

Would it be wrong to look at the makeup of someone else's body without their permission? How many of their secrets would be revealed in the weave of their being? Were Amanda's words giving Brigit's illness power? He blinked and let the magical sight take over his vision, then glanced at Amanda.

She sparkled in the sunlight, golden and bright as if she were made of spun crystal. Tendrils finer than hair reached toward him, touching the darker threads of his body, as if testing his response…and he couldn't stop what happened. He shifted his gaze to the other parts that made up Amanda. Rope-like strands reached for Brigit, pink and pulsing with life and love. There was no dark magic in Amanda, only a mother's love for her child and she was pouring a lot of her life into Brigit without even realizing it.

How sick was the child? If she died, Amanda would be wounded when the bond snapped. He didn't want to see Amanda that hurt. Beneath Amanda's brilliant exterior was an emptiness around her heart he hadn't expected to see.

"What?" She caught him staring.

Dai shook his head and cleared the sight from his eyes. "I was just thinking. It takes a special kind of person to help others."

He didn't want to be admiring her determination to save her child, or her career choice, or wondering why she was alone, because then the random attraction became less random and harder to fight…and he was losing that battle on all fronts. And he knew too well what happened to those who failed. They got punished.

She shrugged as if embarrassed. For a few minutes neither of them spoke. Maybe they'd learned too much about the other to be entirely comfortable.

"The train station is just over there. It'll get you into Perth in about five minutes," she said as she pulled the car over to the edge of the road.

With the car stopped, he took an easy breath. "Thank you for the ride."

"Not a problem." Another smile that held more warmth and was more dangerous than all her previous offerings.

There was a pause he knew he should fill, but he didn't know what to say. A thousand languages and they all failed him. He wanted to reach out and trace his fingers over her cheek, lean in, and kiss her lips.

"I hope you find something you like." Her hand moved from the gear stick and landed lightly on his knee.

"So do I." But he already had. He placed his hand over hers; for a heartbeat, neither of them moved. Her touch held the promise of pleasure he wasn't sure he could reciprocate. It had been a long time since his hands had done anything but kill. When she didn't pull away, he raised her fingers to his lips to taste her skin and test himself. His blood rose, but he released her before desire took control.

Her tongue slid over her lower lip. "Dai…"

"I'll be late." He didn't want to hear her reason why he shouldn't have done that. He had enough of his own. Yet none of them made sense. He was free. Human. He should be able to do what he wanted instead of dragging ancient history along for the ride. "I'll see you soon."

She nodded.

Then he got out of her car and closed the door. He stood and watched as her blue vehicle rejoined traffic. The talons around his heart shifted as if unable to get a firm enough grip to kill him. She might counsel kids, but what would she make of him if she knew even a whisper of the truth? Probably best not to find out. He was enjoying the illusion that she might be interested in a man like him.

The train ride was easier than the car trip, probably because it was on a fixed route and not swerving all over the road—that or he was too busy contemplating

the taste of Amanda on his lips and wondering if he'd
made a mistake. He had no idea what he was doing.

Once in the city, he found the apartment building easily. There were a few of them, all rising up and looking
over the river on one side and the city on the other. The
one he was interested in was a modern mix of metal and
concrete and sharp angles. While it lacked the grace and
solidity of the ancient castles and churches that littered
Europe, it also came without the baggage and history.
The building was only a couple of years old and un-
tangled by its past. It was exactly the kind of the place
he wanted. He walked up the three steps and through
the glass doors. The foyer was empty except for locked
mailboxes, two elevators, and the real estate agent.

She smiled with too much enthusiasm as her gaze
landed on him. "Mr. King?"

He was never going to get used to hearing himself be
called that. He would have made a terrible king, especially during war.

"Yes."

"Verity Jones." She held her hand out as her gaze
flicked over him as if she were there to appraise him,
instead of being there to show him the apartment.

Dai shook her hand. It was her job to make sure he'd
be a good tenant, and he had to play the prospective
renter while he worked out how to buy the place. She
held the grip for a moment longer than he was comfortable with before letting her fingers slide away.

"There are two for rent here. One furnished, one unfurnished. Where would you like to start?"

"With the unfurnished." He didn't want a house full
of other people's things.

Verity smiled, her lips pressed tight, and then took him up the elevator, explaining the security features of the building. She was one of those people who couldn't abide a silence. He tuned her out and made his own assessments. The elevator opened on a short, carpeted hallway. There were three doors, two apartments, and one fire escape. The door was simple, wood with gold numbering.

She swiped the key over the pad and opened the door. "I'll give you a quick tour, then if you have any questions..." She lifted her eyebrows in invitation.

He doubted there would be anything left to say by the time she was finished. As she led him around the apartment she chattered about the benefits of living in the city and that building, as if she could explain why it was perfect if she talked for long enough.

It was. Not even her voice could fill the empty space.

He stopped at the balcony and stared out at the view, partially over the river and partially of the next building. Not the best view, but he didn't care. Below him swirled the humanity he'd been forced to rejoin, yet up there it was quiet. He could fill the living area and the spare bedrooms with his books. Master the magic he'd learned but never used, and all without putting anyone at risk.

Amanda hovered at the edges of his thoughts like a golden-edged blade. Would he cut himself if he reached for her? He walked back inside and made a show of checking the stainless steel appliances that came with the apartment. When the agent paused for breath he took the opportunity to speak.

"Did the owners live here at all?"

"Only for a few months before they went overseas."

He nodded as if carefully considering. "Is there any chance the owners would be interested in selling?"

She giggled and glanced at her file. "I don't think so. They bought this place as an investment."

"Anything similar for sale?"

"There's a new building being constructed, but those apartments won't be ready for another six months."

Too long. He didn't want to rent as if he was borrowing a life until someone took it back. Maybe he could convince them to sell. Dai let his vision slide. Vague impressions of the owners lingered as faint threads with no more substance than a cobweb. They hadn't been overwritten so she was telling the truth.

"It's been empty a while."

"A few months. The economic downturn has opened a lot of rental availability in the city. I have apartments in other buildings, over in East Perth if you'd prefer something else."

He shook his head. He liked that it was walking distance to everything. It meant no more driving and if he wanted to see Roan all he had to do was catch the train. "I'll take it."

"You don't want to see the furnished one downstairs?"

"No."

"I'll need to check your rental references."

Dai stopped with his hand resting on the marble kitchen counter. That could be a problem. He doubted the goblins in the Shadowlands would give him a good reference. After all, they hadn't exactly left it as they'd found it. The rock spire that was their home was one of Roan's creations, ripped out of the dust by the magic that had tried to steal his brother's soul long before they knew the consequences. Dai considered it an improvement on the barren landscape. A landmark, like the pyramids of Egypt.

He looked at the threads that connected the real estate agent to the apartment, searching for something they had in common. He saw the tenuous fibers between his body and the agent. She was trying to form a connection like the one he had with Amanda. Did she think it would make the transaction easier? Would it?

If he used magic to secure the place, would that be wrong? Morally, probably, but it wouldn't contravene any of the laws he swore to abide when being marked by the various lore masters. And he wouldn't ensorcell her, just send her a suggestion—that she could ignore if she chose. With a thought he pushed his will along the connection she wanted to make.

You're checking my outstanding references.

If it didn't work, he was going to have to get Birch to fake some. He probably wasn't their favorite client at the moment, but they weren't his favorite bank either. He held his breath and ignored the pressure at the base of his skull that followed the use of even the tiny piece of magic as if warning him that he was overstepping.

The woman frowned and shuffled her papers as if confused for a moment. She wasn't going to take the suggestion. *Dammit.*

Then she looked up, her eyes bright and her lips smiling as if he'd suggested something else entirely. "That all looks good. How will you be paying your deposit?"

Dai raised a brow. That was too easy. Far too easy. He glanced at the connections she was trying to make and pulled his own back. He didn't want connections with random strangers. If that was the price of getting his way, it wasn't worth it. And yet…he wanted to own the place, not rent.

"Credit card," he said with a smile. He'd work on securing the purchase later. Paper contracts weren't nearly as binding as people thought.

Chapter 5

AMANDA OPENED THE DOOR THAT CONNECTED THE garage to the house and went inside. Behind her, Brigit chattered about her day at Eliza's. Usually Sheriff was running around outside and whining to be let in and be petted. She stopped in the hallway with her stomach knotted tight. The house was silent. Something wasn't right.

Then Sheriff came bounding around the corner toward them.

"Get back in the car," Amanda spoke through gritted teeth. Someone had let the dog in, which meant someone was in her house. There was only one person that could be.

"Mu-um."

"Now…take Sheriff with you." If the dog had already befriended Flynn, there was no point in keeping him with her. But the dog might keep Brigit distracted.

Brigit grabbed the dog's collar and hauled him into the garage. Amanda waited until she heard the car door open and then close.

"Flynn." Her footsteps echoed on the tiles. "I know you're here." Her voice was surprisingly level. Her fingers were wrapped around her cell phone, emergency already dialed. All she had to do was press connect.

"You rang the police." His voice floated down the hallway. He was in her dining room.

"Your parents are worried. They want you home."

An outright lie, but hopefully he would believe her. The police's description of the vicious assault played through her mind.

A man was in the hospital in an induced coma because Flynn wanted his gold watch. Sometimes it was as if he couldn't distinguish between gold and golden colored things. He took them indiscriminately, wrapping paper and pens, ribbon…anything as long as the color was right. An obsessive compulsion to have gold. A human magpie. His parents first noticed his odd habits when he was a toddler and all the yellow building blocks had gone missing. They'd found them under his bed, and he'd refused to give them back.

"They think I'm a freak." Flynn sat at her dining table with an open packet of steaks in front of him. Red blood stained his fingers. In the pale winter light creeping into her kitchen, his skin looked dull and gray instead of white.

"No they don't. They are your parents. They love you." Even if they didn't understand him and were constantly frustrated by his strange behavior. All parents loved their children.

"I'm an embarrassment."

Amanda sat opposite him. He looked so young; the stolen gold watch on his wrist was too large. "You need help."

"Why? What's wrong with lovin' the look and feel of gold?" His fingers smoothed around the face of the watch as he spoke; blood streaked the glass.

"Nothing…but you can't hurt people to get it."

Flynn's white eyebrows drew together as if he didn't understand. Did he remember what he'd done? There were times in the past when he hadn't remembered how he'd acquired his latest find.

"Are you still taking your meds?"

Flynn shrugged. "The police want to put me in jail, don't they?"

How could she tell him the truth? "What they do is up to you. Turn yourself in."

"I've done nothin' wrong."

Amanda swallowed. He'd slipped, gone back to where he was when she'd first started seeing him. Maybe further, since he saw nothing wrong with violence to get his way. How could she help him? She didn't know, but she had to protect her own family.

She got up from the table, and Flynn stood too. He was the same height as her, a boy almost a man and one capable of beating a man senseless. There was a hard glint in his pale eyes she'd never seen before. Was that how he'd looked before attacking? Dazed by the attraction of gold?

His gaze dropped to her hand and the shining gold band on her finger. Her wedding ring. No. He couldn't have that. Matt had placed it on her finger. She put her hand behind her back, but it was too late. He'd seen it and wanted the gold.

"Give me the ring."

"Flynn…" She started backing away. The table was still between them but not for long.

He eased around the chairs and stalked her. Oh God, she was going to have to give him the ring to get out of there.

"Mom, hurry up," Brigit yelled.

Flynn tilted his head as if startled. "Give me the gold."

"You'll let me go?"

"Gold." He held out his hand, still several paces away.

She pulled the ring off her finger and threw it across the floor. It bounced over the tiles, but she was already running. She slammed the door and got into the car. Brigit buckled herself in as they reversed out the driveway.

"Where are we going?"

"I don't know." Where was she going? What the hell was she going to do? Her hand shook as she shifted gears, her finger strangely naked. Her house had been invaded, but the loss of the ring hurt more, like she'd lost her armor against the world.

She stopped around the corner at the park where Brigit liked to play and rang the police. By the time they arrived, Flynn was gone and so was her ring. No doubt he'd add it to his hoard. While she knew it wasn't his fault, she needed someone to blame. And it was easier to blame Flynn than herself. If she'd taken the ring off years before, it would have been safe, but instead she wore it because she was scared that if she took it off she wouldn't think of Matt.

While the police waited, she packed a bag for Brigit and herself. Even though it went against every instinct, she was taking the cops' advice and staying with Eliza. Just for a few days, until they caught Flynn. They kept reminding her how lucky she was.

Lucky.

That summed up her life. Lucky. How lucky she was to lose her father to early onset dementia; by the time she was twelve he didn't know who she was. Lucky her mother quit her job to care for him and left her to sort out herself. Lucky to lose Matt, have his child, have a sickly daughter, and be dependent on the Coulter Trust to make ends meet.

Lucky her.

She clamped her teeth together as another wave of self-pity broke over her back. She forced a breath out between her teeth. It could be worse. There was always someone worse off. She didn't want to believe that. She wanted to wallow, even though she'd sworn long ago not to do that. It was a trap. Once in the mud it had a tendency to cling and suck her down. She couldn't afford to get stuck in the mire.

Brigit was talking the cop's ear off in the kitchen. She was excited to be staying overnight with Eliza. To a kid, everything was a new adventure. To Amanda, it felt like defeat. She worked hard, damn hard to get there. To get to college, to finish college, to buy a house, and raise her daughter. Outrage got her moving again. She would get her life back; there was just a temporary hiccup.

She finished packing, rounded up Brigit and Sheriff, and off they went. The only night she'd ever spent under the Coulter roof was after Matt had a party while his parents were away. His father never approved of her—she didn't have the right background. Yet she knew exactly which room she would be sleeping in—Matt's.

There was nowhere else for her to stay.

Roan and Eliza were in the guest room, the master room having been gutted for renovation. And the study downstairs was being used by Dai. She couldn't say the idea of being under the same roof as him was entirely unwelcome. Their last conversation left her with a desire to know more…and he was more forthcoming than Eliza. So the only two rooms left in the house were the bedrooms Matt and Eliza had used as children. And Brigit would want to sleep in Eliza's princess room.

When they arrived, Brigit proved her right, immediately laying claim to the pink-and-white, rose-patterned room filled with old dolls and soft toys. There'd been a time when she'd first started dating Matt that she'd thought Eliza strange for keeping such a childish room as a teenager, but now she understood her need to hold on to the past. Eliza's mother had decorated that room, and that was all Eliza had left of her. She touched her bare finger; she'd lost another piece of Matt.

In Matt's room, she sat on the end of the bed. The room was the same as it was when he'd died. Surf posters on the wall. His clunky computer was on the desk. Clean laundry in a pile on the chair. Even surrounded by his things he was a memory, insubstantial and untouchable. The love they'd shared was faint and offered no warmth or support. She rubbed her hands together hoping the heat would reach her heart.

It didn't. She was lonely. She didn't want to be by herself. Dai's smile flickered in her mind. He was quiet and mysterious and despite her best efforts she was drawn to him. Something about him sparked an interest she hadn't felt, or wanted, in years. Her body knew exactly what she needed. Her skin ached to be touched. She wanted to be alive again.

Dai set her on edge like she was a desperate teenager. She closed her eyes. What would his lips taste like?

Amanda gave herself a shake. How could she be thinking of Dai while sleeping in Matt's room? No matter what her body thought, she wasn't going to start having flings and introducing strange men into

Brigit's life. With a sigh, she pushed aside all thoughts of men and what her body craved and went to check on Brigit.

She cracked open the bedroom door and waited for her eyes to adjust to the dark. Brigit's breathing was quiet, as it should be. The day off to rest had helped: one more and she'd be back to her usual self. Brigit knew the risks as she'd been hospitalized before. Her teachers knew, and Amanda wasn't far away if anything happened. It was ten minutes from the high school where she worked to Brigit's school. In a few more years, Brigit would be in high school. Her little girl was growing up.

Brigit rustled as she rolled over. "Mom, can you tell me about Dad?"

Amanda smiled. She should've known Brigit wouldn't be asleep after all the excitement. "Sure, honey."

She sat on the bed and smoothed Brigit's hair. "Daddy liked to surf. We used to go to the beach all the time."

"And I was in your tummy." Brigit knew the story well.

"That's right. One day he didn't come back." He'd gone to the aid of another surfer and they'd both disappeared. She'd been on the beach, with every breath she'd expected him to reappear. He didn't, not until the next day when both men's bodies washed ashore.

"Because the angels took him."

"That's right." She'd started the lie for herself so she didn't feel alone, even though she no longer believed it, she continued the story for Brigit. "He watches over us because he loves us and wants to watch you grow up."

"Do angels get tired?"

"Maybe. I know little girls do." She gave Brigit a kiss. "Get some sleep."

She closed the door but let her hand rest on the handle. If Matt were there, he would know what to do. He would've been qualified by now, a doctor who could tell her if she was being too protective of her only daughter. But he wasn't. Matt never even met Brigit. She'd been six months pregnant when he drowned. She'd almost lost Brigit out of grief.

Since then, Brigit was the center of her world.

It had been enough. But she was restless like she wanted more even though she was unsure how to get it, or even what it was. She went downstairs, looking for a distraction. She wasn't tired, and she didn't want to be alone with her thoughts and fears. At the back of her mind she knew the police didn't catch every criminal. They may never catch Flynn. If they didn't, would she be safe?

Eliza was watching TV, curled up against Roan. Amanda hesitated in the doorway, then turned away. She couldn't intrude.

In the kitchen, Sheriff looked up from under the table. The dog spent most of his time under the kitchen table, a habit from when Brigit was little and food had rained from the highchair. He'd made himself at home in Eliza's house very quickly.

Her laptop lay dormant at the other end of the table. She flipped the screen up and restarted it. Almost everyone could be found on the Internet. Maybe she could find the something Dai was hiding, and a reason not to trust him. Something that would kill her interest.

She expected to have to do some digging, but all she had to do was type in his name. Dai King. Language expert, collector of rare books and translator. He'd been to outer Mongolia, Africa, Iceland, and other places to research local legends and lore. He was well traveled, well-educated, and notoriously reclusive.

At the end of an article there was a mention of his parents' and sister's death, but it didn't say what had happened. Amanda bit her lip and stared at the image on the screen. Even on the computer, she could see his eyes held more secrets than the oceans and were twice as dangerous. There was more to him than a deceased family and a bunch of dead languages.

Her life was much simpler if she wasn't distracted by handsome, dark-haired strangers. She should be walking away. She'd made promises to Matt. She had Brigit to care for. But she couldn't ignore the flutter in her stomach when Dai had first looked at her in the church. She wanted to revel in the dizzy thrill and breathless rush of attraction, the tingle of a first kiss. There'd been no one since Matt, and until Dai appeared out of nowhere she'd been fine. Maybe she'd been alone too long. She thought Matt was the one, and if he were alive, he would've been. But he wasn't. And she didn't want to spend the rest of her life by herself. She wanted someone by her side. She pushed her fingers through her hair. What was she going to do?

She didn't need any of the complications a relationship would bring. Hell, she wasn't even sure she wanted a relationship. She just wanted…something. Amanda eased out a slow breath. Maybe she just needed to get laid. Laughter bubbled up; it had been so long she'd forgotten how to do it. Her smile faded. Casual sex wouldn't fill the growing vacuum of emptiness.

––––⁓––––

Dai paused in the kitchen doorway. Amanda was laughing at something on the computer. Her long brown hair was loose for a change. She looked younger, more carefree. Then she looked up and saw him. Her eyes widened and the grin left her lips.

He had that effect on people, but usually only when he'd looked like a goblin. He almost checked his hands to make sure he was still human. "I didn't mean to interrupt."

She closed the laptop. "You didn't. I was just…wasting time on the Internet. You know those videos of cats being silly."

Dai nodded and caught sight of her bare feet tucked under the chair. He'd never seen her so…undressed, even though she was still in her work pants and shirt. It was as if some of her armor slipped and she was a little less walled up.

"You're not into Roan's Bollywood films?"

"Not my thing. I thought you must've been in bed already."

"I went for a walk."

"This late?"

He shrugged. "I like being outside and it's peaceful." He wasn't afraid of being attacked. Nothing could be more terrifying than seeing the might of the Roman army descend on a small town, or a hundred goblins wanting blood. He was pretty sure he could handle any would-be thugs.

The silence stretched between them. He glanced at her. Amanda was watching him; she was waiting for him to ask her a question and continue the conversation.

"I wasn't expecting to see you here."

She sighed and the words poured out like she'd

needed permission to let go. "A student—a patient— broke into my house today. The police suggested I stay somewhere else until they find him. If it were just me, it wouldn't matter."

Why would it matter less if it were just Amanda? Did her safety not matter? "Is he dangerous?"

She shook her head. Her hair shimmied across her shoulders, the ends resting on the swell of her breasts. He wanted to run his fingers through the silken stands and smooth them out. He forced himself to listen to words and not just watch the movement of her lips.

"He never used to be, but the police want to talk to him." She touched her left hand. Her wedding band was missing.

Was her husband no longer at the front of her thoughts?

When her fingers found nothing she glanced down as if surprised. "He took my ring."

Dai raised one brow. "Why would he want your ring?"

"It's gold," she said as if the metal meant nothing.

"Gold?" Gold was everything to a goblin, or even an ex-goblin. Just the word was enough to spark his interest. He sat at the table with her. For a second he thought he saw her eyes light up with the same spark he'd seen when he'd held her in his arms as they'd danced.

"He suffers from kleptomania, so he can't help himself when he sees gold."

How very goblin…yet obviously the kid was human. Over the centuries he learned plenty about the theory that goblins were once humans who had given in to greed.

"Why do the police want to see him?" Dai had a feeling he already knew if the kid was turning goblin.

"He's becoming violent."

"Did he hurt you?" If he had, Dai would hunt him down.

"No. I think he still trusts me." She ran her teeth over her lower lip in a move both innocent and seductive. "He needs help. The longer he avoids the police, the worse it will be."

Dai nodded but didn't agree with her theory. He doubted the police could do anything to save the boy. A human with the compulsion to steal gold was just too great a coincidence. He'd have to see if the kid was on his way to losing his soul. Maybe it wasn't too late to stop him from giving up everything for a chance at nothing.

"You'll be safe here."

"I can't stay here forever." She gave him a smile that barely turned up the corners of her lips.

His lips twitched in sympathy. "I know that feeling."

She leaned forward as if she didn't want to be overheard. "They're a bit intense, aren't they?"

"Enthusiastic, I'd say."

If she knew what Roan had been through, she'd know he had time to make up for. Maybe he did too. Her hand was only inches from his on the table—long fingers and short nails. He'd already felt her delicate touch on his shoulder. Kissed those knuckles. But what would her hands feel like on his skin? He wanted to know—he wanted the touch of another after so long.

Amanda considered him for a moment. "You didn't bring anyone to their wedding."

"I didn't have anyone to bring, but I danced with you." Something he'd do again without hesitation. He liked the way she'd felt in his arms.

Amanda's cheeks flushed pink.

"I meant you no embarrassment."

She placed her hand over his and gave his fingers a soft squeeze. "It's been a long time since I danced with any man." This time there was no mistaking the heat in her eyes. Her hand lingered over his as if she was unwilling to let him go, but there was nothing demanding or harsh in her touch.

"I'm glad you made an exception for me." He turned his hand over so their palms touched. The simple gesture was everything he'd forgotten could exist. Not every action was designed to injure. For a moment he let himself believe that no harm would come.

Her palm warmed against his, but there was more to the simple caress than she could see. A growing number of golden threads slipped from Amanda and into his skin. Without his willing it, his darker strands were meshing with her. When he was around her he couldn't help it. His subconscious sought her out. It was unsettling considering he'd been in control for so long.

For a moment neither of them moved. She watched him, waiting. But he didn't know what to do, or what she wanted from him. He had nothing to give her except the lies about who he was supposed to be. His fingers traced along the fate line of her palm as he reluctantly released her hand and stood.

"Till next time." He smiled to conceal the jumble of thoughts and sharp-edged desire flooding his veins. He wanted her. He wanted her more than he should. More than he could have.

She returned his smile, her eyes dark and wide, but she didn't stop him from leaving. Dai walked to his room and lay down. He let the lust run unchecked through his body, even though he knew it would get him nowhere. She was under the same roof, yet beyond his reach. With a sigh, he sat up and pulled out a law journal. He wouldn't be doing much sleeping; there would be too many ghosts stalking his dreams, waiting to tear him apart.

He slept eventually, but Amanda had left for work by the time he awoke. Eliza invited him on the shopping trip to buy plants with her, Brigit, and Roan, but he declined. He was more interested in studying his magic's effects on the tree in the park.

That morning the tree was dead. Dai walked around it, trying to understand what he'd done wrong. It had grown like spring and summer had happened all in one day, and been stable for several days afterward, yet it was dead. Totally dead with no chance of resurrection, like the weave of the tree somehow became tangled, and choked out its own life.

What had he missed?

He stared deeper into the center of the tree where the fibers clustered like arteries reaching into the heart of the earth, not caring if people stared. Wrapped around the thick central one was what looked like a rope. But the rope wasn't part of the tree and it hadn't been there the day before; he was sure of that. An icy warning rolled down his spine and the circle tattoos on his back prickled. An ancient spell of protection, they sensed the threat, even though he didn't know what it was yet. But it was something to do with the rope knotted around the center of the tree, cutting off its life.

Who would do that?

On the rope was a tag, and on the tag were two words. *Birch Trustees.*

Dai blinked, cleared his vision of the magical sight, and stepped back as if shoved. They were warning him. He glanced around, but the park was almost deserted. A woman ran along the path toward him, but he ignored her. Birch had killed the tree. His mind spun as he tried to work out why.

Because he'd let the growth go out of control?

His gaze took in the curled brown leaves…or because he'd used magic and had healed the tree.

"Such a beautiful tree. Pity it had to die." The woman in running gear stepped from around the other side of the tree.

She wasn't there a moment before, she'd been over a hundred yards away.

He kept his face blank. "Everything dies."

"Some things die sooner than they should." She smiled, but there was no hint of warmth in it. "And all you can do is watch."

Was that supposed to be a threat? The promise of death had seemed like a reward millennia ago. He didn't fear death. He wanted to understand it, to know why parts of the weave ruptured, why others grew strong. And all that knowledge was locked up at Birch as they examined his books and scrolls. He needed the ones on healing specifically, so he could rip the talons out of his chest and erase the scars. And if he didn't kill himself, he'd see what he could do for Brigit.

His heart slowed as he realized what the woman was implying. Not his death, but the death of those he knew. Amanda. Brigit. Roan and Eliza. By staying, he was placing them all in danger, unless he stopped using magic. But that would be like trying not to breathe.

"Will of the gods." He shrugged like the death of the tree meant nothing and he hadn't spent too long gazing at it trying to work out why it was dead.

"If it's the will of the gods, man shouldn't interfere." Her gaze gave him a casual once-over that left him wanting to wash. Then she turned and jogged away.

Dai watched until she disappeared from view.

He frowned and crossed his arms. If Birch planned to kill him and Roan, they wouldn't have furnished them with the papers they needed and the faked backgrounds to satisfy anyone who got too interested. They would've just killed them and pocketed the wealth and his books.

What stopped them?

His eyes narrowed as he watched a boat glide over the river. The spread of water was bigger than the one he'd grown up near. That was the answer. Roan was human; he was as he had been before the curse had been laid.

Dai, on the other hand, wasn't, and he couldn't unlearn what he knew, or quench the desire to learn more. Knowledge wasn't something to be feared; it was something to be used and shared. And he wouldn't be cowed.

He uncrossed his arms and shoved his hands into his pockets as he walked back along the river to Eliza's. Every so often he checked over his shoulder, but he didn't see the woman again. He could defend himself with weapons and without—living in the Shadowlands had taught him more than just survival—but did he know enough magic to defend himself if magically attacked?

Probably not. That, again, was a different type of magic and a study he'd given up on after he realized it didn't work in the Shadowlands.

He stopped in the driveway of the house Eliza had inherited from her parents. Roan had first been there nine years before when Eliza had summoned him to break up a party. They'd never been able to avoid a direct summons, an order compelling them from the Shadowlands to the Fixed Realm that put them in the service of whoever called.

There were obviously rules about magic use that had changed over the years. Where magic was once common, it barely existed. Was there a blanket *no human shalt do magic* rule? If so, why hadn't Birch given him the list of what not to do? He shrugged. He probably would have ignored it anyway. What magic he did in his own house was his own business. If they gave him his books, he wouldn't have had to experiment on trees.

He unlocked the front door and went inside expecting Roan, Eliza, and Brigit to be home, but the house was empty. They were all in the backyard. His brother grubbed around in the dirt like a peasant, while Eliza and Brigit sat in the sun sorting through small plants and seeds. A picture of domestic bliss. The sooner he got out of the house the better. He didn't want to bring Birch to Roan's door.

Yet he still had to tell his brother he was moving out. That was a conversation he wasn't looking forward to, but there was no sense in delaying it. Birch was watching him and he was putting all their lives in danger.

"What are you doing?"

"Planting vegetables. Want to help?" Roan glanced over his shoulder.

No, he didn't want to help. He'd spent more than enough time eking out an existence on the bony, half-starved animals of the Shadowlands that he had no desire to do so again. "They have shops for that."

"I know, but the ground here grows things." Roan picked up a fistful of dark soil. "We're home."

"We're on the other side of the world." Wales was a long way from Australia.

"In the Fixed Realm." Roan dropped the soil and wiped his hand on his jeans.

Dai scanned the pale blue sky. He was so used to looking for a threat he couldn't stop. He was still looking over his shoulder expecting his past to surface and swallow him without stopping to chew.

"You missed a call while you were out."

Dai's chest tightened. Had Birch come looking for him here already? Had they told Roan what was he was doing?

"Your keys are ready for collection."

He let his muscles relax, but the tension lingered in his shoulders. "Great. I'll pick them up and be out of your house tonight."

Roan put his hand on Dai's arm "You don't have to go. Take time to get settled."

Dai looked at the hand on his sleeve. A week ago that would have been enough to start the fight that would've let the curse take their souls. He glanced at Eliza and Brigit and bit his tongue. He was so used to spitting poison at his brother he was struggling to find a common ground they'd never shared even before the curse.

"I need my own space." The trees around him rustled in the breeze. He suppressed a shiver as it stroked his cheek with icy fingers.

Roan pressed his lips together and said nothing. He didn't need to. His hard expression said it all. Disapproval. Disappointment.

"You aren't king anymore. You can't order me to stay."

"I'm still your brother."

"Aren't you sick of having me around?" After two thousand years of living together, fighting together, and hoarding together, Dai was ready for a break. For peace and quiet and the lack of demands on his time. He needed time to work out what to do.

"I know you're still getting used to being back in the Fixed Realm, but you need to enjoy it."

He would, but he'd do it his way and in his own time. It was, after all, his life. And he had control of his life for the first time since he was fifteen.

"I'll enjoy it in my own house."

"You have no furniture."

"And?" Since when had they ever bothered about furniture? For years in the Shadowlands they'd only had what they could carry.

"That's not the way it's done."

"I'll borrow the air mattress." He'd had less and survived.

"Where are you going to put your food? Where are you going to sit to eat?"

"The apartment came with appliances. I'll sort out the rest as I go. I'll be fine." He didn't need Roan as his protector or baby-sitter. He turned to leave. They could work well enough together when life was on the line, but the rest of the time they were too different to get on. No amount of time could change that. They might share blood, but that was where the similarities ended.

"You're locking yourself away."

"Hardly." Dai spun back around, aware they had an audience.

Brigit was watching, her gaze never quite landing on him the way it did on Roan. She put her hand on her chest as if she couldn't breathe. Then she took a small tube out of her back and put it to her mouth. Eliza was talking to her and Brigit was nodding.

Dai lowered his voice as if it was the argument that had upset the child's lungs. "An apartment in the middle of the city isn't isolated."

Roan's lips thinned as if he wanted to press the point. "You're always welcome here," he said instead.

"I know." But he didn't know how to tell Roan about the magic, or what was happening with Birch. It was something only he could deal with because if he told Roan, Roan would jump to his aid, and his brother had more to risk than his own life now. He had Eliza.

"I'm worried about you." Roan kept his voice soft so Eliza and Brigit wouldn't overhear. "How much of the Shadowlands have you brought with you?"

"I'm fine." Dai forced what he hoped was an easy smile. "Just getting used to day and night again."

He wished it were that simple. Daytime was all right. Nighttime was filled with a darkness he couldn't fight. Nightmares of his own making. It was hard to fight himself and win. But he'd be damned before he'd forgive and forget.

Roan didn't look convinced. His eyebrows had that

pinched look like he really wanted to say something but didn't want the argument that would follow, as if they were still dancing around the curse and trying to avoid a fight that would make them surrender their souls and become goblin.

"It'll all work out fine. Have faith."

Dai wanted to believe him, but what was wrong with him was harder to break than a curse. The scars didn't wash away as easily as the dust of the Shadowlands. But it wasn't just that. Eliza knew who Roan really was; she'd seen goblins, the caves, and the gold. She'd saved Dai from fading and fighting Anfri to the death by offering her gold earring.

"Birch is still holding my books."

Roan frowned. "Do you need them?"

"They are my life's work." He'd spent centuries amassing knowledge instead of gold while searching for a cure. The lust for gold he'd been able to ignore until the very end—yet once he'd given in it had been a glittering slippery slope to soulless goblin.

"They're relics best suited to museums."

"Like us." Where did people who'd lived ancient history belong? "Go back to your planting," Dai said as he walked away.

"The plaque is ready," Roan called after him.

Dai stopped. He hadn't expected it to be engraved so quickly. He turned slowly.

"Will you join me this evening to remember?" Roan's face was impassive and revealed none of what he was thinking.

"What will your guests think?" Surely burying swords would raise suspicion?

"Eliza is taking them out for dinner. We will be alone."

Dai nodded, his gaze on the ground. Roan had planned this. Brac, Fane, Anfri, and Meryn would be put to rest a final time in the Fixed Realm. They should have all survived the curse and be experiencing life in the world of men again. His lips turned in a sad smile. Fane wouldn't be considered a man in this time. He was only sixteen when he was cursed. He'd taken his own life, unable to cope with the harshness of life in the Shadowlands and the prospect of eventually fading to goblin.

Meryn had faded to goblin after the first summons, that first awful night at the beck and call of the general while the last of the Decangli were slaughtered. Brac had been pulled apart by the druid centuries later, and Roan had killed Anfri. He'd faded only a handful of days before the curse broke.

And Dai was jealous of them. They got to die and be reborn with no memory of the Romans or the Shadowlands or goblins. They got a fresh start, not just a second chance.

"I will." Maybe he could bury his past along with his sword and torque.

Chapter 6

THE COLD PRESSED AGAINST MERYN'S BONES AND squeezed. They ached in a way he hadn't felt for…he paused. He couldn't remember his bones ever aching and yet he knew they must have or why would he have thought it? He curled tighter into a ball to preserve his body heat as the need to survive that fueled his flight left him shivering in the dust. Above him, his gray stained cloak hid him from the casual sight of a goblin scout and blocked out the dull, never-ending twilight.

How long would he have until the goblins heard the beating of his human heart and found him and ate him? That's what they did to humans who found their way to the Shadowlands or who were caught during the Wild Ride—the only time those who'd turned fully goblin could escape the Shadowlands and roam the Fixed Realm. The fear of being found wouldn't let him close his eyes, even though he was exhausted. He was so tired his muscles shook. He'd only stopped because he was too weak to go any farther. He didn't want to be human.

He wanted to be goblin. Maybe he was being punished for being different, for giving himself a name. Goblins didn't have names. Yet he did, and he didn't remember a time without one. He didn't remember ever being alone either, but his troop had turned on him when his skin had become pink. He'd been forced to flee or die.

They would come after him. They no longer knew

him or wanted him because he was human. A crushing weight settled on his throat, making it hard for him
to breathe.

Human and in the Shadowlands. How had it happened and what did it mean?

Memories rose like infected blisters, pushing pain-
fully on his mind. Meryn pushed them down, unwilling
to examine them or the hurt they caused. There was no
pain or conscience when he was part of the goblin troop.
Now every death, human or goblin, committed by his
once-gray hands hung like a barbed hook through his
skin, dragging him down.

He tucked his hands against his body to keep warm
and tried to sleep for just a little, knowing the strange
dreams would come again. Battle and blood. The things
a goblin lived for—except he was no longer goblin,
and in those dreams he was also a man. Fighting, but
he fought for more than gold and glory. But what was
worth more than gold?

Meryn closed his eyes to stop the strange tears that
burned his skin, dampened the dust, and swelled in his
heart, and he prayed for mercy. For the oblivion of gold
and greed.

To wake up goblin.

Dai's breath clouded in front of him as he looked up at
the tree with the little house wedged in the branches.
At his feet was a bundle of ancient swords and torques
wrapped in an oilcloth and a shiny new plaque.

"It's freezing out here." In Wales it was either going
to be sunny and cold or rainy and cold. Here in Australia,

on the other hand, it could be sunny one moment and bitter the next as if the country couldn't make up its mind about seasons. Not even the trees knew if it was cold enough to drop all their leaves, some, or none.

"Remind you of home?" Roan huffed out a breath.

"Yeah, except this would be summer." He forced out a laugh and raised his beer.

His brother drank too. Who'd have thought cold beer would become popular? Or that there would be so many kinds? And that none of them needed to be eaten with a spoon.

Roan squatted down and lit the four little candles at the base of the tree. He marked on the bark where the plaque was going, but neither of them was quite ready to attach it. They stared at the bundle on the ground and drank in silence. There was nothing that could be said that would change ancient history. They were at the end of their lives as Decangli. The end of the Decangli. Though in truth, their tribe was wiped out the night the rebellion failed.

The Romans had made sure there would be no further uprisings. All the men who'd survived the fight were captured and killed. The women were taken for slaves— assuming they didn't raise their swords in retaliation. With the death of their sister, the last princess, the routing was complete. If nothing else, the Romans were efficient. Maybe rebelling wasn't the smartest of moves, but at the time it felt like the only option; giving in went against the grain. With the wisdom of history on his side, Dai knew they'd been lucky to hold out as long as they did. The whole of England had fallen under the boot, as had most of Europe and northern Africa. In this time, there would've been criminal charges and war-crimes tribunals for most of the things that had happened.

Dai finished his beer and put it on the grass, then picked up the shovel to begin digging the hole for the old weapons and the memories that went with them. At least he'd get warm. As Dai dug, Roan hammered the plaque into place, the steady tap-tap like the beating of a solid gold heart. Dai paused, his cold hands chaffing on the shovel. He wasn't used to the manual labor. He glanced at his brother, but Roan's attention was on the hammer and nails.

If he could move beer, could he move dirt? He looked at the layers of web that made up the earth and the plants pushing through it. Then he imagined scooping out a handful. At first nothing happened, then the ground trembled and a clod the size of a large dog jumped out and landed at his feet with a whoosh of air and a thump. He gave it a cautious nudge with his boot and the soil fell apart so it looked like the other, smaller pile he'd dug out by hand.

"Finished already?" Roan said as he turned.

"Trying to stay warm." Dai gave him a tight grin, hoping Roan hadn't seen.

"Deep hole."

"Don't want anyone digging them up by accident. How would the archaeologists explain finding old Celtic weapons and jewelry in Australia?" Probably by concocting a tale about Celts traveling farther than first thought and then they would spend vast amounts of money searching for a nonexistent settlement.

Roan nodded and picked up the swords. One for every man cursed. Six in total, but the sword for Meryn was a stand-in. When their cousin faded to goblin, he took his weapons with him. The sickly, gray thread still connected Dai to his goblin cousin. Meryn deserved so much more than an eternity of roaming the Shadowlands. He was Roan's second, a battle planner to match the Romans. Dai shuddered as if the cold from the Shadowlands was still chilling his blood. Maybe burying their swords wasn't a good idea.

"You sure you want to part with it?" Dai raised an eyebrow.

The blade hadn't left his brother's side in nearly two thousand years. While he'd acquired others, that was the one he'd been cursed with.

"I've got to." Roan cradled the bundle, holding the memories for the last time.

Dai had surrendered his sword, but he'd kept his throwing knives. He couldn't bring himself to be totally defenseless. There had been too many years where he was forbidden to carry any weapon in case he slit his master's throat. He still wanted to hear the bastard beg for his life, but that chance was long gone even if the nightmares of Claudius weren't.

Roan placed the swords in the ground. The clanking was muffled by the cloth. It felt like they were burning the corpses of the men again. If Dai hadn't told Roan there was a traitor and suggested they stall the rebellion, the druid wouldn't have argued with Roan about the delay and the curse would never have been laid.

"Do you ever wonder what would've happened if we hadn't been cursed?"

"We'd be dead and I wouldn't have met Eliza."

True, the rebellion would have gone ahead as planned and the Romans would've been waiting. But at least they wouldn't have had to live as goblins. "She made two thousand years in the Shadowlands worthwhile?" *All the fighting, all the death?*

Roan sighed, a puff of cloud in the cool night air. "I have to believe it was all for something."

Dai nodded; suffering had to be for something. What had he got? A library he couldn't touch, magic he couldn't use, and a wealth of scars not even the ink on his skin could hide.

"What about you?"

"I was ready to die." That was no secret. While for years he was the one who'd urged Roan to keep fighting the curse's grip while Dai searched for a cure, in the end it was Roan forcing Dai to stall when Dai's fear of turning goblin was turning his thoughts to suicide.

"Don't waste your second chance. Live for those who died." Roan stood up.

None of the men had deserved to die, yet he envied them their peace. Fighting to stay human in the Shadowlands was like trying to hold a handful of water. It didn't matter how careful he was—drops escaped, some evaporated, and eventually there was nothing left but a thirst for gold that could never be slacked.

Was it his responsibility to make up for their lives? What about his life? His life was over long before the curse. It had ended the day he was taken hostage, a good behavior bond to make sure his father, and then Roan, did as the general asked. In return, Dai was educated in all of Rome's vices. At first their sister, Mave, was too young to be of any use to the invaders. If the Decangli hadn't tried to rebel, she would have married a Roman and they all would have died in a quiet corner of Wales centuries ago. Who would they have been reborn as if that had happened?

Amanda's daughter lingered in his mind. "Have you noticed how much Brigit looks like Mave?" he asked.

Roan shrugged. "I guess, a little." He lifted his gaze and looked at Dai. "You're not thinking she's come back?"

Dai looked at his hands. The first life he took had never left him and still haunted his dreams. Maybe it was his guilty conscience searching for soothing. As if through knowing his sister had been reborn and was happy, he'd be forgiven. "She would've had many lives in between then and now."

"You still believe." Roan frowned as if he couldn't understand Dai's faith in the old religion.

Dai nodded. He did, even though it clashed with so many others. He held on to the belief that everyone got another chance to have a better life. He had to. It was all he had. He wanted the chance to have what every man wanted. He wanted a life untainted by the poison of the past.

But Brigit wasn't free. Her father had drowned before she was born and she suffered from a breathing condition. He'd researched asthma and was now interested in whether the illness would show up in the weave of Brigit's body. If it did, he might be able to heal her, and Amanda would no longer have so much worry. He liked it when Amanda smiled. He'd like it even more if she were smiling at him for healing her daughter. The breeze rustled the leaves in the tree so they whispered in his ear, mocking his desires. If he couldn't fix himself, how was he going to help someone else?

"So do you. You didn't want to kill the druid."

"I didn't want more bad luck." Roan stared at the

dirt as if he didn't want to admit he still clung to the old beliefs after centuries of existence. "I hope Brac and Fane had better lives the next time around."

They, too, would've had many lives since escaping the Shadowlands in death. Anfri wouldn't be reborn for a while. And who knew what would happen to Meryn, a goblin who was damned to run the Shadowlands? If he died, would he get the chance to live again as a man or was he damned forever?

But their ritual wasn't about the lives they could be living, but about the lives they had led. Fierce and fearless. They were half wild at first, as if the Shadowlands made them mad just by breathing the air. Brac's death forced them to reevaluate how they were living and how they were going to survive.

Roan took the shovel and backfilled the hole. "It doesn't feel like two thousand years, does it?"

No, it felt like four thousand or more. It was hard to quantify that amount of time even after living it. Months and years bled to one gray, amorphous mass.

His brother stuck the rosebush in the much smaller hole and pushed dirt in around the bush. "It wasn't all bad. There were good times."

Dai closed his eyes. There was a time when they were able to fight the commands, travel to the Fixed Realm at will, but still had a grip on their souls and were safe in their castle. Yet even then he'd never had peace. He couldn't let his guard down and let the truth slip out. When Roan brought women back, eager for a silver slice of goblin wealth, it had been easy enough to pay them off and talk like the others. But he could never bring himself to let another touch him, or see the scars. His fingers curled as he remembered the touch of Amanda's hand. She was making him want the impossible.

The candles guttered, casting the names of the other four men in darkness. But he knew them and would never forget them. Without his poking and prompts, the rebellion would never have taken place. His thirst for revenge resulted in the slaughter of his tribe, and the general still had the last laugh. The one time Dai held a sword in Claudius's presence, he was unable to kill him. With his goblin body bound by the curse he was forced to obey once again. The final order was worse than anything Claudius had done to him as a slave.

Dai shivered like ghosts were caressing his skin. He didn't like remembering his past. There was too much of it, and too much he didn't wish to think about. The breeze swirled around him, creating shadows at the corners of his vision. If he succumbed, he'd never find his way out of the dark.

The candle on the desk didn't stop the shadows from closing in, but it kept them out of reach and was softer than the electric light. Maybe having some light while Dai slept would keep his nightmares at bay…maybe, but not likely. He doubted even Amanda sleeping upstairs would be enough to bring him pleasant dreams. He stared at the little flame and stifled a yawn.

In the Shadowlands he'd been tired, but not sleepy. Before that, as a slave, he'd slept with one eye open, jerking awake at the slightest sound. He must have slept peacefully as a child before the Romans had first arrived and the battles had started.

He had vague memories of being held by his mother—sharper memories of the tiny baby who survived after she died. His father and Roan were busy, and no one worried about him, the second son, so he made sure she was okay and well looked after. He just needed to feel as important as his older brother, so he became Mave's protector and made sure she was treated like the princess she was. He was thinking of his sister as he fell asleep, but Claudius still claimed his dreams.

Not even the curse, and the ugly goblin body, had saved him from General Claudius's attention. Like Roan, Dai was compelled to answer all summonses. He was called to the general's private chambers, as the Decangli rebellion surrendered and died, to find eleven-year-old Mave held in one of Claudius's hands, and a sword in the other. On the floor was the body of Drem, his cousin and Meryn's younger brother, his face slack with death as his blood seeped into the rugs. While every other man had been fighting, trying to throw the Romans off Decangli land, Drem had been with the general.

Dai knew why. The traitor was killed by his own greed. But being right was a bitter reward, Drem had been a trusted friend.

"Your sister is quite pretty, don't you think?" Claudius squeezed her arm until her skin was white beneath his fingers. "How fast do you think I can make her cry?"

Mave didn't flinch. She didn't even scream when she saw him. Did she recognize him? Did she know what had become of her brothers?

"Leave her alone. She's a child." The rasping goblin voice scratched his ears. Was it his?

Claudius caressed her cheek.

Rage burned like acid in Dai's veins, but he couldn't move. He wanted to rip Claudius's heart from his chest and force it down his throat and see how he liked to choke. But the curse kept him immobile in the presence of his summoner. Was that what it was going to be like? Never free, always a slave to whomever called them to the Fixed Realm?

"You get to choose her fate. Think of it as my last gift to you." Claudius stroked her hair. *"It's fitting. The last Queen of the Decangli making peace with Rome. Something your brother wasn't smart enough to do."*

"Would you befriend a two-headed snake?"

Claudius smiled. That smile alone woke a thousand unpleasant memories. *"Choose. Her life, or her death."*

There was no choice. He wouldn't let Mave suffer the way he had. *"Death."*

The Roman general tossed Dai the sword. *"Then go ahead and kill her."*

His gray, gnarled hand caught the sword even though he wanted to let it fall at his feet. He watched his arm rise, unable to fight the order. Mave stared into his bulging yellow eyes; she didn't blink or cower. Even if Claudius wasn't holding her, she was true to her bloodline. The last queen standing proud.

Her lips moved as she whispered her final words, *"I forgive you."*

Then his hand slit her throat while his mind screamed.

Claudius dropped her as if she were a sack of rags. Dai couldn't move to catch her and lay her down gently.

"You're dismissed."

—⁓—

Dai woke with a jolt. Nausea from the sweet scent of blood rolled in his stomach, and his skin was cold as if the Shadowlands had invaded his sleep to keep the nightmare alive. He hated that dream. Even being in the Fixed Realm didn't remove the sharp edges of Mave's death. He'd never been able to tell Roan what had happened that night.

When the six of them had regrouped in the Shadowlands after that first summons to the Fixed Realm the night of the rebellion, no one had spoken. It was bad enough to have been cursed by the druid, but to be summoned back to the Fixed Realm to watch the massacre was devastating. They were in a state of shock after watching the slaughter of their kin. Then they all had their own private summons, the final punishment for daring try to throw off the Roman yoke, but they didn't share what they were compelled to do. It was bad enough Meryn faded to goblin as they watched. It was easier for Dai to let Roan think he was summoned to kill the traitor, Drem, than to speak the truth. He'd discovered later that Roan had been forced to kill the remaining men who were loyal to their king.

Dai sat up, turned on the light, and blew out the candle. There would be no more sleep, so he pulled out a law book that dealt with property contracts. Study was always a useful distraction from the horror going on around him. It would be useful to know what he was dealing with before he attempted to manipulate reality and buy his apartment.

Chapter 7

DAI LOCKED THE DOOR BEHIND HIM AND PAUSED, enjoying the silence. One suitcase and an oversized shopping bag held all his possessions. He moved them to an empty bedroom where he wouldn't be able to see them and nothing spoiled the emptiness. The space he craved echoed around him; it was nice. Peaceful. He toed off his shoes and walked around barefoot, enjoying the feel of the thick ivory carpet instead of the rock or cold dust of the Shadowlands.

He opened the sliding doors that led from the dining room onto the balcony. From there, Perth stretched out along the Swan River. The only people out were too far below him to be a nuisance; they marched along the footpaths on each side of the traffic. The world was there, only a short drop away if he wanted it. He tapped the railing, unsure what to do next with his freedom. Then he remembered the six-pack of beer in his bag and went inside for a bottle. He'd have a drink and watch the sunset. He hadn't grown tired of that, or watching the sunrise—not that he could see both from his balcony. Would he ever after missing so many?

With a beer in hand, and the others in the fridge, he went back out to watch the sun melt away and be replaced with velvet blue. There were fewer stars visible than when he was born, and they were different in the southern hemisphere, but he didn't care. There were stars. There was a moon—hell, there was weather. It wasn't until they were gone that he realized how much they were a part of living.

His life had been on hold, yet in that holding pattern he learned. He had the knowledge of many lifetimes. And nothing to do with it. He couldn't correct the errors made in history books. No one would believe him, although he'd left hints to be found over the years. Sometimes they got picked up, most of the time they were ignored. The healing magic he wanted to use, he couldn't control well enough…that, and Birch was watching him. He glanced over his shoulder as if expecting to see someone, but his apartment was empty and everyone below him was getting on with their lives. No one cared about one man having a drink on his balcony.

He leaned on the railing. The building had been designed so he had no view of his neighbor's balcony. It was one of the reasons he chose it—that and it was the reality most easily altered to suit his needs. He drained the last of his beer and went inside, leaving the door open to let in the breeze—even the movement of air was worthy of notice simply because his life had lacked it for so long. The curtains fluttered like the delicate wings of a newly hatched moth.

How was he going to follow up on his books when Birch knew he was using magic? He couldn't plead innocence and curiosity. His lips curved in a bitter smile. It had been a bloody long time since he was able to claim the former, and the latter had been with him all his life.

He closed his eyes. In the quiet he heard music and car engines. He let it fade away until it was just him, the carpet beneath him, the wall at his back, and the cold beer in his hand. From around the edges crept a scent like summer and the sea. Salt and heat. His mind strayed from the blankness until it found the answer. Green eyes and a smile that could melt gold. It lingered in his mind and couldn't be pushed aside.

He needed a distraction. Something else to focus on. He may not have his books, but he could still experiment with the magic.

Dai opened his eyes so he could see the threads around him. His place was a web. Solid items were woven tight, but even the air was crisscrossed with strands and fibers, some no thicker than a hair, others like rope. Some were smooth, others uneven. He'd yet to remember the subtleties between the different kinds. He was sure he'd learned something about them, but he'd forgotten when he couldn't manipulate them to break the curse.

He glanced around his place looking for something he could practice on, something with no life, something he couldn't kill. He saw the empty beer bottle, then looked at the mesh that made up the fridge. Could he get a beer out without opening the door? Inside the web of the fridge, he could feel those that belonged to the beers. He grabbed one and tugged. The bottle slammed against the solid reality of a closed fridge. Glass exploded against the door and his concentration broke.

"Damn." Three beers left and a mess to clean up. Solids couldn't pass through each other. But magic could beat physics any day of the week. All he had to do was alter reality instead of blindly groping around like a novice. He should've known better. He chided himself, knowing that if his old teachers saw him, they'd be shaking their heads. It had taken a long time for him to earn their respect as a goblin and he wasn't about to fail their memory now—or himself.

If he wanted a beer, he was going to have to get it with magic, or go without. He refocused his vision and studied the weaves for longer, and while he could've opened the door with magic and brought a beer to his hand, that wasn't what he wanted to do.

With a thread of thought he took hold of the beer and as it approached the door he let it slide against the fibers of the fridge. Instead of trying to break the weave, he let the beer slip through a gap too small for the actual bottle, lifting so it cleared the kitchen island, then the bottle slapped against his palm. Whole and undamaged and full of beer. With a grin he twisted off the cap and brought the bottle to his lips, then paused.

If the beer could come to him, why couldn't he go to the beer?

Dai stood. While his apartment was tangled with threads, he could have easily stepped over and under them without touching them. But that would be boring. He wanted to be able to cross the room with a thought. Except the kitchen island was in the way and getting stuck in the carpentry would require a hell of a lot of explaining, if it didn't kill him. He walked around until he had a clear view of the fridge. It wasn't far to travel, ten feet tops. He rolled his shoulders and thought about where he wanted to be.

The thought became a fragile thread no thicker than a hair traveling out from him to his destination. Then he let his body be pulled along the delicate strand. Pressure built at the base of his skull and the thread snapped.

Carpet solidified under his feet. The room wobbled—no, that was him as he struggled to hold his balance. After a couple of breaths, the room stabilized and he realized something was different.

He looked around.

He'd moved four feet.

He had moved.

It had worked. The spider tattooed on his chest shifted in her web. He was the spider spinning a web, altering reality to suit himself. Flickers of knowledge he'd learned centuries ago resurfaced. All he had to do was remember, and the best way to jog memories was with use. He took a swig of his beer and placed it on the floor. He'd do it properly this time, with full focus. With a thought he was in front of the fridge. Back to his beer. Picking up his empty bottle and putting it in the bin. All without taking a step. All without crossing the kitchen island.

Excitement and adrenaline pumped in his veins. He could actually do something useful. He ignored the tightening at the back of his neck and tension building in his temples. A headache was nothing; he'd lived with worse. He had to see what else he could do. He turned to the kitchen island with its polished marble top and oak doors. It wasn't about forcing his way through; it was about flowing through the same way water changed shape to fit the container. Nothing was so solid there weren't gaps for other threads to pass through. He threw out a thought line straight through the island to the fridge. It thickened with his will and he jumped.

Dai's hip hit the oven. He grunted as searing pain jolted through the bone and tightened his stomach, but he ignored the agony like so many other times. He had reason to celebrate.

He'd moved through something. He ran his hands down his legs even though they felt fine and wriggled his toes. Aside from what would be an awesome purple bruise in the morning, he'd done it. He could move through solid objects.

His celebration was cut short by the pulsing in his temple as his vision blurred into a confusing mess of web and normality. He reached out a hand to steady himself, as the room spun with increasing speed and threatened to send him sprawling, and blinked to clear his vision of magic. It took two tries to see the way a man should without the tangle of threads. Magic and beer didn't mix. He was drunk and hung over at the same time. And it really, really wasn't good. The room canted to the side. He lowered himself to the floor and lay down on his back. One arm rested over his eyes as if he could block out the lights dancing on his eyelids as he tried to center his breathing.

It was about the same as when they'd first learned to slide through people's nightmares into the Fixed Realm. The brain didn't like the idea and the stomach didn't like being taken for the ride. No…actually, this was more like being ripped out of the Shadowlands with a skin-peeling summons—the gut-wrenching loss of ground and the suffocating spin as reality shifted.

It was almost as bad as being in a car.

The slow, deep breaths didn't help, and the room moved even without him watching, which only re-inforced that he hadn't eaten any dinner and that beer wasn't a good substitute. He was human and he needed to eat. After not needing to eat for so long in the Shadowlands it was a hard habit to get back into. He would get food after he finished lying down.

Without magic to distract him, his thoughts wandered off and found their way back to Amanda and the way her lips curved when she smiled. His headache receded as blood was redirected. He fisted his hand, his nails digging into his palm. How could he want something that had only ever brought pain?

While he knew that wasn't always the case, the only memories he had of Seiran's touch were smothered with what had happened after. He knew being touched by another wasn't supposed to be bad. But knowing it and living it were two different things, and he couldn't separate the pain and fear that came with thinking of letting another get that close to him. If she was close enough to caress, she was close enough to kill.

He'd made himself sit up. He'd rather have the headache and dizziness. His pulse echoed in his ears like a drum. Of all the things he'd thrown into his bags, painkillers weren't one of them. He pressed his fingers against his temple as if to reassure himself his head wasn't about to crack open. Then with a wrench of will he stood and placed his hands on the kitchen counter for support like an old man not sure of his footing.

He'd had a concussion before…but this was something else. And it wasn't improving.

Around him, his apartment was like an empty cell closing in and there was no end to his sentence. He needed painkillers…and family. One more night in Eliza's study wouldn't hurt. Could he travel that far? Could he travel that far at the moment? His head pounded in time with his heart, a throbbing beat, but the alternative of staying here alone without the prospect of pain relief was worse. And if he couldn't get there? He'd probably be unconscious so it wouldn't matter. He sent out a tenuous thread, the way a spider might when looking for an anchor for the web. Dai forced himself to step forward.

Green eyes flashed in his mind. A split second of distraction and his path was altered. The room he stood in wasn't Eliza's study. He was in a bedroom. He blinked and glanced around confused, as the room danced around him in time with the pounding inside his head. He caught himself with the wall and tried to stay upright. He'd pushed himself too far. All he wanted to do was slide onto the floor and pass out—not necessarily in that order.

A sigh that wasn't his drew his attention to the bed in the center of the room and he knew why he was drawn here. Amanda was sleeping in the bed, curled up on her side. The blankets stirred and she stretched like she was about to wake. Her long legs, bare to mid-thigh, were revealed. Dai looked away, but the image was already embedded in his brain like shrapnel. The room turned around him like a child's spinning top.

His gaze was drawn back to her sleeping form. He shouldn't be there. Yet for a heartbeat, it was where he wanted to be more than anywhere else in the world. He wanted to be next to her, his body curled against hers. No bed had ever been to tempting…or so wrong.

What was he doing? Staring, creeping around like a bloody goblin instead of facing her like a man. A gray dog lifted its head off the floor at the end of the bed. It tilted its head as if deciding if Dai were real. He stared at the dog; it wouldn't dare bark and give him away. The dog opened its mouth.

Dai didn't have time to walk out of the bedroom— even if he could've walked in a straight line. All he knew was he didn't want Amanda waking and finding him watching her. Adrenaline flooded his system and gave him a moment of clarity. People pulled stronger than places. One thought. One chance to get it right, or he was sleeping wherever he landed. His brain felt like roadkill. Killing himself by getting stuck in a brick wall was beginning to look very attractive.

Roan.

He fell along the thread, a bark echoing in his ears.

Dai landed flat on the floor on his stomach. White tiles pressed cold against his cheek. He closed his eyes and enjoyed the personal fireworks display on the inside of his eyelids complete with sound. *Ridiculous.* He needed his books. Not everything could be learned on instinct. If he kept experimenting, his head might just explode.

There were painkillers in the kitchen. Eliza kept them on the top shelf of the pantry. All he had to do was get them. What was going to be worse—getting up or bringing them to him? He groaned. He had to get up. He didn't want Roan or Eliza finding him sprawled on the floor; explaining why he was here was already going to be hard enough. He'd use the lack of furniture as an excuse, say he caught a cab. He didn't care.

He waited another two breaths then forced himself up and used the wall for support and balance. In the kitchen he helped himself to four tablets, two more than he should take, but he had an extra strong headache and he was pretty sure the manufacturers hadn't taken magically induced brain implosion into account when they thought up the recommended dosage. He washed them down with a glass of milk and helped himself to bread, ham, and cheese. After his second sandwich, the vertigo was gone even if the headache wasn't, and he was almost ready to face his brother. As he walked past the living room, he tried to look nonchalant in bare feet, like he'd walked over for a visit.

Eliza and Roan looked up from the television show.

"How'd you get here?" Roan frowned.

"Long story." Dai didn't stop walking, hoping Roan would let it go and let him sleep.

Dai went into the study, closed the door, and lay down on the floor. The air mattress was un-inflated in his apartment, even though Eliza had lent him the vacuum cleaner to blow it up. The study door opened.

Dai lifted his head and glared at Roan. "I'm not up for talking."

"You can't sleep on the floor."

"Yes I can. Done it plenty of other times." He closed his eyes, waiting for the painkillers to kick in. Rapid action wasn't nearly fast enough.

The door closed, but Roan hadn't left. "You're using magic, aren't you?" Roan said softly.

"Yes." It required too much effort to deny the obvious. He didn't walk from Perth to Peppermint Grove without shoes.

Roan made himself comfortable on the floor, so Dai forced himself to sit up. The headache lodged in his temples was like a jack pushing his skull open so his brain could be examined. He was going to have to give up beer or magic. He already knew which one had to go.

"Is it safe?" his brother asked in Decangli, the language they had always spoken with each other.

That depended on Roan's definition of safe. Safe as in it wasn't going to kill him instantly, or safe as in it would never harm him?

He shrugged. "Safe enough."

"You manipulated to get your place."

"It was for rent."

"Not sale."

"A simple suggestion." He lifted his hand to stop Roan's argument. "I'm paying top price." But it still wouldn't be his for another month. Settlement took longer these days; there was more than just the exchange of money involved. And it was more complicated than he'd first thought.

"With your soul."

"No. My soul is mine. Fixed Realm magic has no price." Not for the things he was doing anyway. And Birch hadn't bothered him again so he was pretty confident he was sliding under their magical radar. All he had to do was convince them to give back his books, even just some of them—he didn't need the ones for black magic and curses anymore, and he'd be set.

"There's always a price." Roan's voice didn't hide the scars of how close he'd come to losing his soul to the curse because of his use of Shadowlands magic.

"You would have me stop?"

"I can't make you stop. But as you urged me, use caution. Do you not think there is a reason Birch still holds your books?"

They were just examining them. That's what they said—the headache spread and slithered down his spine like a snake made of ice. "What do you mean?"

"How many people do you see using magic? When was the last time you saw real magic in the Fixed Realm? Two hundred, three hundred years ago?"

"You think they are deliberately withholding my books?" Anger rose and increased the throbbing in his brain. They were his. Amassed over centuries, they were the world's biggest occult library.

"I don't know. There is a lot they don't say. Just look closely at the world. We have to fit." Roan fixed him with a stare that would have made a loyal subject squirm. He'd seen it too many times for it to have an effect.

"We don't fit." Well, maybe Roan did. He didn't.

Roan scrubbed his hand over his short hair like he was looking for a familiar dreadlock, but his fingers came away empty. "We have to try."

"I don't know how. Maybe I'm not even human? Maybe I'm something else that shouldn't be here." He was too tired to talk about it.

"You belong here. You need to find something to ground you and occupy your time."

"Someone," Dai corrected. He knew exactly what his brother was thinking, he'd had similar thoughts, but he didn't need a lover to break a curse.

Roan nodded. "Without Eliza I'd be adrift."

"Without her you'd be goblin."

Roan got up. "I know what I was, but I also know who I want to be. Do you?"

Dai had no idea. In part because he had no idea who

he was; a Decangli prince, then a slave to the general, finally a prisoner of the curse. He'd become scholar by default, a monk out of necessity, and a mage by accident. He'd learned to control his body and now, with a bit of practice, he would be able to control the world. But none of that was him; they were roles he'd been either born into or forced to play.

Dai didn't answer. He didn't have one Roan would like.

Roan looked away as if he were interested in the floor. "I'll bring you a pillow and blanket."

"Thanks." Not that he cared. If he'd had the strength left, he would have dragged his ass home and slept on the floor there.

"Just be careful tonight. I don't want to try explaining to Amanda why the lights come on randomly." Roan got up and left.

Amanda? She was still here? Dai lay back down on the floor. The sight of Amanda sleeping remained. She was upstairs, so close, yet so far away. He allowed himself a weak smile. Maybe he'd see her tomorrow.

The door pushed open, and Roan tossed a collection of blankets and two pillows at him. "What are you grinning for?"

The blankets landed on top of him.

"Nothing." Dai gave his head a small shake that he immediately regretted as his brain bounced against his skull. He started pulling the blankets around him.

Roan watched like he wanted to say something but didn't know what.

Dai tucked a pillow under his head and hoped Roan would get the hint before his head shattered and sent shards of skull flying around the room.

"We'll talk in the morning." Roan closed the door
and the room was thrown into darkness.

For the moment, Dai didn't care. He closed his eyes,
but the headache followed, hunting him like a wounded
beast. He'd overdone it, pushed himself too hard, and
reveled in the new skill. Like learning to throw knives,
once he'd grasped the concept, he'd practiced until his
arm ached, then he'd used his other hand until he was
deadly with both. He was never going to be a victim
again. But tonight, magic had got the best of him. He
wouldn't make the same mistake again.

His dreams were a tangled mess of lust and fear and
panic. Amanda's long, tanned legs drew him. Instead
of waking and screaming at his presence in her room,
she beckoned him closer and into her bed. And he went
to her without a second thought, his skin craving to be
touched by hands that wouldn't hurt. Their lips met. Her
fingers traced the scars on his body. He tasted the sweetness of her skin. But before he could lie with her, the
eagle of Rome appeared and dragged him away, tearing
him from her embrace and dropping him onto the gray,
flat, endless plain of the Shadowlands.

―〜―

*The eagle soared through the twilight, hunting him while
goblins crept through the twisted trees. Dai swung the
sword that appeared in his hand, loosening his wrist,
ready to fight. In his other hand he held a knife, ready
for throwing at the first thing that rushed him. The goblins for his gold and then his flesh. Claudius for his flesh
and then his submission.*

He didn't want to be there. He wanted to be back

in Amanda's warm bed. But the nightmare wouldn't release him. He couldn't escape; he never did. But he wouldn't surrender either, not this time. So he stood and waited for the attack to begin—last man standing to the bloody end. He'd kill the nightmare—and everything in it to get back to Amanda.

His heart pounded in his ears. Battle calm was a myth. He'd never found peace before a fight. Thoughts of death and vengeance kept him on edge. Who would reach him first tonight?

The goblins?

He could fight them. He'd done it for years. They weren't smart. They fought for greed, but there were always more climbing over the bodies of their fallen comrades to fight him until he got too tired to lift his arms. Then they would swarm over him like ants on honey, stripping off weapons and gold and then skin. He always woke before he died.

But it was easier to fight the goblins than Claudius. Claudius knew him too well...and the general never tried to kill him. That would be too easy. Too painless. There were worse things to do to a man, and Claudius knew all of them. Unfortunately, so did he. Even in his dreams there was no escape. How did he fight a memory of his own creation when the Shadowlands fed on fear and gave it life?

He turned slowly, one eye on the eagle above, waiting for it to land and become the general, the other on the creeping shadows sliding between what passed for trees. There were only two. One following the other. His eyes narrowed. One of the goblins didn't seem right. Something was wrong with this dream.

The eagle screamed and swooped, then dropped to the ground. Dai threw the knife hoping to skewer the bird, but the blade glanced off the gleaming bronze armor of the man. Claudius drew his sword and marched forward, a smile on his face like he already knew the outcome. He did. They'd had the fight too many times. Every time the end was the same.

Dai cut the air in front of him. The sword was light in his hand as he hoped he could finish what he'd started centuries ago.

Vengeance and freedom.

He drew another knife and this time aimed more carefully. He needed the knives he'd made from goblin bones. The dark magic in them always ensured their flight was true. Maybe it would take Shadowlands magic to defeat a nightmare.

Claudius laughed, knowing he couldn't be defeated. "You'll never be a man until you have a woman."

Chapter 8

Dai woke with desire corroding his veins and hardening his flesh. Revulsion at his own weakness crawled under his skin like the poisonous legs of a hundred centipedes. Immediately he tried to smother the lust with the monk's chant, but he stopped after the first few words, the echo of his Roman master's taunt ringing in his ears.

The longing for Amanda had woken him. But no woman would want him—not once they saw what was under his clothes.

White scars and black ink. Neither of which he could readily explain.

But that didn't stop him from wanting Amanda. He let the thought expand, reliving every touch they'd shared. Their hands linked, her palm warm on his thigh. She'd wanted to touch him and had expected nothing in return. The idea of taking it further, of caressing her skin and tasting her lips grew without giving rise to the old fear.

The talons wrapped around his ribs moved, running nails over the bones as if trying to keep hold. Dai grunted and rubbed the center of his chest to ease the persistent ache. The talons hadn't let go, but they'd shifted. Were they less invasive now? He tried plucking at them again, one fiber at a time, to see if he could remove the hateful grip of Rome. But they tightened as if his old master was still unwilling to release him.

Unwilling but not unable.

If they fed on hate, then the easy solution was to stop feeding them with the bitterness he'd brewed over too many years. But even for him, it was too much to ask. No. He would find another solution, a way to pry them from his body be truly free of Claudius.

Dai unrolled himself from the blanket. He couldn't lie there all morning, not if he wanted to get out of the house before anyone else woke. Would Amanda be up? He hesitated, torn between wanting to see her and being unsure about what to do next...that and he'd accidently been in her room. He glanced out the window to see the sky was still gray. Not Shadowlands gray; the sky there had too much depth and too much color variation.

He folded the blankets and placed them on the desk with the pillows. Even though he'd slept most of the night through—which almost counted as a miracle even though it was brought on by beer, magic, and pain-killers—he didn't feel up to traveling by magic. At the thought of magic his brain slid to the base of his skull like it was trying to escape. He massaged the back of his neck as if the slight throbbing was simple tension and not a lingering magic-induced hangover.

Maybe some tea and a couple more painkillers, but he'd go before Roan insisted on driving him home. Just because his brother was learning to drive didn't mean Dai had to suffer along with Eliza's car.

He padded out to the kitchen, his bare feet silent on the tiles. Around him, the house was quiet. It was a different type of quiet knowing there were people around, sleeping, than being alone. He frowned. Had he ever actually spent a night on his own? Not as a child, certainly not as a slave, or in the Shadowlands. Huh. No wonder the idea appealed.

In Eliza's jar of assorted tea bags he rummaged around until he found peppermint. Automatically he went to flick the kettle on, but he paused with his fingers resting on the switch. The kettle was noisy...he glanced at the tap. He'd only promised Roan no magic during the night. Dai shrugged and filled his cup from the tap. It was technically morning since the sun was on its way up.

He let his vision shift so he could examine the water. In the Shadowlands he and Roan had been able to purify the black liquid that had passed for water with a thought. It had taken time to learn—but the Shadowlands was always true; it responded to fear. Fearing the water was polluted made it so. Believing it to be pure, and holding no fear in his heart as he drank, turned the water from black to clear. Easier said than done when thirst was riding him ragged.

But in the Fixed Realm, water was different. Reality had a different construct. While he wasn't up to attempting any big magic, he was willing to try something tiny. He wrapped his hands around the cup and concentrated on heat and friction. Bubbles formed as the threads became active. He stopped before the water began boiling hard. No ill-effect followed. He had to master the little things, and then the big ones would follow. He knew that, but practicing it was hard.

With his cup of magically boiled tea in hand he wandered back to the living room. He looked at the sofa where Roan and Eliza had cuddled up and changed his mind; instead he grabbed the blanket off the study table, because he didn't have a coat, and went outside wearing his makeshift cloak.

Dew glistened on the grass and steam rose off his cup. In some ways the world hadn't changed too much. In the tree birds were waking, snails were creeping over the path leaving silver in their wake. If not for the faint rumble of cars, he could've been the only person in existence. He eased back into the chair of the outdoor dining set to enjoy the peace of the living world.

The tension in his shoulders eased, and he sighed. In the yard the tree with the plaque attached shook in the light breeze. The leaves whispered as if he was intruding on the morning when people should be sleeping. In his time, people would've been up, breakfast would've been cooking, kids would have been playing. He could almost hear the sounds of the tribe waking.

The door opened behind him and a gray dog bounded out. Dai sat up straight. That was the same dog that had been by Amanda's bed. The dog stopped and looked at him as if recognizing him, then took off, with a shake of its head, to the grass to relive itself. Where the dog was, Amanda was. He turned a little more in his chair, shadows dancing in the corner of his vision.

"I wasn't expecting to see you here." Amanda stood in the doorway, as if unsure whether she wanted to come out and join him at the table.

He wasn't sure if he wanted her to join him. It was one thing to dream of her, another to see her in the flesh—even if she was bundled up in a jacket against the cold. The memory of her bare legs lingered, something he shouldn't have seen without invitation.

"I wasn't expecting to see you either." So much for being gone before anyone arose.

The dog ran back and sniffed Dai's toes and up his leg. Dai offered his hand to the dog's wet nose. The dog snuffled and licked and it was disgusting. He kept his face neutral, since Amanda was watching with a faint smile on her lips, and he hoped he passed the dog test. He never had as a goblin, since dogs would attack him—hell, everything had attacked him, a creature born of shadows and misery.

"He won't bite." Amanda snapped her fingers and the dog trotted to her side and lay down.

Dai wiped his hand on his jeans. It wasn't the dog he was worried about. It was the woman who'd slipped into his dreams, and made him question the vow of chastity he'd taken over a thousand years before, who was now within touching distance. His fingertips whitened on the cup. Gods help him, he wanted to touch her. While he was sure the god who had taken his vow would release him, he didn't know if he was ready to release himself. He wasn't sure he knew what to do anymore. Was he ever?

Amanda sat so they faced each other across a corner. "So, you're staying here still?"

How to explain? The truth was probably not the best option. He took a sip of his tea as he thought of an answer.

"I stopped by late last night to pick up a few things, then crashed." More literally than she needed to know, but he wanted to tell her. He watched as an arrow of birds flew over the garden. How could he ever be honest with Amanda when there was so much he couldn't say?

It didn't seem fair to either of them. While he knew life wasn't fair, love should be.

He glanced at her bare finger, where the gold band should've been. "Do you miss him?"

Amanda's answer rolled off her tongue before she had time to think.

"Yes." It was her automatic response, and today it was empty and tasted like a lie after the thoughts she'd been having about Dai.

She looked at her hands instead of at him. "I think I do." Then she sighed and glanced back up at Dai. "I don't know anymore. That sounds bad. After Brigit was born everything was different, and while I tried to put Matt in our lives…he was never really there." It had always been just her and Brigit. "I sound horrible, don't I?"

Dai shook his head. "Maybe I shouldn't have asked."

Maybe he shouldn't have, but Amanda was glad he did. If he'd hadn't appeared in her life she'd have never noticed that her life was passing her by while she told her daughter stories about the man she'd once loved and lost before they really had a chance.

"I'd rather talk about it, have it in the open. I don't want you thinking…" God, what did she want him thinking? This was a very dangerous line of conversation after her dreams of him. Her dreams should've kept her warm for days. Skin on skin, hungry lips, greedy hands wanting more. She woke with a tightening in her belly she wasn't able to ignore, yet unable to satisfy. She hadn't had *those* kinds of dreams for years. But dreams were no longer enough to keep her happy. She wanted more out of life than imaginings of what it could've been like. He watched her with those dark eyes, and heat crept up her cheeks like she'd told him exactly what they did in her dream.

"I haven't dated anyone since Matt. Most men aren't interested when they realize I have a daughter...then if they are, I wonder why."

Amanda held her breath; she didn't know what she wanted him to say. Only that she hoped he wouldn't prove himself unworthy somehow.

Dai sipped his tea, then calmly said, "Brigit reminds me of my sister."

He'd opened a door she wasn't ready to look through. And now that it was open she was tempted. She was tempted every time she saw him, but instead of doing something, they both circled as if waiting for the other to act. There was so much she didn't know about him. But none of it mattered when all she wanted was to feel his hands on her skin.

"Eliza mentioned you had a sister."

For a second his features tightened as if he were in pain. Then it was gone, but he was too well composed. "She's dead."

Those two words said more about her death than he realized. Whatever happened wasn't easy. She doubted it was natural either. What was he seeing when he looked at Brigit? Did being around her daughter make him uncomfortable? She began uncovering more reasons why seeing Dai was a bad idea, and yet she didn't want to listen to any of them.

"I should get going." He stood, swathed in the blanket he'd wrapped around himself like a cloak. "I've a list of things to get done around my place today."

Amanda got up too, cursing herself for killing the conversation. "Maybe I'll see you around."

"I'm sure you will."

But instead of walking away, he raised his hand and his fingers grazed her cheek as if he couldn't leave without touching her first. She knew the feeling, but was resisting as if she could prove to herself she didn't want him. It was a lie.

Amanda turned her head into his touch, wanting the moment to last for as long as possible, seeking to feel the heat of his skin while awake instead of only in her dreams. She wanted to step closer, slide her hands under the blanket, and feel his arms wrapped around her. She needed to feel his lips on hers. The same need was mirrored in his eyes. But they couldn't get close because their pasts were standing in the way.

His hand fell away as he stepped back. Her fingers curled as she resisted the urge to grasp his hand and keep him with her for a moment longer. With a smile and a small incline of his head, he turned and left her standing alone.

He strode inside with the blanket like dark wings flapping behind him. He didn't move like an academic; there was something else. She frowned and touched her cheek, but the warmth of his fingers was stolen by the cold air. She snapped her fingers and Sheriff followed her inside. But while Dai's cup was in the sink, he was gone, as if he'd flown away.

—⁓—

The skeletal deer toppled over with an arrow hanging like a misshapen limb from its flank. Meryn sprinted over and tore into the carcass. He sliced open the belly and pulled out the liver, gorging on the warm flesh. Then he hacked into the wasted muscle on the haunches.

He had to move fast otherwise the deer would rot before his eyes, spoiling whatever he didn't eat. And he was starving. His stomach was tight and hollow. He couldn't remember the last time he was hungry for something other than gold.

Blood turned his hands red, washing away the gray dust he'd rubbed into his skin for camouflage. As he ate, swallowing chunks of raw meat as fast as he could put them in his mouth, he glanced over his shoulder, searching for a movement that didn't belong, a flicker on the landscape that would give away the presence of a scout on his trail. He was always looking for goblins on the vast plains of the Shadowlands.

So far he'd been lucky. He'd seen no one. But he didn't stay in one place for more than one sleep—as much as it could be called sleep. His body exhausted from running, but his mind alert to any sound and creating vivid nightmares of what the goblins would do to him when they found him. Nothing tasted better than tasty pink human, and once they smelled him they would be after him. Meryn spat out the deer meat he was chewing. He was human now.

His stomach convulsed and bile defied gravity, flowing up into his mouth. He couldn't lose the meal. It had taken too much energy to find and hunt. He swallowed hard and turned away from the already discoloring carcass. How many humans had he eaten as a goblin? He scowled as he sorted through disjointed memories.

None. He'd never joined in the feasts. Why eat when not hungry?

Yet he knew hunger and the satisfaction of a full stomach. The same way he knew thirst, and tiredness.

All weak human traits. He thrust aside unwelcome thoughts and tossed dust over the carcass. Leaving it exposed would be another clue for the goblins to follow. His hands became gray again, hiding his hated pink skin. Gray was an easy color to live with.

As a goblin he'd never been cold. He'd never thought of anything but battle and gold. As a human, all he thought about were food and warmth. If he wasn't thinking like a goblin, how could he be one?

He had to act goblin—maybe then the nightmares and screams would leave him in peace and he'd wake up gray and goblin. He knew that was a vain hope. Whatever magic made him human was going to take more than a wish to undo.

Meryn turned away from the deer's grave. He had to keep moving and put some distance between him and the kill before he stopped to rest. In the distance rose the rock spire that pierced the heavy, starless twilight.

That was where he was going. The only blot on the perfect landscape.

But in the spire dwelt a goblin so powerful he could cross between realms at will. His caves were laden with more gold than all the other goblin kings possessed. He was so strong, human queens went willingly to his side. All other goblins wanted to kill him and take his place, but none could get close enough because he lived in a fortress, surrounded by loyal goblins who would never try to usurp him.

The Goblin King was his last hope.

Chapter 9

DAI LET THE SHAKING IN HIS HAND SUBSIDE AS HE stood in the center of his empty living room. The curtain flapped where he left the balcony door open all night. He risked stepping though the fabric of reality to get home instead of being tempted by Amanda. He couldn't be around her without wondering what it would be like to kiss her, even though she was very clear that she didn't date.

That was okay. Neither did he. He wouldn't know the first thing about dating, or women, in this time…or in any time. But he'd stop questioning what he could've done differently many years ago. Seiran and he would've been found out eventually and the result would've been the same. After that he tried to become an invisible slave so no woman's gaze landed on him. He couldn't stomach the loss or the punishment. Somehow he'd failed, and Amanda's gaze had landed on him and now neither of them could look away.

And for the first time in many years he didn't want to. Didn't have to. There was no one watching and waiting for him to step out of line. The only person holding him back was himself. He ran his hand through his hair. As he moved the skin on his back rippled as if tickled by an unseen hand. He shook off the feeling. Now he was imagining her hands on him while he was awake. He wanted to hate the idea of her fingers trailing over his skin, but he couldn't. His dreams came back to taunt him. Daring him to go farther. He shouldn't have left; he should've stayed and seen what happened next. She didn't shy away from his touch. Would she have balked at his kiss?

He was half tempted to go back, kiss her, and see what would happen. But only half. Was he a Decangli warrior or a cowed slave?

Pale winter sunlight illuminated his apartment. He was neither anymore. He could be whoever he wanted. Was he what Amanda wanted? The only reason she wasn't wearing her husband's ring was because it had been taken. While he knew Amanda would want the ring back, would she put it on again if he found it?

The kid was probably just human, even though he stole gold compulsively, as the chances of finding someone actually turning goblin were slim. But he couldn't let the thought go. If the kid was truly on the path to becoming goblin, he'd be avoiding daylight as it would hurt his skin and eyes. Damn, he wished he had that linen roll he'd recorded the conversation with the priest on. This kid could be the evidence he needed to prove the old man's claims.

But he'd also recorded ways to save a human soul. Although how effective they were he didn't know since none of them had helped in breaking the curse, and he couldn't remember a single one. That was the trouble with having two millennia to learn things. He'd forgotten more than he could remember.

It was why he needed his books and scrolls and tablets. But that would mean facing Birch again, and after their veiled threat at the dead tree, he wasn't sure that was a great idea. He didn't want any danger falling at Roan's feet. He needed a better plan; so far all he had was they could keep the darker, more dangerous information and he'd get the rest. He didn't see them going for that option, otherwise they would've already handed over some of the most innocuous books. A smile twisted his lips; maybe they were having trouble reading them. Hopefully they wouldn't take as long as he had. He didn't have twenty centuries to waste now that he was human.

Around him his house remained silent. It lacked the life that Eliza's house had, her house was a home. He stared at the cream wall where shelves and books should line the room. Books he knew, and there were books written about everything. He'd even written some on goblins and curses and obscure occult practices.

"Books and bookshelves." That was what he needed to make this place his.

He showered, and as he dried he peered into his chest with the sight to examine the taloned hands gripping his ribs and piercing his heart. They had definitely moved, but had their grip eased or tightened? It was hard to tell, but if they were moving, maybe they'd drop out of their own accord like a full leech. He doubted it, though. They'd fed on him for so long, why stop? He slung the towel over the rack and dressed in his usual long sleeves and jeans, then added a jacket as an afterthought. Perth might have mild winters when compared to Wales, but the mornings were still bitter when the wind was funneled up the street.

The footpaths were already busy as people made their way around the city. Cars and buses clogged the

streets. Dai shook his head; sometimes it was quicker
to walk. He joined the people on their way to work as
they pushed into the center of the city. People veered
around an obstacle. As Dai drew level he saw what
people were avoiding. A man sat against the wall of a
takeaway shop, a hat in front of him and a few coins in
the bottom.

Dai walked past a couple of paces then turned back.
The man had the same expression he'd seen too many
times on the faces of men trapped in the Shadowlands.
One part resignation, one part futile wish that something would change; all he needed was a chance. A
quick glance at the weave of the man's body was all Dai
needed to confirm that it wasn't how the man normally
lived. The man wasn't reaching and grasping for a hand-
out; he was embarrassed and trying to be invisible—no
wonder no one else was stopping.

He couldn't go past and do nothing, so Dai opened up
his wallet and pulled out the diamond and gold earrings
Eliza gave him, one in the Shadowlands and one in the
Fixed Realm. They'd stopped him from fading to gray,
and the man could use the same luck. He dropped them
into the hat along with a few bills he had in his wallet.
He'd spent years collecting wealth and had more than
he could ever spend.

"Thank you," the man called after him.

But Dai didn't pause. He hadn't done for it for thanks.
He didn't like seeing people trapped by circumstances
they had no control over. Sometimes where planning
and praying failed, simple luck came to the rescue. If
Eliza hadn't summoned Roan, and then fallen for him,
he and his brother would be dead. Eliza was the luck he

hadn't been able to predict or manufacture despite all his study.

A couple of blocks up, Dai reached the shops. Two streets had been closed to traffic to create a pedestrian mall. Most of the stores were for clothes with a few coffee shops scattered among them, but he passed them in search of books.

The idea that a whole shop could be devoted to books was decadent considering that when he was born, none of his tribe could read. Druids had learned their craft and committed it to memory. When the Romans had arrived they'd brought their writing with them. It wasn't hard to learn.

Roan struggled, but they had years to waste in the Shadowlands so it hadn't mattered. Learning to read and write was the one good thing that had come out of being the general's pet. Knowledge was power. Power meant he was no one's slave. His lips twitched in an almost smile. He was free.

So why did he feel like he was always looking over his shoulder, waiting for his past to catch up with him? Because he could never tell Amanda the truth, and it would always be between them no matter what he did or didn't do. It would be forever lurking, waiting for an opportunity to strike. But the idea of bringing it into the light was too terrifying.

He went into the first bookstore he found and browsed the shelves. Out of curiosity and a little bit of hope he scanned the titles in the incorrectly named New Age section. There were plenty of books claiming to be about magic, but none held any real magic. There were books of spells, which if the right thought was applied could produce results, as a spell was just a focus for the magic the same way a prayer helped the follower focus his faith.

Divination was popular and probably still as inaccurate as it was in his day. Very few people could accurately predict the future, and those who could usually went mad, or gave their answers in riddles no one could decipher—not even with centuries to waste.

He gave up trying to find something that would help him get a better control over the Fixed Realm magic and instead went to look at the fiction books. There was plenty of magic in them. He'd read to escape the Shadowlands. In books, people succeeded, they beat the gods, broke curses, and defeated mythical beasts. There was a speck of truth in many of the old myths. He picked up a book about the son of a Greek god.

Guess he was one of those myths now, a tale two thousand years in the making.

"Can I help you?" A dark-haired woman smiled as her gaze slid from his eyes to the toes of his boots and back up.

Dai shifted uncomfortably. "Um." He had been enjoying wandering around instead of skulking in the shadows. "Just browsing."

"Okay, but if you need some help you only have to ask." The sales assistant paused a moment before turning away.

He walked along a few more aisles filled with history, languages and warfare before finding something that might be useful. Self-help was full of books on everything that could possibly bother a person, including three titles on dating. He knew he had issues, but did everyone? Amanda did, but that was because she'd had her heart broken when her husband had died. He wanted to be the one to put it back together, but to do that, he had to sort himself out first, and there was no book written for recovering ex-slaves who'd spent the best part of two thousand years in the Shadowlands.

He knew Amanda was interested. But as much as he liked the idea of seeing her naked, the reality was it wasn't going to happen. She might smile at him, but once she saw under his clothes…he wasn't ready for that kind of scrutiny. No one had seen his scars except him and a handful of witch doctors, wise women, sorcerers, and one dragon who'd offered to eat him when he was ready to die.

He'd outlived the dragon. Returning to her lair and finding her bones turned to stone was painful. He'd never expected to see her die. They'd had many conversations about hoarding, magic, and humans. But not even she knew half his life story. That was for him alone. Not every story should be told.

The books closed in around him. He was surrounded and he didn't know what to get. Once he would have taken everything in case he needed it later. Now the words were empty. Their promises hollow. There was nothing in these books to help him. He'd rather face the Roman army empty-handed than show Amanda his scars.

The corner of his lips curved. What he needed was a book on conquering fear.

He checked the titles again and found several, including one written by an ex-soldier—war he understood, so he selected that one, plus one on insomnia.

The tension between his shoulder blades eased. Books never failed him; he just had to know what he was looking for. He took his reference books, plus the novel about Zeus' son, and went to the register.

The sales assistant rang up the total, and he pulled out his wallet, realized he no longer had any cash, so he pulled out his credit card. Roan and he had spent their first day free arguing as only brothers could. Roan thought the name King was as much his as Dai's because the same blood ran through them. In the end it was concede or tell Roan the things that had gone on behind his back.

He forced his hand to sign, but it was still stiff and unnatural. The woman made a quick check between card and paper. To Dai's eye they didn't match—one signature a scrawl made in anger to stop a fight, and the other one that hadn't been used enough to look natural. But she smiled as she handed the card back.

"Do you know where I could buy bookshelves?"

"You could try the department store over at the mall." She handed him the bag of books.

"Thanks."

"Anytime."

Dai strolled over to the multi-story shop. They wouldn't have the kind of shelves he was used to—antiques polished from years of use. He should've brought them from the Shadowlands along with the books. They'd be wasted on the goblins. Still, any shelves were better than no shelves.

Two hours later he had a set of shelves assembled and in place. They were pale and flimsy. He crossed his arms and looked at them. They weren't even real timber, just a laminate. They certainly weren't sturdy enough to take his entire collection. He'd replace them later, when he found something more suitable, but they'd do for a time. He unpacked his purchases and put them on the top shelf.

That looked worse.

He couldn't remember the last time he had so few books. Maybe he should go back and buy some more just to fill up the space. He shook his head. He'd need the room when Birch gave back his books. The more he thought about it, the more he thought Roan had a point. There was no magic in the world anymore; he frowned. Maybe it died with the last dragon, or maybe she died when magic was replaced with science. If Birch thought that he wouldn't do magic just because he didn't have his books, they were wrong. And if they thought he'd give up, they were going to be unpleasantly surprised. He'd ring them today…he'd have to get a phone first. Damn it. He'd pay them a visit. They couldn't be that hard to find; even though he didn't have their address, he'd never had a problem locating a branch as a goblin.

His front door buzzed and jolted him out of his book dilemma.

Dai pressed the intercom. No one knew he lived here, so who would come looking? Hopefully not the real estate agent. "Hello?"

"Come downstairs and help me with the boxes." Roan's voice came through with a metallic edge. Of course, he'd taken the call from the agent and had no doubt extracted as much information as he could from her.

"Boxes?" He didn't need boxes. He glanced at the bookshelf and with a thought sent the books into the cupboard in the kitchen. He didn't want Roan checking the titles.

"Hurry up. Eliza's in a loading zone."

Dai clenched his jaw and went downstairs. Whatever Roan did, he no doubt thought he was helping. Eliza's car was parked out front of the building with a trailer on the back, loaded with ready-to-assemble furniture. Eliza waved from the car. Dai forced a smile and waved back. The house was about to be full of things he didn't need.

"You left so early this morning I didn't get a chance to talk to you." Roan handed him a box taller than he was. "We should have this done in a couple of trips."

"You shouldn't have gone to all this trouble."

"I knew you wouldn't." Roan thrust another box at him. "Have you bought any furniture?"

"Yes." Did Roan think he was incapable of living in the Fixed Realm?

"Really?" Roan hefted a couple of boxes and they went inside.

"See for yourself," Dai said as he pressed the button in the elevator.

In his apartment they put the boxes on the floor.

Roan looked at the empty shelves and shook his head as if he were gravely disappointed. "You bought bookshelves."

"It's furniture." It was his house and he didn't have to please anyone except himself.

"It's not how it's done. This isn't how people live."

"I'm not expecting company."

"You have nowhere to eat, to sit…and what are you going to sleep on? The air mattress forever?"

Dai shrugged. Better that than the furniture Roan had bought to clutter up his house.

They made a couple more trips to the car in silence then moved the boxes into the correct rooms.

One bedroom he left empty on purpose. He didn't want every space filled. Without speaking, they started assembling the bed. Then they moved onto the bedside tables. All the while Dai could see Roan running through the options of how best to get answers to his questions without starting a fight.

"I know this isn't what we're used to. I thought you could replace it when you find pieces you really like."

Their caves in the Shadowlands were furnished with stolen items from castles, items that had become antiques. Things that couldn't be replaced. He didn't care what they were worth; he liked them because they were beautiful and built to last for centuries.

"I left them in the Shadowlands." Regret was starting to creep in. If he'd expected to outlive the curse, he would've brought them. Then he'd be surrounded by familiar furniture. He was starting to miss the place—no, not the place, but the life he acquired there. He understood it, knew what was expected of him, and knew how to survive.

Roan frowned and put down the sheet of instructions. "Is there something you'd like to tell me?"

"The English instructions are on the other side."

Roan flipped over the paper, not that it mattered when the pictures were self-explanatory. "About last night."

"I won't crash the house again. I'll knock first."

"That's not it. You looked wrecked."

He had been wrecked and unable to take another step. "Beer and magic don't mix."

"You're not going to give up the magic, are you?" Roan crossed his arms. A sure sign he wasn't going to concede his anti-magic position.

"I can't. It's part of me." Dai ripped open a bag of screws and unpacked the pieces of wood. "Watch this."

Ignoring Roan's scowl, Dai put together an image of the finished bedside table in his mind. As he did that, the pieces of wood began pulling themselves together like metal to a magnet. The screws fell into place. And the table formed.

His brother stood, his lips pressed tight. "Are you sure this isn't Shadowlands magic?"

"Yes."

"How?"

"I can see how things are put together."

"So can I, but I can't make them dance like a scene from *Fantasia*."

"I can see how things are made. How they fit in the fabric which makes the world. All those texts and the knowledge. It makes sense now."

"I knew all that study wasn't a good idea."

"That learning kept me alive." The air between them shook with static. "It kept me sane and it kept me human." He'd had a purpose and reason to live when he should've quit and given into the curse.

"This," Roan pointed at the table, "isn't human."

"Well it sure as hell isn't goblin. So what does it make me?"

Roan didn't answer.

"All those people we sought help from. They could do magic. I've had the benefit of millennia of study."

"Why couldn't you break the curse? Why did you do nothing?"

Dai shook his head. How could Roan not understand? "Because I couldn't. It wasn't my curse to break. I could see how enmeshed you were in the Shadowlands. But I couldn't find a way to separate you without killing you…it's why you needed Eliza. She replaced the Shadowlands."

Roan looked away, but not before Dai saw the uncertainty and distrust. Magic caused the curse. And while Roan had used magic in the Shadowlands, it was for survival. Dai wasn't using magic to survive; he was using it because he could.

"I didn't ask for this."

"So don't use it."

Dai laughed, his hair falling around his face as he stared at the floor. He sighed and raised his gaze. "You know better than me about the lure, the temptation."

"What will you become?"

Dai spread his arms. "A hermit in a tower."

"I spent too long trying to break the curse and get my men back. All so you could have a life. You don't get to opt out."

"You're not my king anymore. I'm a free man."

Roan grunted and picked up the instructions, flicked the paper once, and went back to assembling the other bedside table.

Dai went into the living room and unwrapped the plastic from a blue sofa. He sat down on a cushion and without moving he assembled the rest of the furniture. Whether it was the lack of alcohol in his system or he was getting used to manipulating the threads he didn't know, this time his brain didn't try to crawl out of his ears. It merely pulsed and threatened a migraine if he pushed too hard, so he worked methodically, taking his time. When he was done he blinked and cleared his sight

of magic, yet the headache remained. A reminder that
working magic took energy.

When Roan came out of the bedroom Dai was waiting.
His brother looked around the now furnished apartment.

"You didn't need me."

"I'm not your baby brother anymore."

"I suppose not." Roan leaned against the door frame.
"But you're still my brother. You're family."

"I know." They would always be brothers, but they
weren't tied by duty or curse anymore. They had to find
a new way to relate to each other.

A knock on the door interrupted their awkward
conversation.

"That'll be Eliza with lunch." Roan looked grateful
for the distraction.

Dai stood, a knot forming in his gut. "I didn't buzz
her up."

Roan reached to his side, but there was no sword to
grab. And Dai had no knives handy ready for throwing.

"Don't suppose you bought any cutlery?" Dai ginned
at his brother hopefully.

"You don't have plates either, do you?" Roan moved
out of direct line of the door, his fingers curling into fists.

"Not yet." Dai opened the door, unarmed but ready
for battle.

A man in a navy blue pinstripe suit waited on the
other side. He held a briefcase in one hand, yet he was
no salesman. There was something about him that wasn't
right. The tattoos on Dai's back prickled as the protection
spell activated at the perceived threat. Power rippled up
his back, through his shoulders, and tingled at the ends
of his fingers. He knew the spell worked. It saved his ass

when he was goblin and attacked in the Fixed Realm. Was it strong enough to help him now, and what could he do with the power buzzing in his blood?

"Can I help you?" Dai blocked the door so the man would have to force his way in.

The man's tongue darted over his lip. "I think I can help you, Mr. King."

Dai didn't move. The man didn't blink.

"I'm here on behalf of Birch Trustees," the man added as if that would make a difference.

"I'd figured that." It was probably a bad idea, but Dai stepped aside and let the man into his apartment.

The man slipped past. When he saw Roan he dipped his head a fraction in a sign of respect. Word about breaking the curse must have been the talk around the office. Bet Birch had never counted on that—or having to pay out the wealth they'd amassed.

Roan's eyes narrowed. "What do you want?"

"I've come to make you an offer." The man spoke to Dai. As he did his tongue kept flickering over his lip the way a snake might taste the air. "In recognition of your generous donation, Birch would like to offer you a token of appreciation."

He opened the briefcase. Inside were neat stacks of green one-hundred-dollar bills.

The muscle in Dai's jaw twitched as he fought to remain calm. "What donation?"

"The books."

"I haven't donated them," Dai said through his teeth. The tattoos on his back warmed. He'd never used magic as a weapon, but he had no doubt he could. However using it to kill would also break one of the many vows he'd taken. He took a breath and exhaled. Calm didn't follow.

"Yes, you have," the man said slowly, as if his words could convince Dai that he had indeed donated the books.

An enchantment? This suited employee was trying to enchant him and muddle his mind? He almost laughed. Birch would have to do better than that.

"They are my books and I'm going to get them back."

"I would advise against that." His gaze didn't waver as he stared into Dai's eyes.

The enchantment rippled over his skin and beaded off like water. He could maim the man, which wouldn't technically break the oath. But it would still be wrong, and he knew it. A self-defense plea wouldn't work, as the man could stare at him all day and it would have no effect. If Birch was trying to ascertain how much magic he could use, it was probably a good idea not to show off.

He smiled, the way a wolf might at dinner. "Is that right?"

"Dai—" Roan tried to intervene.

He ignored his brother. "Why's that?"

The man took a step back as if realizing the threat. His words tumbled out as he gave up on the enchantment. "You're already using magic you shouldn't be. You are marked by more than one thread. We can track you. We know what you are doing. We are watching you." He closed the briefcase. "Been busy today, haven't you?" His tongue swept over his lip. Then he turned and faced Roan.

"A generous gift your brother is making, wouldn't you say?"

"He has nothing to do with my books." Dai tried to draw the man's attention away from Roan.

"I know, but he is here, surrounded by the remains of magic. It would be a shame for him to be implicated." The man's thin lips turned in a too-wide smile.

"For a bank, you're very interested in books." His blood was hot, fibers clouded his vision ready for him to rip the world apart and remove the man from existence. It would be so easy to do. If Birch tried to touch his brother, or Eliza, they would find out just how many sacred vows he was willing to break to protect his family.

"Magic is knowledge. Knowledge is wealth. We deal in wealth of all kinds. Take the briefcase."

"Take the case, Dai." Roan's voice was low.

Dai couldn't look at his brother without thinking betrayal. Roan should be on his side. But he wasn't. Was he affected by the enchantment, or just hoping he'd quit using magic?

"It's not a donation." He forced the words out. Birch couldn't blackmail him, and he couldn't be bought. He would go over this lackey's head and talk to someone else. He didn't need all of his books, just a few that dealt with the practicalities of magic he never had to worry about in the Shadowlands.

"I see." The man nodded.

Dai opened the door for him. The man paused and looked at Dai with his black eyes. The enchantment slid once more around him like oil on water. Then Dai realized what was odd about the man—he hadn't blinked once.

"You are playing with forces you don't understand."

"Oh, I understand." He'd forgotten more about magic than this man, if that's what he was, had ever learned.

"It doesn't matter how far you go. We can follow." The implied threat was clear. They knew he was traveling.

"What I do in my own house is my business."

"Make sure it stays that way and we won't need to talk again." The man headed for the elevators.

Dai shut the door. Putting together the furniture had used enough magic to attract Birch's attention. They'd sent someone to check on him like he was a bloody acolyte who didn't know what he was doing. He knew what he was doing, sort of, but he needed practice to relearn or remember the intricacies he'd forgotten.

"Guess I'm not getting my books." He made his words light as if he didn't care he'd lost his life's work. He glanced at Roan to make sure the enchantment hadn't stuck. It hadn't. Roan just didn't like magic, and he didn't understand what it was like to be powerless. He was born to be king and no one ever questioned his role. Dai, on the other hand, was Plan B, a bargaining chip. He was never surrendering anything to anyone ever again.

"What did he mean you're marked?" Roan stood with his arms folded and his face hard.

He wasn't going to be able to glide past with half-truths this time. Yet he tried anyway. "I have a few magical tattoos."

Roan gave a nod. "When did you get them?"

"Researching magic and curse breaking." Some people would only share knowledge once a certain level was achieved, so he'd studied and achieved and been marked as reward. A few had only marked his goblin skin. The powerful ones marked more than skin and had hurt worse than anything Claudius had ever meted out.

Dai pulled up his sleeve so Roan could see the

Sanskrit wrapped around his forearm. It wasn't magical but Roan wouldn't know that. None of the masters had had a problem teaching a goblin once they realized he had a human soul—but they'd watched their gold with the eyes of a hawk. He didn't blame them, yet once they knew he hoarded knowledge, not gold, they'd been able to freely trade ideas and systems of magic. Amongst other practitioners he'd had a degree of acceptance and respect he'd never had. Many masters of the art had tried to help. Some out of pity, some had hoped to break the curse to increase their own status. All had failed.

Roan studied the marking without touching the ink. "And the rest."

"It doesn't matter." Dai shrugged and covered his arm.

"It does matter if Birch is tracking you by them."

"Don't make me show you."

"Why can't you show me? What other secrets have you hidden?"

"If I show you, you will blame yourself." It wasn't the tattoos he didn't want to reveal. It was the scars underneath.

Roan frowned. "I already blame myself. I shouldn't have left you with the responsibility to break the curse."

"I was the obvious choice." He could read and write Latin, he had studied a little of druid law before the Romans had invaded, and his father had refused to allow him to join. He couldn't lose his second son when he might be needed if the first was killed. "I don't regret any of the tattoos; I'm proud of them and everything I did to get them."

"Then show me why Birch is targeting you."

"Not targeting, tracking."

Roan raised one eyebrow. Dai wasn't going to win

the argument unless he stepped out of his apartment and into Siberia, and Roan would probably still wait for him. That trick never worked in the Shadowlands. In his heart he always knew he'd have to face the problem. Avoiding it for close to two thousand years wasn't bad going.

Dai lifted his shirt so his brother could see the black ink and the old scars beneath. His back was worse, so he didn't turn.

When Roan said nothing, he let the shirt fall and cover the marks. Tension thickened between them as Roan digested what he saw. It wasn't the cuneiform text, or the glyphs on his ribs Roan saw. It was the scars made by a knife. The same wound reopened after it had barely healed. Shallow enough to do no damage to a useful slave, deep enough to draw blood and cause constant pain. They were just the ones made for fun. The ones made in anger or for punishment…he was lucky to have kept his balls after Seiran.

"You should've told me." Roan forced the words out between gritted teeth. He looked ready to kill, his eyes frozen shards of ice blue.

"No, brother. I couldn't. That knowledge killed our father. He saw the result by accident and launched the first rebellion." Seiran had been sold and sent away, and he'd been beaten, then his father had launched into the ill-planned battle that killed him. In that battle Roan was severely wounded and became king. If Roan had known, they would have fought before they were ready, again. Staying silent and plotting revenge was all he could do. And all that kept him going.

"You've had centuries to tell me."

"What difference would it have made once we were cursed?"

"I could have gone after the bastard."

"He was dead before we had that kind of control. It doesn't matter." He almost believed his own words. The number of times he'd planned to kill Claudius and make him suffer. The different ways he could've killed him, all of them slow. And he'd never gotten the chance. He'd never got the vengeance he needed.

"I should've protected you."

"No one could've protected me." Every scar made him who he was. All he had to do was learn to live with himself. Easier said than done when his past still gave him nightmares and was stuck in his chest and wrapped around his heart.

"So are you going to tell me about the tattoos?"

"Can't. I'm bound by oaths I have no desire to risk breaking."

Roan's lips turned into a grin. "So, you really are a powerful sorcerer."

"Possibly the last one." When he died, magic in the Fixed Realm would die with him.

The buzzer went off and Dai pushed the button.

"It's Eliza, with lunch," the female voice said.

"Come up." Dai released the button and glanced at Roan. "You swear never to tell anyone. Not even Eliza."

"I can't tell anyone. What kind of man lets his little brother take a beating in his place?"

"One who was king and had to keep his people together. I don't blame you. Be angry at Claudius, not yourself." Dai would never tell Roan the full extent. There was no point. He didn't need people feeling sorry for him. He hadn't felt sorry for himself for a long time. Better to be angry and incite rebellion.

That plan hadn't worked out so well.

But he was alive. Maybe Roan was right about one thing; he should be making the most of his second chance at life. He should see how deep Amanda's attraction ran. Dare himself to cross lines he swore never to step over again. Around Amanda, his thoughts were far from pure and celibacy lost its appeal…even though the alternative was fraught with more danger.

He opened his front door as Eliza got out of the elevator.

She looked around the apartment. "That was quick."

"When Dai puts his mind to it he can do anything." Roan kissed Eliza on the cheek and took the bags from her.

"Thank you for organizing the furniture." He smiled. His apartment was looking more like a home, like he had a life and belonged in the Fixed Realm.

"Not a problem. Roan needs the extra driving practice."

That wiped the smile off his brother's face. Mr. I'm-Fitting-In was having problems.

"You'll get there. You just have to be one with the car." Eliza gave Roan a wink as they shared a joke that didn't get a laugh out of him.

Suddenly the burger and chips were making him really hungry, so he turned his attention to eating and ignoring the happy couple getting reacquainted after only being apart for a couple of hours.

"Roan says it's your birthday on Saturday." Eliza raised her eyebrows and bit into a chip as if daring him to argue.

He didn't want to disappoint. "According to the ficti-tious driver's license."

"No, it's your birthday. I made sure Birch got it right," Roan added.

Dai kept the surprise off his face. Roan knew when his birthday was. "But not the age."

Centuries of existence in the Shadowlands had been compressed into just thirteen years. He was barely nine-teen when cursed. He'd be thirty-three instead of twenty. Birch had kept the eighteen-month age gap between the brothers and as much as they could from their old lives to make the transition easier. After living for centuries, counting years didn't seem important.

"Can you imagine an eighteen-year-old becoming king now? Or picking up a sword to defend his home?" Roan said.

Dai's lips curved up on one side. "Maybe his cell phone."

Boys were boys for much longer than they were when Roan and he were growing up. That was a good thing. No one should have that much responsibility so young.

"Birthday party at our place at six," Eliza said between bites.

"You don't have to." Really. He'd hoped it would slide past with no one noticing, the way birthdays al-ways had in the Shadowlands.

"Yeah I do. It's the first of many as a human again." Roan gave him a grin. "I assume you can get there on your own."

Dai nodded. "Six o'clock."

How many people would Roan invite to the party? Even, as he thought it, he didn't care. He only cared that Amanda would be there. And he would be ready.

Chapter 10

ELIZA SPREAD THE CHOCOLATE ICING ON THE CAKE. A proper birthday cake.

"You made a cake?" Amanda leaned against the kitchen counter.

"It's a birthday." Eliza plopped some more icing on and smoothed it around the sides. "Besides, who doesn't like cake?"

"He's an adult." She tried to remember the last time she had cake on her birthday. It was a very long time ago—and she'd made it herself because her mother didn't have time.

"Yes, but Dai's been out of civilization for so much of his life and missed so many birthdays."

"And Roan too?" Amanda waited for Eliza to brush off the question. She was very good at evading anything that came remotely close to digging into the King brothers' lives.

"For some of it." Eliza put down the knife she was using to spread icing and looked at Amanda. "Roan is *the one*."

Amanda wasn't sure she believed in *the one* anymore. Matt was supposed to have been that man. She thought he was, even after his death. Now it seemed like an empty fairy tale. There were no Prince Charmings and no such thing as undying love. Love died. Or at least faded into something less fulfilling. What she'd thought would last a lifetime burned away quickly without anyone to tend it with until she was left holding cold cinders.

"You've only known him for a few weeks." And while she'd initially encouraged Eliza to take a chance—anyone was better than Steve—now she wasn't sure. The brothers were changing everything. Roan had swept Eliza up, and Eliza wasn't even looking at the ground. And Dai...he was haunting her sleep and making her count the hours until she saw him again. But all she could think about was falling and breaking her heart. She wasn't sure she could survive that again.

"I feel like I've known him all my life." Eliza's eyes glistened.

She knew that feeling. When it didn't matter what anyone else said. When logic didn't mean a thing. She missed that. A ripple of envy coursed through her body and tightened around her heart. Eliza had a freedom she would never have when it came to men. She couldn't jump like Eliza, even if she wanted to. She had Brigit to think about. She forced a smile. Eliza deserved to be happy. "I don't want you to get hurt."

"I won't." Eliza picked up a tube of white icing and carefully began drawing a symbol on the top of the rectangle cake. "Do you think the cake looks like a book?"

"Add some lines around the sides for pages and you'll be right." Her eyebrows lowered as she realized what Eliza was drawing with the icing. "Why are you drawing a pentacle?"

"The cake's supposed to look like a book of magic." Eliza paused and glanced at Amanda. "Dai has an interest in the occult," she said as if it explained everything. Instead it raised more questions.

"What kind of interest?" Was he a nut who ran around naked under the full moon casting spells? What would he look like naked? She pushed the thought to the side. Or was he a practitioner of new-age therapies? Would he be able to help Brigit or offer any advice?

"Research."

"Oh." He wouldn't be able to help Brigit. She was just a little disappointed she wouldn't have an excuse to talk to him and see what he thought about some of the things she was trying in an effort to heal Brigit.

Eliza gave her a grin. "If you give him half a chance, he'll bore you with the rituals of a forgotten tribe. And if you're really lucky he'll tell you in their language."

"Really?" That actually sounded rather interesting. The study of people and their beliefs wasn't too far removed from what she did. While she would have loved to study something less practical, she needed to be able to get a job at the end of college because she refused to be totally dependent on Coulter money. "Doesn't it take years to learn a language?"

And Dai wasn't old enough to speak the hundreds he claimed.

"Not if you're him." Eliza turned the cake to admire her artwork. "What do you think?"

"Looks great." What did she get a man who researched mystic rituals and spoke weird languages for his birthday? "Any suggestions for a present?"

"Books."

"What kind?" She glanced at the cake again. A giant book of magic.

"Any. He loves to read. Fiction about magic or treasures or lost civilizations. He's just finished reading the Harry Potter series."

Right, about a boy who could do magic and went to school in another realm. Was Dai turning thirty-three or thirteen? Something about him didn't add up. Her search had turned up a few references to his studies and a short mention of his family. But huge chunks of time were unaccounted for, and while he could've been off in some foreign land doing something, the excuse didn't sit right. It was like she was looking at the edges of a puzzle and trying to guess at the picture. But instead of running she wanted to solve the mystery.

—◆◆—

Night slid over the city and the buildings lit up as though they could hold back the shadows. Dai waited until the sun was completely gone from the sky and no trace of its passing remained. Then he stepped through the fabric of reality and into Amanda's backyard with hardly a stumble. His inner ear was getting used to the rapid change in place, but his body was still struggling. Fingers of pain gripped his temples. He ignored them, knowing they would fade in a few minutes if he resisted the temptation to use more magic.

Amanda's house was easy to find. It was linked to her, and he could find her far too easily. Half a thought and he was halfway to her. Her house and yard were smaller than Eliza's, but filled with children's toys, from the plastic cubbyhouse to the bike and trampoline. Amanda was giving Brigit everything she could.

He turned his attention to the house and walked slowly around. Through the glass sliding doors he saw a figure sitting at the dining table, and he was ready to bet a pile of goblin gold that the person inside wasn't a cop. He took a step and appeared in the house.

A kid in a black hoodie and pants sat at the dining room table. His hands were playing with a gold chain as if it was a rosary and he was praying for salvation. It was the kid's hands that made Dai pause. They were white, whiter than skin should be, like he had no color. Dai walked around the table.

The kid jumped, and his hood fell back as he stood.

It wasn't just his hands. His hair had no color either, and his eyes were pale, so pale they could hardly be called blue. They were more like puddles of water reflecting a pale winter sky.

"What you starin' at?"

"You. This isn't your house."

"'S not yours either." His white-lashed eyes narrowed. "You Amanda's boyfriend?"

"Friend." He hadn't been a boy in a very long time. "She's worried about you."

And so was he. With the sight he could see a red thread wrapped around the boy's throat like a noose, but that wasn't the worst thing he saw when he looked at the weave of the boy. The Shadowlands ran through this kid like an extra circulatory system bleaching the color from his body and life, until only gold remained. It was like he was experiencing their curse while living in the Fixed Realm. His soul was slowly corrupting until he had no option but to give in to the greed. Dai frowned. How was that possible?

"Why isn't she here?" The boy rubbed the chain between his fingers as if holding the gold gave him comfort.

A feeling Dai was too familiar with and had come too close to giving in to. How far gone was this kid? Too far gone if he was willing to hurt people to take more gold.

"You took her ring. You scared her."

The kid's face scrunched and he dropped the tough act. "I can't help it. It was gold." His hands stopped moving as if he realized what he was doing.

"Gold's nice, isn't it? Pretty, shiny."

"Yeah. I can't help it. I always want it." He cocked his head. "You klepto too?"

Dai placed his hands on the back of a dining chair as he faced the boy who was halfway to goblin. There was something about this kid he should recognize.

"No. But I used to hoard gold."

"Where?" His pale eyes got wide as if he hoped to steal it.

The kid was goblin. All he lacked was the gray skin and yellow eyes. Why would a human soul give into greed so young? Did he not realize what would happen to him? That once he became a goblin, a true goblin, he would be soulless and condemned to the Shadowlands forever.

Dai shook his head. The gold the last of the Decangli had hoarded had been left in the Shadowlands for any goblin who could hang on to it. "I gave it away."

"You got better." The kid's eyebrows rose.

"I didn't need it anymore." No amount of gold could give him what he wanted. There was no price that could be put on freedom...or the way Amanda looked at him.

"I don't need it. I just can't stop." He dropped the

gold chain and stared at his hands. "I don't want to live like this."

The kid's words echoed in the empty house, chilling the marrow of his bones as only the Shadowlands could. Dai had heard those same words once before in Decangli—in the Shadowlands. They were the final words of a young warrior before he took his own life.

"Fane?" Dai looked more closely at the boy.

There was no physical resemblance except for the age. But the web of lines that made up his body suddenly made brutal sense. Fane had slit his throat rather than live on in the Shadowlands at the command of all who summoned them. The harsh life had broken him down until all he thought about was escaping in death. But death didn't bring him the relief he hoped for. Fane was still living the curse. Trapped in a nightmare he couldn't be free of. How many lives had he lived with the shadows chasing him?

"Flynn," the boy threw back.

"Sorry. You reminded me of someone I knew." This wasn't Fane anymore, even though he'd been fighting the curse ever since.

"Did he like gold too?"

"No." Fane had never got that far into the curse. "But he was young, about your age, and no one noticed when he was in trouble." They had all failed him and his death had been another wound for them to bear.

And here Fane was again, still dealing with the Shadowlands because he hadn't faced it the first time around. Dai studied the red thread; it was too thick to mark just one suicide. As he looked closer he saw that like a rope it was made of many fibers. With each life cut short it had thickened. The realization hollowed his stomach. Fane had taken his life many times over in an effort to be free of the curse, but that wasn't the way reincarnation worked. If the lessons weren't learned in one life, they had to be repeated. Issues would carry through and tarnish the next life. And the one after that.

He looked at Fane and saw a warning of what his future would be like if he didn't overcome his hate of Claudius. He would carry that with him. The weight of every year he lived pressed down and made breathing difficult. But knowing what he needed to address and being able to move on were two different things, otherwise he would've done it years ago.

"I can't force you to do anything." He gave the threads in the kid's body a pluck to see if they would unravel with some help, but they were stuck fast. He couldn't remove the red noose, or the Shadowlands threads, without unraveling the boy's life. Whatever was wrong with him he had to fix himself, much like when Roan was cursed. He would do more harm than good by interfering with magic, but that didn't stop him from offering advice.

"Only you can make the right choice. But if you don't go to the police, you'll find no peace. They'll keep looking for you." Dai didn't add that until he faced the effect of the curse it would be bound to him. This kid would have no understanding of any of his previous lives.

"You gonna call them?" Was Flynn looking at him hopefully?

He could, but it would change nothing. He couldn't unravel the mess Fane had made centuries ago. He wished he'd paid more attention, or done something back then. Maybe Fane would have faded, but the curse would've been completed and in death he would've been free. Instead he was stuck in limbo. The curse may have broken, but the damage lingered.

What did that mean for Anfri, Brac, and Meryn? Anfri and Meryn had given in and Brac had chosen to go down fighting. Would they be free of it or haunted by it in their next life? What damage was done to them that had to be undone? He had no way of knowing. Only that Roan and he had been lucky, very lucky. If they had taken their lives as they planned, they would've been forced to face the consequences of dodging the curse in the next life.

Dai shook his head. "You have to help yourself, Flynn."

"You came 'round to tell me that?"

"And to leave Amanda alone. Stay away from her house." He gave the kid a friendly smile, and forced out the words. "Any chance I can have her ring back?"

"I can't give it to you."

"Trade?"

"Nah, can't." Flynn pulled his hood up. "I'll be seein' you, Amanda's friend."

"Dai."

The kid stared at him for a moment too long. Did he recognize him? For a moment Dai saw the young warrior, a man old enough to swear rebellion, and then he was gone. Replaced by an uncertain kid who didn't understand why he wanted gold more than life. Then Flynn turned and slipped out the back door and into the night.

Dai locked the door and stared out into the dark yard. Around his pale reflection was black, like an extra shadow. His chest ached as if the claws were sliding over bone and rubbing them raw. He pressed his hand to his chest where the talons should poke through, but it didn't ease the pain.

The idea of having to repeat the life lessons made him sick. Despite all the knowledge he'd accumulated over the centuries, he had no idea how to break free and no idea how to help Fane. His forehead touched the cool glass. He didn't want to carry his past through to his next life, yet at the same time, letting go didn't feel right. He hated the four years he'd spent as a slave. He hated the fear, and the loathing that Claudius had created. He still hated Claudius. Forgiving him was like granting a mass murderer parole for good behavior. He closed his eyes. He knew he had to do something or he would be trapped like Fane, forever damned to repeat until he learned and changed the outcome.

Before the goblin could raise his horn, and summon help from the rest of his troop, an arrow pierced his throat. The goblin wrenched it out and removed a chunk of flesh at the same time. He had a moment to stare wide-eyed at the gore before he collapsed, his black blood staining the gray dirt.

Meryn crept over to the corpse with his eyes on the horizon, searching for other goblins. Goblins never traveled alone; there would be other scouts. He closed the goblin's eyelids, then paused. The scar on the gray face was familiar, slashing down the cheek in a puckered line. His finger traced the scar. He knew this goblin. He'd made that scar in a fight. This goblin was a scout for the troop he'd been in before he'd turned human.

Was his troop searching for him? Or was it an accidental run-in? He couldn't be sure there had been recognition in the bright yellow orbs of the goblin's eyes. Definitely shock. Had his life meant so little to the troop that he was already forgotten by his comrades?

With a numb heart, he stripped the body. He'd never mourned the loss of a goblin before and he couldn't start. Goblins didn't feel loss. He had too much feeling. Like the surface of his skin had been removed and had left him raw and unhealed. His gray skin protected him from hurt like armor. Without it, he was naked and vulnerable.

Pink in a land of gray. Human in a land of goblins.

And he needed the supplies. He could use the goblin's knife to make more arrowheads from the bones he found. He pulled the muck off his arrow and wiped it clean and checked it for damage. He grunted in satisfaction. He could re-use it. It was hard to find straight limbs on the twisted trees. A bowl made out of a bleached, white skull hung from the scout's belt. It fitted neatly into the palm of his hand. He frowned. It was a child's skull. He'd never seen a child in the Shadowlands.

How did he know what children were? Yet he knew. They were little people, little humans yet to grow up. His heart constricted in a loss he couldn't define. There was no such thing as little goblins. The frown deepened. If humans made little humans, where did goblins come from?

He didn't know the answer. And he didn't like the thought that followed. If he couldn't have been born goblin…had he once been human? His heart lurched against his ribs and the screaming in his head grew louder.

No. He couldn't give in to such wonderings.

He snapped the string attaching the skull bowl to the goblin's belt. He needed it more than the scout. He needed anything he could get his hands on since he no longer had the protection of being in a troop. A lone goblin was a dead goblin. Meryn tossed the skull onto the pile of clothes and weapons. He would go through the haul later when he'd run as far as he could.

Lastly he took the scout's pouch of gold. There wasn't much there. Not enough to give the Goblin King in payment for getting his gray skin back. He shook his head. He was prepared to give away gold to become goblin again. That didn't make any sense; he should be doing everything in his power to get more gold. He blinked and looked at the few coins. The gold shone but didn't beckon. It didn't fill him with the joy and a desire for more. He didn't want the gold. What kind of goblin didn't lust for gold? The need that had filled him, warmed him, and kept him alive was gone. It was replaced by the knowledge of what he'd done to get gold. Fighting, killing, stealing.

All were activities he'd enjoyed at the time. He was good at fighting. The best warrior in the troop. He could've become a king, each goblin troop had their own, but he didn't want that responsibility. He'd been happy keeping his troop safe, and making sure they won any battle they started. None of the others could think far enough ahead to run a campaign, but they followed orders well enough—until they saw gold. His shoulders sagged as a heavy sense of failure settled around him; he'd never been a good goblin. A good goblin would have fought and killed to become king and seize control.

He set his jaw and slammed the emotion away. Goblins didn't have emotions. They had greed. Meryn snarled. He had to act goblin, even if he didn't look like one, or he wouldn't survive the Shadowlands. He hefted the bundle over his shoulder and ran. The next goblin he came across would meet the same fate. And the next one. And the one after that. He would kill them all if it meant he could lose the human heart that pounded in his once-still chest, and feel nothing.

Chapter 11

"HOPE I'M NOT LATE." ALL EYES TURNED AT DAI'S SILENT entrance.

He was getting better at traveling. His accuracy was improving along with the distance he could cover. But translocation was a small trick compared to what he needed to fix Flynn. He risked a glance at Amanda. He'd been tempted to try and find the boy again that day and tell him the truth about the curse. But would that help or make it worse? He didn't want to cause more damage to an already unstable kid. Without his books he was guessing.

Bloody Birch.

"Not at all. Besides, we couldn't start without the guest of honor." Eliza handed him a glass of wine. "Happy Birthday."

"Thank you." He took a sip of wine but knew he wouldn't be drinking much—not if he wanted to get home without giving himself a migraine.

His brother slapped him on the back. "It's good to have birthdays again."

Roan's voice was low enough that the others didn't hear. Roan would have to wait another six months before he got to celebrate a human birthday again. He was doing everything in his power to be human and belong, and that meant dragging Dai along for the ride. How much of this was Roan doing for himself as a reminder that they were free? And how much was to celebrate Dai being another year older? Like he needed reminding.

"We've had too many," Dai said with a smile for the benefit of those watching their conversation.

Knowing too much about someone didn't always bring them closer. A little distance was a good thing. A man was entitled to secrets, but since becoming human, Dai was itching to shed the heavy cloak he'd worn for so long. He glanced at the people in the room. Eliza, who knew more than enough about goblins, Roan, who wouldn't be able to stomach any further revelations, Amanda, who he didn't want to know anything about his past in case she stopped looking at him like she was waiting for a chance to get him alone, and Brigit, who looked too much like his murdered sister for him to feel truly comfortable in her presence.

He couldn't tell any of them. He would have to keep his silence the way he always had. Be more like Roan, and act like it never happened.

Roan handed him a small package wrapped in gold paper. Not that long ago they would have been fighting over the paper simply because of its color.

"I've had it for a while." Roan's words were weighted. A while, meaning decades or longer.

Dai carefully opened up the present. A real gift. On his birthday. His throat closed as he looked at the book. *A Christmas Carol* by Charles Dickens. An old copy, but unused. The pages were crisp and the spine unbent. He opened the cover. The pages smelled of ink and glue. He scanned the inside cover; the book was a first edition. And it had been signed, by Mr. Dickens, but it was addressed to Dai. The book had been in the Shadowlands since it was signed.

"How did you get this?" It was a gift Roan had prepared for when they were free, or maybe for their death. Either way Roan had put more thought into this one gift than anyone had ever bothered over his whole life.

"A friend owed me a favor."

And it was a story for another time. His brother still had his own secrets. "Thank you."

"Me next!" Brigit rushed forward with a scroll trussed up in multiple ribbons. "Open it."

Dai dutifully untied each ribbon while Brigit hovered. He unrolled it with a flourish that would make a town crier proud and revealed his gift to everyone. It was a picture of a fairy prince, complete with wings, crown, and wand. The only fairies he knew were the ones best avoided unless he was willing to bargain with his soul. His had been spoken for by the curse, so the fairies weren't interested in helping or hindering his search for a cure.

"It's lovely. I'll stick it to the fridge." In the same way Eliza had kiddie pictures stuck to hers. That seemed to be the way these gifts were displayed.

Brigit beamed and fished out a much smaller present from her little handbag and handed it to him. He unfolded the paper, aware Amanda was watching every move he made. He lifted his gaze and gave her a small smile, which she returned, her eyes wide as if he'd caught her off guard. He didn't need his magical sight to feel the threads of attraction thickening between them. He promised himself he wasn't going to fight it; he was going to see what happened. Claudius was dead, so indulging in a little desire wouldn't get him killed no matter how unnatural it felt, or how many memories tried to spoil it.

He glanced back at the present. Tucked inside the paper was a tiny sun with a smiley face. He frowned, not sure what it was.

"It's a magnet so you can stick the picture up." Brigit took the magnet and drawing and stuck them to Eliza's fridge to prove the point.

"Excellent." This was obviously how people accumulated stuff in the Fixed Realm; they were given it for their birthdays. And it beat the hell out of stealing.

Amanda stepped forward and handed him a chunky parcel that felt like a book. "I took a guess. I hope you like it."

Their fingers touched for half a second, but the contact shimmered over his skin like a wave of heat. The look in her eyes was one he wouldn't forget, naked desire. One of them had to make the next move…it should be him. But he was enjoying the slow dance; there was no risk of failure, only the promise of what could be.

"*Viking Gold.*" A golden dragon longship, decorated the cover. For a moment, all he could do was stare. The last longship he'd seen was Brac's funeral pyre. Of all the books she could've bought, she picked one too close to truth.

He flipped the book over and read the back. As he did, his lips curved. Treasure hunters and ancient civilizations, obviously Eliza had given Amanda some hints—but how many? Had she told Amanda how she'd met Roan? Nothing Amanda had said would indicate she knew anything, and if she did, she was in safe company to talk about it. He realized he was surrounded by the only people who wouldn't think him crazy for talking about goblins, curses, and the Shadowlands.

"Thank you. I look forward to reading it." When he did he would think of her.

Her smile widened for a second before she remembered herself and drew back as if she overstepped a line. "It's the first in the series, but he writes lots of other adventure books."

Dai kept his grin in check. He doubted anything could come close to some of the tales he could tell, but it was always fun to read about someone else getting into trouble and escaping instead of being the one in danger and scrambling to survive.

"And lastly…" Eliza handed him a box.

Too light to be a book. He lifted the lid and wrinkled his nose. A cell phone. There was a reason he wasn't going to get the landline connected—he didn't want calls. Still he had to be gracious—she'd broken the curse and was making his brother very happy.

"I thought you might need a new one," she added in case he didn't got the hint.

"Yeah." Like a knife in the back. Although now he could call Birch on Monday and make an appointment before turning up at the office he'd failed to locate while walking around the city. It was there, he knew it was.

"I've programmed in some numbers already."

"Thanks." He put it on top of the books on the kitchen counter.

There was a pause and the adults all looked at their drinks as if trying to come up with a safe topic for conversation. If it was just Roan and Eliza, things might have been less awkward. Hell, if it was just him and Amanda, it would have been less uncomfortable. The way Eliza kept glancing between him and Amanda, he was beginning to feel like some kind of social experiment.

He took a drink of his wine, knowing he could always crash in the study again. "So what's for dinner?"

"Roast lamb," said Eliza.

The tension in the room dissipated, and everyone moved as if freed from the bonds that had held them in place. Brigit began setting the table with Eliza helping with the glassware. Roan shooed him out of the kitchen. There was nothing for him to do but wait.

Amanda followed him into the lounge room. "So, what did you do last year for your birthday? Where were you…Mongolia?"

Dai studied the reflection as light cut the crystal glass and scattered in the red wine. She was searching as if she knew he was hiding something. The truth hovered on the tip of his tongue; he'd been in an ice-bound tomb looking for black diamonds, but he swallowed it down.

"I don't remember too much, just sampling the local fermented yak's milk." Not a total lie, just not last birthday. He had gotten drunk on their lethal brew more than once. It was kind of expected.

She nodded. "Must be nice to have that kind of freedom. To up and go on a whim."

The wistful tone made him glance up. She was watching him. Their gazes met, then she looked away, her eyes skimming down his body before turning aside. With his scars hidden by clothes, he didn't flinch at her attention. He never thought of his travel as a freedom. It was a requirement, a duty to perform as part of his quest. But he'd seen things no one living had. Drank chocolate laced with chili in the Andes before the Spanish invaded. Joined forgotten rituals. Been to every continent. Raided tombs of heroes and villains. Shared a kill with a dragon. Sworn vows to gods no one remembered. Watched magic be worked and spoken with the dead. Left fingerprints on the pages of history—and he couldn't share any of it with her.

"It was." His life hadn't been on hold in the Shadowlands; it was just different.

"Where's your favorite place?"

"I don't know." No one had ever asked him. "Every place is unique."

Could he visit those places again? Could he still cross continents with a thought? What would she think if he told her he could take her anywhere she wanted to go?

"You've traveled the world and yet you're settling here." She raised one fine, dark eyebrow as if she found the thought to be beyond belief.

"Roan wanted me here for the wedding." If not for that, he'd never have met Amanda.

She twisted the stem of her glass. "But this isn't just a visit. You've bought an apartment."

"My family is here. Plus Perth makes a good base."

"A base?" Amanda frowned.

Before he could answer Roan appeared in the lounge room.

He smiled at Dai and then Amanda like he was breaking up an important discussion. "Come and sit. Don't let the meal grow cold."

Or rot.

But they weren't in the Shadowlands. Food didn't

decay soon after it was killed or served. And eating
would be a welcome break. Amanda couldn't ask questions with a mouthful of food. Every time she glanced
his way, or she opened her lips, he expected a question
to follow, the one that would catch him out saying something made with less truth and more lie.

Brigit wasn't as recalcitrant as her mother, for as
soon as she'd finished eating she started. "Can you do
fairy magic?"

Roan coughed as he choked on his last mouthful of food.

"No, just tricks and illusions." Dai glared at his brother.

Did Roan really think he would bandy about something
as bizarre as real magic? He picked up his fork and wiped
it clean on the napkin. Then he rubbed his fingers over the
tines for show; as he did he twisted and turned the threads
of the forks to change its shape. Amanda watched, her
breath held and lips parted. When he was done the prongs
were tied in a bow. He handed the fork to Brigit.

Her mouth hung open as she took the fork and
examined with a reverence only a child could have. His
sister wore a similar expression when given her first
real sword. Everyone else just stared as if they didn't
believe what they saw. He smiled, as if to convince
them it was all in fun.

Damn. Knotting the metal might have been too
much; he should've just bent the fork, but it was too
late now. Roan flicked him a cold glance that made the
Shadowlands seem warm and welcoming. Dai knew
what he was thinking. But as long as he kept the magic
indoors and didn't just pop up all over the place in
front of people Birch wouldn't interfere. He hoped they
wouldn't. Ice prickled between his shoulder blades. He

should've thought about that before showing off. He didn't want Birch to pay a visit to any of the people here.

"If magic isn't your specialty, what is?" Amanda found her voice again, but her eyes were wide as she looked at him as if seeing him for the first time.

"Myths. *The Occult Practices Amongst Indigenous Populations of the Northern Hemisphere* was the last book I had published." And it had been widely decried as being new-age rubbish dressed up as fact. He had cited some of his earlier, more obscure books as references, but given that some of his sources were older than he was and written in languages humans didn't live long enough to decipher, it presented a problem.

Amanda nodded and he could see her thinking. "So, you believe in magic."

"Of course. If I didn't believe, how could I have knotted the fork?" He wasn't going to lie and say magic didn't exist, because Amanda would see straight through him and explaining why magic did exist after denying it would be harder than admitting outright that it did exist.

"See, magic is real, Mom."

Amanda nodded, but her eyes didn't leave him. Her gaze hadn't lost any heat; if anything the interest he saw burned brighter.

Eliza smiled at her niece. "Of course magic is real, sweetie, but only if you believe." Her gaze lifted to Roan.

"How are you going to continue your research living in Perth?" Amanda leaned her cheek on her hand.

The cheek his fingers had touched. He wanted to feel her skin against his again…but not with all these people watching. Whatever was growing between him and Amanda needed space and privacy and time.

Dai leaned forward. He'd already decided what he was going to do with his newfound life. "I'm writing the companion book for the Southern Hemisphere." Some of the lore he needed was in his books, but he could make a start and maybe find new texts.

"Really?" Both of Amanda's eyebrows rose in graceful sweeps.

Was she interested or being polite? At least she didn't roll her eyes. Not everyone was as enthusiastic about lost cultures and lore as he was, but then his life had depended on the obsession for many decades. It was nice to talk openly about his work, instead of publishing work and hearing about its reception secondhand through reviews.

"He might be able to speak a hundred languages, but he can still kill a conversation." Roan raised his glass.

"A skill that took years to develop," Dai countered.

Roan leaned over and kissed Eliza's ear. She blushed. Amanda glanced away and her gaze met his. Her eyes were a mirror for the loss he felt. For something he'd never had and something she'd lost. Could they create something beautiful out of old hurts? The talons tightened as if they didn't want to let him go. His breath caught at the crushing pain.

"I need some air." He got up without waiting for a response, and no one rushed after him as he went out into the backyard. He shoved his hands into his jeans pockets and gazed up. A handful of stars were visible in the blue ink puddle of the sky. This spot on the well-trimmed lawn was where he'd stood a little over a week ago, knife in hand determined to beat the curse while Roan and Eliza had said their farewells. He didn't believe Roan had the strength to leave, and Dai didn't want his brother to fade and take him with him. He was glad his hand had been too slow.

Fane's battle with the curse had continued through many lives. And every time he failed. Would he break free or succumb? Dai took a breath; he had a chance to really be free, really free, and all he had to do was take it. Only he wasn't sure how.

He wasn't sure of anything anymore. Amanda was changing the fabric of his reality with just a glance and a smile. He drew the cold night air into his lungs, but the chill didn't cool the warmth in his blood. He knew what he wanted with Amanda, but did he have the courage to pursue it when it went against everything he knew? He wanted to erase the old memories and replace them with something else. He wanted to know what her kiss would taste like and what it would be like to lie with her—outside of his dreams.

Dai forced out the breath. Amanda had experienced enough grief in her life. She didn't need the weight of his ancient history on her shoulders. And whatever existed between them would have no substance without her knowing the truth. He swore in Decangli.

There was no easy way. He couldn't drop his past and be something he wasn't—no matter how tempting the idea. Maybe he should give up on the idea of trying to be normal. Around him, the trees whispered and groaned. The metal plaque on the base of the tree glinted as the leaves moved and moonlight danced across the surface.

Those men never had a chance. He closed his eyes. He was such a coward. As long as he feared himself,

Claudius would still be laughing and inflicting pain. He shivered in the cold night air. How did he remove the grip of a wraith?

———⁘———

Amanda watched Dai leave the room. It was easier to look at him than Roan and Eliza. They were so obviously in love. She could see the fire but never feel the heat. The love that she'd thought would warm her for a lifetime was now lukewarm ashes that did little to repel the cold. Until meeting Dai the embers' glow had been enough.

He lingered in her thoughts. When he spoke, she watched his lips and wanted to be kissed by him, to feel his hands on her body drawing her close. Those fingers had worked magic on the fork—she cut the thought off, but her body finished it without words. The tightness in her belly had nothing to do with how much she'd eaten, and everything to do with the man who'd slipped outside.

"Come on, Brigit, I'll pop in your DVD."

Her daughter slid off her chair and skipped into the living room, magic fork in one hand and handbag swinging from the other. The pretty pink bag looked cute, but it was all that protected Brigit from a life-threatening asthma attack. She hoped the healer they were going to see next week would be able to help. She wasn't naïve enough to think there was a cure, but she'd take even a lessening of severity. She'd take any improvement, anything to prove the doctor wrong. Brigit's asthma wouldn't kill her. She wouldn't let it. Maybe if Dai could bend a fork, he could fix Brigit's lungs.

"Which one did you pick, sweetie?"

"*Cinderella.*" Brigit took it out of her bag and handed

it over. It was her favorite. Like all little girls she believed in fairies, princes, and magic.

A sad smile formed as Amanda got the disk going. Once upon a time so did she, but the clock struck midnight, and her prince had turned into a pumpkin. Brigit was her glass slipper. A beautiful, fragile reminder of the life she could've had. She kissed the top of her daughter's head.

"No shoes on the sofa." Cream-colored sofas and children didn't mix, something Eliza would learn.

"Call me for cake." Brigit kicked off her shoes and lay down.

"I will; you can even lead the song." Because there was no way there was going to be cake without a song. Brigit would sing by herself if need be.

Brigit nodded. "But quietly because Dai has a headache."

Amanda paused. Yeah. If only it were a headache, they were easier to fix than heartache and she'd seen the look in his eyes. One she saw too often in her own.

With Roan and Eliza laughing and cleaning up, she slipped outside. She almost convinced herself it was just to make sure he was all right until she saw him. A tall silhouette in the moonlight. His back was to her, head tilted to stare at the sky as if he looked for answers to questions she hadn't asked. Her heart gave an extra beat and she knew she just wanted an excuse to be alone with him.

Her foot touched the grass with barely a whisper, and he turned. His eyes were dark wells of trouble.

"Escaping your own birthday?" she asked as she joined him.

"Guilty."

"I didn't think men worried about getting older."

Dai gave her a quick grin that didn't reach his eyes. "It's not that so much."

Amanda stayed silent, leaving him an opening he could fill, or not. Her toes gripped the inside of her low-heeled boot as she hoped he would share something with her. Something more than his love of languages and belief in magic. They were the things he showed the world, but they weren't him. They weren't what she wanted to know. She suppressed a shiver as a tendril of longing coiled around her.

"I've been out of touch with the world for too long…too obsessed with the dead and obsolete…" Dai shrugged as if changing his mind.

"I know the feeling." She'd wanted him since the moment she saw him in the church. That first glance woke her and she couldn't go back to sleep and ignore what she'd tried to forget. Desire.

He turned to face her, the moonlight catching on his cheekbone and lending him a sharper edge. But instead of running, she leaned closer. The heat of his body lessened the chill of the air. Her pulse pounded in her ears as if her heart remembered how to beat after too many years being still and was making up for lost time. Their eyes met, and for one painful moment she thought he wasn't going to kiss her and she'd misread all the signs.

Then he stepped closer. His fingers trailed up her arm and caressed her neck so softly it was as if he expected her to break. His hand slid into her hair and cradled her head. She tilted her chin to meet his lips. His mouth moved against hers, teasing and tempting. Offering a hint but not satisfying the lust that was unleashed and raging in her blood, demanding more. She didn't realize how hungry she was until she tasted him. Her lips parted, tingling from the lightest touch, and her tongue flicked against his lip. Her hand slid up his chest, hard with muscle she hadn't expected to find. Her fingers pressed against him, enjoying the sensation of feeling a man.

Dai pulled back, breaking the moment stolen out of time and place. "I'm sorry."

His gaze remained on her as he drank in the sight of her as if she was a mythical creature he shouldn't be near.

"Dai." She reached for him but it was too late. The magic was gone.

He turned and without a word he stalked back into the house. Amanda exhaled and hoped the chill of the night would cool the fever in her skin. What the hell happened?

Had she forgotten how to kiss?

No. It had barely been a kiss. An experiment, a testing of desire. Did he not like her after all? She frowned. He'd kissed her. She pressed her lips together, but the memory of his mouth remained and couldn't be erased. Why had he walked away?

The wind whipped her hair about her face as she glanced back at the house. But Dai had disappeared. What was she doing? She was playing games in the dark with a man she hardly knew while her daughter was inside watching a movie.

And yet she wouldn't take it back. For the first time in too long she felt alive instead of going through the motions and living for everyone else. She wanted something for herself. And he hadn't brushed her off. He'd apologized, as if he thought she didn't want to be kissed. No, she wanted so much more. She bit her lip.

But maybe he didn't, and that was why he'd apologized. It didn't make sense. None of it did. They were adults dancing around each other like teenagers.

She hadn't been on a date with anyone but Matt since she was eighteen.

"What do I do?" she whispered into the night. She couldn't go back, but should she, could she go forward?

Chapter 12

DAI CLOSED THE LAUNDRY DOOR TO KEEP THE CHILL out and the heat in. Amanda's touch as she'd pushed him away was burned on his chest. Why had she done that? Because he'd helped himself to a kiss. He wanted to taste her lips to see if they were as soft, as sweet, and as yielding as he thought. They were everything he dreamed. Everything he was always denied.

He leaned against the wall and pushed his fingers through his hair. He was defenseless against Amanda. One glance and he was captivated. Resisting left him shaking, but giving in was worse; like a goblin, he craved more.

More. But unlike the lust for gold or knowledge, it was hot and fast like a wildfire let loose to destroy. Destruction was all he would bring Amanda. He didn't want to know if years of cruelty soured his blood. He couldn't risk hurting her or any woman. Taking a kiss when none was offered was a sign of his poison.

Screw being normal. He wasn't even close.

He held his hand up and let his vision slip. The damage was worse than he'd thought. This was no tentative connection; instead a silken thread of sunlight passed through his hand, wove through the door and out. He knew where it ended. Amanda.

Could he pull it out like a splinter?

It didn't hurt. He turned his hand over and examined

it closer. It pulsed and glowed with a life of its own. Dai gave the thread a tug, but it remained enmeshed in the weave of his body. The bond between him and Roan was loose and pale. The bond between family was weaker but more permanent than those connections made willingly. The tie between him and Meryn was both a family bond and more, but it was gray, tainted with the Shadowlands.

He frowned and looked at the golden thread. She hadn't pulled it back despite the stolen kiss. If she hated him, the thread should've snapped.

"Why don't you like birthdays?" The little voice jarred Dai back to reality.

He looked up with his eyes still clouded by the sight and saw the tattered cloth that made up Brigit's body. Across her neck was a cut and from the cut her body unraveled. The fabric around her chest gaped, the damaged threads unable to hold her together. When they snapped she would die. Not even the long colorful threads that Amanda had wrapped around her daughter would help—no matter how much love Amanda pushed through them.

But that wasn't the worst thread he saw. Between him and Brigit was a wispy strand as fine as spiders silk. A faint blood tie. But that shouldn't be possible. Then he realized where it joined her body. Her throat. For a moment he couldn't breathe and the world seemed to stop. Brigit reminded him of his sister for a reason...she was Mave reborn and still carrying the wound he'd caused. It was no accident she was in his life again. But he wasn't sure that was a good thing. The last time they met it had ended in her death. If Mave was there to teach him a lesson, he had to learn it or he'd be damned to repeat it in his next life, and so would she.

How many lives had she lived unable to breathe properly? Waiting for him to come back and make amends? What was he supposed to do? How could he ever make up for taking his sister's life?

Heal her. Save her. She doesn't have to die this time.

"I like birthdays. Just not mine." With a slow blink he cleared his vision.

He couldn't save Brigit. His magic was unpredictable. Something as delicate as a child's body could be ripped apart with a stray thought or a misplaced string. And if he touched her, Birch would no doubt fix the outcome like they did with the tree. The image of the tree with its life cut off remained burned in his mind. Would Birch really kill a child because they didn't want him using magic? Even if they didn't, their threat was clear. They would hold him and Roan responsible. Once again their fates were tied, and he was damned no matter what he did.

"Why?" She never looked right at him. Her gaze always slid away like she couldn't bear to acknowledge his existence.

He didn't blame her after what he'd done. In the background the TV was talking to itself. "Aren't you supposed to be watching a movie?" And not talking to him.

Brigit shrugged as if she was used to getting her own way. "Why don't you like your birthday?"

Dai considered her for a moment. What could he tell her that wasn't a lie, but would satisfy her curiosity?

"It's been a while since I had a happy one." Claudius made each birthday memorable for all the wrong reasons.

"But this one is a happy one?" She smiled and nodded encouragingly.

And he was obliged to agree. "Yeah, I guess it is."

As he spoke he realized it was. He was human, with family, and a thousand miles and two thousand years away from the life he'd had. If he ever got the feel for his new life, he'd be all right. But all he wanted to feel was Amanda. He didn't care where they were. But she would. She had an established life. She had Brigit and he wouldn't do anything to upset the life of the girl who'd been his sister. He owed her that much.

She glanced behind him. "Do you want to watch *Cinderella*?"

When Dai hesitated, she snatched up his hand and pulled him into the living room. She let go when she plunked herself onto the sofa. Dai sat at the other end, but it was already too late. Another creeping tendril had invaded his body. Brigit was trying to befriend him, to strengthen the bond that already existed. Did she sense the connection they shared as brother and sister?

The movie ran unnoticed. Sitting with her, after all the time that passed, he had to remind himself that she wasn't Mave; she was Brigit now. She'd been plenty of other people over the years. Had she suffocated in every life the way Fane was lured by gold? What did it mean that they were both part of his new life? Maybe he could find a way to save them both and heal himself in the process. But that was too simplistic, and if he voiced that to any mystic they would've laughed. They were separate, yet tied events; there was no chance it was mere coincidence his past was re-forming. He'd escaped it once by being cursed. He'd have to face it. He wasn't ready. He'd never be ready.

Brigit took her eyes off the screen where the girls were getting ready for the ball. "Are you an angel?" She stared at him, challenging one of the heavenly order to lie.

"No." Those who met angels didn't tend to live long. He'd wanted to break the curse, but not that badly. Not even Roan had wanted to try that cure.

She scrunched up her face as if trying to understand. "Then why do you have wings?"

Brigit lifted her hand and pointed to a spot just over his shoulder, the place where her eyes were drawn every time she looked at him.

Dai's blood became iced mud in his arteries. He turned his head slowly. At first he saw nothing. He blinked and saw nothing with his magical sight either. But he knew children saw some of the other planes that made up existence—the ones where ghosts and shades existed. He hoped he had no extra shadow.

He relaxed as his heart pounded hard against his ribs, then stretched and glanced away. From the corner of his eye he saw the silhouette of wings. Eagle wings. He glanced at his chest where he knew the thick ropy talons wrapped around his bones. They were there, and they were attached to the ghostly wings like they were feeding them, feeding off him. Beads of frozen sweat rolled down his back. He didn't need any magical training to know the wings weren't a good sign. He had the eagle on his back. Rome was still riding him and wouldn't let him go.

Brigit waited for an explanation. He couldn't tell her it was his very own angel of death waiting to rip out his heart.

"Must be my guardian angel standing close by." Like hell. Where was it two thousand years ago when he'd needed a protector?

She smiled knowingly. "Mommy says Daddy is my guardian angel and that he'll never leave me."

Dai wished that were true, but he saw no one by her side watching over her except her mother.

"You're a lucky girl," he said, unable to look at her as his lie reinforced her belief. He stood up as Cinderella began crying in the garden. "It must be time for cake."

In the doorway Amanda stood watching them, her face unreadable. Dai drew in a breath ready to defend himself. Would she mention the kiss he stole or let it go?

"Is it time for cake, Mom?"

"It must be since it's Dai's birthday and he said it was." Amanda gave her daughter a smile.

Brigit picked up her bag and ran into the kitchen.

Amanda's green eyes assessed him. Confusion had replaced the heat. Yet, every time he looked at her lips he would remember and hunger. He'd have to live like a starving man again. He was used to that, but he didn't want her thinking he was a cad.

"I…" What did he say? "I should've asked first."

She shook her head. "You shouldn't have stopped."

"You shouldn't have pushed me away." If she hadn't, he was sure they'd still be standing in the garden and he'd be cursing himself for not being able to walk away.

Her gaze flickered over him. "I didn't."

Then she closed the distance and placed her hand on his chest the way she had in the garden and right over the talons. His breath hitched in his throat. This wasn't a good idea. He covered her hand with his not wanting her to pull away. She was close enough that he could smell the cold still clinging to her skin, feel it seeping through his shirt and into the talons that bound him to the past. He wanted her to reach in and rip them out regardless of the price. The talons scrabbled as if unable to keep a hold of his heart.

For a heartbeat neither of them moved.

Then her tongue moistened her lip. He tracked the movement. Was she waiting to be kissed again? But Amanda leaned in and kissed him.

His hands moved to her hips and drew her close. Her body against his offered all the temptations he'd denied himself out of fear. With Amanda, those old doubts wilted. Her touch was every kindness he'd forgotten existed.

Her lips brushed his for only a second before she pulled back and looked up at him smiling. "They'll be waiting."

Let them wait. But they couldn't linger. He didn't want everyone walking in and finding them like that. Yet he placed another light kiss on her lips and when she didn't stop him, he stole another. For a moment longer, they remained nose to nose. Then he released her before he lost the strength to let her go.

"Another time." Whatever was going on was on hold, not over. But the weight of the ghostly wings he was carrying remained. It was many, many years since he'd been this close to a woman—back then he'd been so young. This was different. They both knew where this was leading.

Together they walked into the dining room. On the dining room table was a chocolate cake shaped like a book. The symbol on the front was an ancient symbol of protection that most people now mistakenly associated with witchcraft and the devil. Dai raised a brow and looked at Roan. No doubt that was his idea of a joke.

If only it was a real book and he could open it up and find out what he needed. All he needed was one skin scroll on healing. He'd avoided handling it too much as he'd had suspicions he didn't want to entertain about where that skin had come from. With the scroll, he could help Brigit and Fane and maybe himself.

Eliza dimmed the lights and pulled out a lighter.

Dai glanced at Brigit. "Let me."

He snapped his fingers for effect, not out of necessity. The gold candle in the center burst into flame. When nothing else caught fire he let out a sigh. He was getting better.

Amanda smiled at him, her eyes molten in the shimmering candlelight. "Make a wish."

Dai closed his eyes, but her image stayed with him. A wish. Just one and it had to be specific. Wishes were bite-sized pieces of magic. One wish with enough intent behind it had a real chance of coming true. Eliza's wishes summoned Roan. What could he wish?

Feathers shifted and brushed against his back with a ghostly chill. Gooseflesh spread down his limbs.

To be free of Rome.

He blew out the candle.

He didn't need a wish.

He needed a miracle.

Chapter 13

AMANDA UNCLIPPED SHERIFF'S LEAD AND WATCHED AS he ran after Brigit into the playground. The dog did a lap of the equipment before settling at Amanda's feet, happy to observe while Brigit went up and down the slide. Staying at Eliza's was like a holiday for Brigit. New room, new yard, new park down the road. For Amanda it was like falling through the looking glass and into a world that was familiar yet alien. Right house, wrong man…except kissing Dai didn't feel wrong.

She leaned back on the park bench. The winter sky was blue and clear with the promise of summer not far away. Usually as she sat with the sun on her back, watching Brigit play, she was content. This morning she couldn't find calm or peace. She was an outsider in her own skin.

Her body created dreams out of one kiss that was more intense than anything she'd ever felt, even though their lips had barely touched, and turned them into cravings she hadn't experienced or wanted for years. Had she ever felt like this before? Her skin ached, her heart rushed, and a stray thought could steal her breath.

It was illogical to be attracted to a man she barely knew.

And thrilling.

When Dai looked at her, he *looked* at her. Not her clothes, not the color of her hair or the size of her boobs. Her.

Men didn't do that.

Had Matt?

The smile left her face as she scrambled through faded, scattered memories. She couldn't remember how Matt looked at her. The details of their love were blurred, so only impressions remained. No matter how hard she tried she couldn't bring back the memory. It was lost. Her throat closed and tears formed. But none fell. She'd finished crying for Matt years before. And when she stopped grieving, the edges had lost their sharpness. They couldn't hurt her, but they couldn't fill her either. When had she moved on? When had acceptance taken the place of grief? When had her heart healed enough to beat again?

Brigit came down the slide with one hand on her chest. Her lips more blue than pink. Amanda grabbed the bag and ran over, Sheriff bounding by her side as if it were a game. She helped Brigit with her inhaler and stroked her hair.

"I'm okay," Brigit said, sitting on the slide as she caught her breath.

"We should go back to Eliza's."

Brigit shook her head, her brown eyes solemn. Sometimes she looked so much like Matt it made her heart ache. Not from her loss, but his. He never had a chance to know his daughter. Amanda kissed Brigit's forehead as her panic subsided. This time it hadn't been anything to worry about, but next time…

It was her fault. They shouldn't have come to the park so early. In another hour the day would have warmed up a little more. Winter was the worst—colds, cold air, they could both trigger an attack. But Brigit wanted out and saying no had been too hard. Sometimes it was easier to go with the flow, plus getting away from Eliza and Roan for a few hours was nice. She was in their house, and they needed their space.

"Push me on the swing?" Brigit was so used to asthma that it was just a part of life.

She would never get used to watching her daughter struggle to breathe. Hopefully the healer would be able to do something. The halotherapy wasn't helping as much as she'd like. It treated the symptoms, not the cause. If the healer couldn't help there were other remedies, older and more expensive. So far they worked their way through the easy things, diet, and medication. Oils and crystals. They got through the winter with only one trip to the hospital. But it was one too many.

"Sure." She smiled, but at the back of her mind in a corner she didn't want to acknowledge she knew that she had to make every moment with Brigit count. Just in case the doctors were right.

"High."

"Yep." She slung Brigit's bag over her shoulder and followed her over to the swings. Brigit sat and let her get the swing going. Amanda fell into the easy rhythm of pushing and rocking back. Sheriff got bored and pranced over to a beagle, his tail whipping from side to side with enough force to shake his bum. He wouldn't go far, so she didn't call him back.

"Mom?"

"Mmm."

"Hailey's mom is getting married."

That would be Hailey's mom's third marriage. She never worried about what would happen if she fell in

love and got her heart broken. Maybe some people's
hearts were better built and more resilient.

"And Hailey is going to be a flower girl."

"You were just a flower girl and ring bearer for
Eliza." And she'd managed to drop the ring halfway
through the ceremony. Not that anyone minded.

"I know, but if Hailey's mom can get married again,
why can't you? Then I could be your flower girl." Brigit
looked over her shoulder, as if it were a perfectly natural
question. Perhaps it was to a seven-year-old who just
saw her aunt marry.

Sheriff came back and lay down, his sides heaving.
Amanda pushed the swing in silence.

"Mom?"

"I might, one day, if I found the right person." Could
she be that lucky twice?

"How do you know if you've found the right person?"

If adults knew the answer to that, there would be no
divorces and every marriage would be perfect and no
kids would sit in her office torn up by custody battles.

"How did Cinderella know the Prince was the
right one?"

"That's a DVD, Mom; it's not real."

Amanda missed a push as the realization her little girl
wasn't a baby anymore hit her hard, like a shove to the
chest. She didn't know what to say. The little white lies
she told Brigit were no longer working. How much longer
until she stopped believing in the tooth fairy, Santa, and
that Matt watched over her? Brigit only knew her father
from old photos and the stories Amanda had told her. She
sighed. There was no fairy godmother to help out when
things got hard, or when she didn't know what to do.

With the swing going again, Brigit was quiet for a couple pushes, but Amanda knew the next question was coming.

Brigit tipped her head up to stare at the sky. "Can we go to the beach after school tomorrow?"

"If it's not raining." In summer they'd spend every weekend at the beach. At first it was a way for Amanda to be at the places Matt had liked. It made her feel closer to him, then it'd become a habit.

How much of her life was habit and routine she'd set up to get through each day? She'd stopped living when Matt died, and she hadn't noticed. It took Dai coming along to make her see what she was missing.

Her tongue slid across her lip, remembering the soft touch of his mouth. Their first kiss. She smiled to herself as a hundred butterflies exploded in her stomach. Maybe seeing him again would break up the night's magic and reveal some of his secrets. With Brigit there, watching, they would only be able to talk and while she wanted more than that, but it was a start. To know if what they had would survive in sunlight, she was going to have to invite him to the beach.

―⁓―

By sleeping in daylight, Dai's nightmares lost some of their intensity. They became wasted shadows that let him sleep, but they denied him any pleasant dreams. The eagle shrieked and swooped.

Dai turned to face the coming attack, but instead of being in the Shadowlands about to fight he was in a room filled with sunlight. He squinted and tried to orient himself. His living room. He was on the sofa where he fell asleep. Maybe in his dream he could've killed Claudius before history repeated and his knees got dirty. Probably not. It wouldn't be a nightmare if he succeeded.

On the coffee table, his new cell phone rattled and rung. He reached out to shut it up, but the name on the screen stopped him.

Amanda. His heart paused as he remembered the kiss. Why couldn't he have dreamed of her instead? He picked up the phone and answered, wanting to hear her voice again, even though it had only been a few hours.

"Hello." His voice betrayed him; he sounded half-asleep.

"Ah, hi. It's Amanda. Did I wake you?"

He should say no. Normal people weren't stretched out on the sofa in the middle of the afternoon.

"Just catching up after last night." He could let her think he'd stayed up late to celebrate being another year older. One thousand, nine hundred and seventy. He could burn down the house with those candles.

"You stayed up?"

She'd gone to bed just before midnight and he'd left soon after.

Dai pushed his hair back. "For a bit." The truth was more unpalatable, and for Amanda unbelievable.

"I was wondering if you'd like to see some of Perth's beautiful beaches tomorrow."

Why?

The word rested on his tongue, but he swallowed it down because he knew the answer. Amanda wanted to see him. Heat blanketed his skin as it remembered her touch. Blood pooled in his groin. How could he say no when his flesh craved her touch? He didn't need to see the threads she was spinning to feel them reaching for him. Tentatively they reached out, waiting to see if he would brush them away. He didn't. He wanted to feel them run through him. Watch as they threaded through his body, leaving only pleasure, not pain. Strands no thicker than spider's silk, but a thousand times stronger. He fisted his hand. Amanda was Mave's mother in this life. His past was tangling his future and he didn't know what to do.

"Dai?"

He blinked and shook his head. "Sorry, still waking up. Which beach?"

"Cottesloe...do you want me to pick you up?"

"No." He spoke too fast. The tenuous threads pulled back like he'd slapped them. He winced. He hadn't meant to push her away. Yet a part of him whispered that would be the best idea.

You don't deserve anything; you were born a prince but you will always be my slave.

Damned if he'd listen to a man who'd died while trying to destroy the Celtic tribes of Wales. He may not be able to kill Claudius, but he didn't have to listen anymore.

"There's no need for you to come into the city. I'll meet you there."

"Okay. I'll meet you at the tea house then, say...two-ish?" The golden threads reached out and took hold. Slipping past his skin and holding on tight.

"That sounds good." Could he spend an afternoon with her and not screw it up?

"I'll see you there."

"Yeah."

Neither of them hung up. The silence rested and rose like dough with each breath.

"Thank you for inviting me." *For trying. For thinking I'm worth a try.*

"I'll see you tomorrow." Amanda hung up, and the original gold strand through his palm thickened and pulsed like a stray vein linking them together, growing stronger each time he let Amanda a little closer, building a connection that would wound them both if broken.

If he didn't want to see her hurt, he was going to have to be careful. Even that was a lie. He wanted to kiss her again. And a kiss would lead to other things. He glanced at the ink on his arm.

What he wanted was as out of reach as the sun. There could be nothing else without him first exposing what the ink failed to hide, and he wasn't sure he'd ever be ready to do that. There was too much. He rolled his shoulders and feathers rustled softly at the edge of his hearing. Some shadows didn't dissolve in sunlight.

―――∿―――

Dai looked at his reflection and shrugged. It was as close to beach wear as he got—a long sleeved shirt, jeans, and weird rubbery shoes. He wasn't taking his leather shoes anywhere near saltwater and sand. At least it wasn't summer. Not too many people would be in shorts and a T-shirt, so hopefully he wouldn't look too out of place.

He picked up his sunglasses and his cell phone. He'd discovered a new feature on it that was actually useful while trying to locate Birch's office. With a few touches he could pull up a map of anywhere in the world. With the cell phone he didn't need to have been there before, or know anyone there, to travel there. He'd failed to locate any branch of Birch Trustees—secretive thieving bastards—but finding Cottesloe beach was easy. At his thought reality opened, and he simply followed the thread to the map location and stepped out into sunlight. Someone sidestepped him but didn't question his sudden appearance. He put on his sunglasses and walked down the footpath to the tea house.

As he walked he studied the other people around him. He didn't stand out; he didn't even rate a second glance. The tension in his back eased with each step and tightened in his chest. Nerves. He could control reality, yet he was nervous about seeing Amanda without an excuse to protect him. They were meeting for no other reason than that Amanda wanted to see him. It was enough to make him want to step back into the safety of his apartment. The only thing that stopped him was knowing that Claudius would still be controlling him if he didn't face up to the attraction that slid through his blood like liquor every time he saw Amanda.

"Dai!" Brigit waved from the park bench that overlooked the beach from its own grassed terrace.

Amanda turned her head and smiled, but her lips were tight as if she was no longer sure about inviting him. That made two of them. He wasn't sure about coming.

"You found it okay?"

"The magic of technology—the globe on a phone." He gave his cell a shake. It was almost the truth. If Rome had developed that kind of technology, the world would be speaking Latin and wearing togas.

They walked down to the sand without touching, but he was aware of the swaying of her hips as she walked and the slight turn of her head as she looked at him, the sunlight catching in her hair so it shone like gold. On the beach, Brigit tipped out a bag of buckets and spades and set about constructing a castle.

Kids had it so much easier. At eight he could swing a wooden sword and hunt down dinner. He'd still had a mother then, and was eager to see if the child she was carrying would be a brother or sister—and if baby would survive. He didn't like to see his mother sad, and she always was when a baby didn't live to be named. He was glad she wasn't around to see what happened to her children. He wouldn't have been able to look her in the eye after his father's death.

Dai rolled up the cuffs of his jeans, took off his shoes, and sat. The sand was warm, not like the desert at night where the temperature dropped away to be almost as cold as the Shadowlands. He'd missed the sun. As a goblin in the Fixed Realm he was only ever able to see the world at night, because sunlight hurt. It boiled the marrow of his bones and, unless a shadow other than his own was nearby, escaping was impossible.

He leaned back on his elbows and tipped his face to the sky, but his gaze slid to the woman next to him. Amanda sat cross-legged with her eyes on her daughter. Her back was straight as if she couldn't relax. She glanced at him and caught him looking. He wanted to look away but was trapped by her gaze—he knew her sunglasses hid the heat in her eyes. But if he couldn't see her eyes, she couldn't see his. He tried creating a conversation that two people getting to know each other might have. He hadn't done that in a couple of centuries and it was a well rusted skill.

"Do you come to the beach often?"

"Most weeks. In summer Brigit has swimming lessons. The saltwater is good for her asthma."

Dai nodded. He'd read a little about asthma and understood the damage he'd seen in Brigit's body. But he also understood the cause. It was manifestation of damage done many lifetimes before. What he didn't understand was why she held onto it. There was no reason—he glanced at the child—except him. Mave had waited for him to return to the Fixed Realm and undo the damage he caused. He shivered despite the warmth of the sun.

"How are the treatments working?"

She frowned. "Eliza told you?"

"Yeah, a bit." That was better than telling her he could see the fibers that made up her daughter and that he knew she was dabbling in things older than modern medicine.

"Not good." She watched Brigit add another level to the castle. "You've been around the world and believe in magic; you must have heard of something."

Dai pressed his lips together. He should know something...well he did know what needed fixing. All those loose and broken threads needed to be mended back into a tight weave. He looked at his hands. He just didn't know how to do it. What use was magic when he couldn't help those he needed to?

"I don't know."

Amanda stared at the sand as if he'd delivered awful news. She desperately needed hope to hold onto and he'd taken it away—he couldn't do that to her. He knew that feeling, when grabbing at anything was better than holding nothing.

"I'll see what I can dig up. I'm waiting for my books, still."

"Thanks. I'm taking her to a new-age healer later this week. She specializes in aura cleansing." She flicked him a grin. "You are probably thinking I'm a little crazy."

Dai blinked and was glad the sunglasses hid most of his surprise. "No. Many cultures believe illnesses are caused by damaged to the non-visible parts of the body." Maybe this woman could help Brigit where he couldn't. If she was a true healer, he wouldn't mind going to see her and asking how she worked. And if she wasn't…how much harm would she do? "Let me know what happens."

"Really?"

"I'm curious about that kind of stuff." He shrugged, trying to make light of it. He hoped it worked. For Brigit, for Amanda, and for himself. But if his sister had carried the wound through multiple lives, there was a bigger reason. He hated not knowing what was going on.

From the corner of his eye he watched as Amanda dug her toes into the sand. He followed the line of her leg, the curve of her ankle as it peeked below her jeans.

"You know the kid I was telling you about?" Her face looked strained, like she was holding onto the news, waiting to tell him.

Dai nodded, the sun suddenly losing its warmth. He'd seen Fane, and he knew it wasn't going to be good.

"The police called me this morning."

"He turned himself in?" Dai asked, trying to hope he'd broken free and started the path to healing. Even as he spoke he knew how hollow his words were. Amanda was pale and drawn, not out of anxiety but out of sadness.

Amanda shook her head. "His father found him in the garage. He'd used a hacksaw blade to cut his throat." Her voice quivered as she spoke.

Dai closed his eyes, the sun was too bright for such a dark day. The weight of every year he spent under the curse pressed hard against his chest and stole his breath. A thousand years of study and he did nothing for Fane. He should've done more to help him. Should he have called the police and forced him to get help? But what good would that have done when every time Fane was given a chance to be free he killed himself?

How many times would he have to die before he changed—or succumbed?

If Fane failed, would Dai do any better? Or was he damned to repeat his mistakes forever?

He opened his eyes and looked at Amanda. Her mouth was turned down and her shoulders were slumped. His hand twitched, wanting to offer comfort. She'd known Fane better in this life than he had. He let his hand move so it landed lightly on her thigh.

"There wasn't anything more you could've done for him." Fane's mistakes were his own to fix. But that knowledge did nothing to quell the fresh loss clogging his throat. Amanda wouldn't understand his grief, so he swallowed it down and let her indulge in hers.

Amanda didn't brush him away; instead she laid her

hand over his, her thumb sweeping over his skin. Then she laid her head on his shoulder. "He was getting better."

She sniffed, and her body trembled as she drew in a breath.

He said nothing. There was nothing to say, so he rested his cheek on her sun-warmed hair, wishing he could've done something to save her the pain. They sat without moving, drawing strength from each other as they watched Brigit play. Amanda's fingers moved in a small circle against his wrist as she examined the ink on his skin.

"That's interesting," she said as if looking for a distraction. Her finger touched his arm and traced the line of text that wrapped around his forearm and disappeared up his sleeve. She shifted to look up at him. "May I?"

Dai resisted the urge to pull down his sleeve. His tattoos were personal. A testament to survival and magic long forgotten. He nodded and let her push the sleeve up farther.

Her fingers moved over the black letters, tracing the shape, as if she could unravel the meaning, and leaving heat in their wake. "What does it say?"

"It's Sanskrit. Roughly *forgiveness is sharper than the sword of vengeance*."

"And is it?" Her eyebrow arched over the frame of her sunglasses. She made no move to withdraw her hand.

Beneath her fingers, his skin was starting to burn as if her gentle touch could erase the words etched into his skin or soften their meaning—it was harder to forgive than to seek vengeance.

"I don't know. I was denied one and have failed at the other."

"Forgiveness is a process, not a state of being." She lifted her hand off his wrist. The words were as black and sharp and as fresh as the day they'd been pressed into him.

"That may be true, but it feels like I'm letting him off the hook," he said through clenched teeth. He didn't want to share that with Amanda. He didn't want her to see how damaged he was on the inside.

"No. Forgiving is about freeing yourself. Until you do *he* still holds the power."

He shook his head and glanced out over the ocean. "You're right."

It was a conclusion he'd been in the process of drawing. He couldn't defeat Claudius; the man didn't exist anymore. All he could do was let go of the hate. But it had kept him warm for so long, it had become part of him. If he let go, what would be left?

"This is about your sister."

"Yeah." He glanced at Brigit now digging a moat out for the castle which was more of a pointed spire reaching for the blue sky.

"Can I ask how she died?"

The secret was too heavy to hold on to, so he let it fall. "Her throat was cut."

She closed her eyes and looked away. "I'm sorry. Roan never said."

"He wouldn't." Roan was raised to be a king, not a brother, and he pushed that part of his aside as easily as he'd shaved of his dreads. "I should've protected her better."

It didn't matter how many times he'd thought it over; once he was cursed, there was nothing he could do to protect her. Before then he'd done everything he could to keep her safe.

"Were you there?"

Was he there? How did he answer that without betraying himself?

"Yes. I was there." He'd never forget the feel of the sword in his hand, or the way it cut through her flesh with too little resistance, and the coppery scent of her blood. "I should have done more."

"You can't change the past." Amanda touched his hand again, her fingers lacing with his. "Only move forward."

The breeze stirred the feathers of the wings at his back. All he had to do was let go, forgive, and be free. And he couldn't do it. He knew if he ran into Claudius on the street in another body, living another life, he would be hard pressed not to run him through with a blunt, rusted blade. A stupid thing to do. Then he would spend another life tied to the bastard. He didn't want to end up like Fane, fighting without knowing why.

Dai stood up. He'd never told the truth to anyone, and he wasn't about to spoil the day by starting now. But if he stayed and let her pluck at the strings holding him together it would be Pandora's Box all over again. Once seen, the horror could never be put back.

"Brigit, would you like some water for your castle?"

"Yes, please." She held up both buckets.

Dai took them and walked down to the sea. The water was sharp and cold, reminding him that it was winter and that summer was an illusion. He took some deep breaths and longer than required to fill the buckets. Being happy wouldn't last. Nothing good came for free, and he was damn sure he couldn't pay the penalty for falling for

Amanda. He turned around. Mother and daughter were excavating a moat for the water. He blinked slowly. When he opened his eyes, Amanda was a shining sun in the weave of the world. Next to her, Brigit wanted to shine, but her light was hemorrhaging out the tears in the fabric of her being.

Dai made himself walk up the beach. He placed the buckets down next to Amanda.

She stood, sand clinging to her jeans. "I didn't mean to open old scars." She touched his hand, her fingers finding his, and this time he returned her grip. "I know what it's like to think they are healed only to find them still raw."

"Maybe they never heal. We just learn to live with them." If she could see the blood that was on his hands, she wouldn't reach for him so readily.

Amanda kept her gaze on him. "You're going, aren't you?"

"I should." He lifted her hand and pressed her knuckles to his lips, for longer than a gentleman would. "Thank you for inviting me."

She smiled, as pink flushed her skin, and glanced down at her daughter.

He released her hand and squatted down. "That's a great castle, Brigit."

She smiled as if she knew all his secrets. "It's a goblin castle."

Yes it was. A miniature version of the rock spire Roan had ripped out of the Shadowlands to protect them from the goblins that roamed the dust. He nodded and stood back up, sure the thread between him and Brigit was growing stronger.

"Mmm, and that's the last time I let Eliza make up a bedtime story," Amanda said in a voice low enough only Dai could hear.

He couldn't keep the smile from creeping over his lips. Eliza was slipping Amanda tiny bits of truth wrapped in a bedtime story suitable for a child. "You believe in magic but not in goblins?"

Amanda laughed, then stopped when she saw he was serious. "Goblins aren't real."

"Most tales have some basis in fact once upon a time." He wanted to be able to tell her everything, but the way she was studying him, he knew that would be impossible.

"Next you'll be telling me dragons and fairies are also real."

Dai shrugged. "Every culture has dragon lore."

She opened her mouth as if to argue, and he was tempted to lean in and kiss her so he wouldn't have to listen to her deny his existence. But Brigit was watching so he did nothing, and then he hated himself for still second-guessing everything he did.

She shook her head, her hair golden in the sunlight. "True. But goblins still don't make appropriate bed-time stories."

"Agreed." While he was sure Eliza gave Brigit a highly sanitized version, goblins were quite literally the stuff nightmares were made of. "So, you'll be back home tonight?"

"I think so. I want to be. I'll see you around?" Amanda asked.

"Yeah." He hesitated, then leaned in and kissed her cheek. For a second he felt the warm brush of her lips against his skin as she returned the kiss. "I'd like that."

They looked at each other a moment longer, then he turned and walked away before the moment became too much more awkward.

He walked until he was steady enough to stop and step through the fabric into his home. His heart pounded as if he'd run the whole way. He pushed up his sleeve. Where Amanda's hand had overlaid the words ribbons of pale gold went into his skin and slid into his body. He wanted to see her light run through his veins. To see if it felt better than the bitter blood that had fueled him for so long. He wanted his heart to be in her hands, not the grip of the eagle. He sank to his knees and held his head in his hands. Her words chased his thought. He had to free himself or Claudius would always control him. The whisper in his soul echoed in his skull.

Let it go. Just let it go.

Dai reached over his shoulder. He knew the wings were there and that the talons lodged in his chest were preventing him from healing. His fingers closed around air, but he tried again. In his mind, he held the glimpse of what he'd seen. His fingers touched a silken feather with no more substance than a sigh. He pulled and it came free.

So he used both hands to rip out more, tearing at the ghost that wouldn't let him sleep. The more feathers he ripped out the more substantial they became. Blood welled. His blood since they fed off him. He didn't stop until the floor was coated in crimson blood and black plumage. It wasn't enough. His hands closed over the bones of the skeletal wings that still hung from his back, their roots in his heart. He tightened his grip ready to pull them free. The muscle of his heart gave a twinge. A stab of pain. Every tug would do him damage.

Ripping them out would kill him.

Claudius and Rome would win. And he'd have to repeat the lesson in his next life. Once was too much.

He released the bone. How did he forgive the man who took first blood? Tears formed but never fell. His vision wavered and the feathers vanished, invisible to the average human eye. His breathing rasped in his throat, pain burned in his chest as he fought with himself.

He couldn't let go.

But he could make amends. He had to fix Mave and let Brigit breathe, and in doing so he would free himself from his past. And he would give Amanda respite from worry.

He raised his eyes to his empty bookshelves. He had to speak to Birch Trustees. He needed to at least view his books and work out the intricacies of healing.

―――∾∾∾――

"What do you mean my books are in a sealed collection?" Dai paced his living room.

"Well, it's a matter of content." The voice on the other end of the line tried to soothe.

While ringing was easier than locating the office, getting a straight answer was proving difficult. He'd been shunted around and was now being stonewalled.

"What's wrong with the content? All of those books originated in the Fixed Realm. I collected them and I should have the right to view them as required for my research."

"I'm sorry, Mr. King; that's all I have in front of me on your case."

Dai gritted his teeth as the speaker's lie rubbed over his skin like wet canvas. The man didn't believe what he was saying.

"I need to view my books." One specifically. Healing Brigit was his responsibility. She had suffered the curse along with her brothers, without knowing why for too many lives.

"Ancient knowledge can't always be reintroduced into the modern world."

"I'm not introducing it. They're for private use."

"Just a moment, sir." Before he could argue further, hold music filtered down the line.

Dai stared at his empty bookcases. Well, they were almost empty. One book sat alone on the top shelf; the others were still out of sight. He touched the spine of the book Amanda bought for him. A gift given without the expectation of anything in return.

"Are you there, sir?"

"Yes." He turned his back on the gift. Amanda did want something. She wanted him. How could he give her that when he couldn't tell her the truth?

"Mr. Vexion is willing to discuss your books with you, *if* you can come to the Birch Trustee office." The speaker's smirk traveled cleanly to the cell phone.

Birch was well guarded with magic and wards that turned humans away. They only catered to clients with special needs. Banking was a real problem if one was immortal, or cursed, or couldn't go out and mingle with the human public. There were enough beings that weren't human to keep Birch Trustees busy.

"When?" Not that it mattered; he hadn't been able to find the office. He knew there were offices in all major

cities, but he also knew it wouldn't matter where he
went. He would have the same problem.

"Tomorrow at four."

Dai scribbled down the time. "Are you going to give
me an address?"

"No." The line went dead.

Chapter 14

MERYN USED THE SKULL BOWL TO SCOOP WATER FROM the dark, slick river. In the surface rippled the face of a man. He stared, and the man in the river stared back with his dark eyebrows that were drawn together beneath shaggy dark hair.

His fingers traced the shape of his face, his nose, and his beard-coated jaw. The reflection copied. He wasn't just the wrong color, he was the wrong shape. His ears were too small and round, and his nose was too short, and his eyes were too flat. He looked like a man.

A man he should recognize.

The screams from his nightmares filled his ears. He couldn't be that man. He had vanished long ago with good reason. But the reaching hands of his memories clawed at the inside of his head, wanting to be remembered. He gritted his teeth and raised his eyes to where the horizon blurred between land and sky. He was goblin, not human. Whatever thoughts broke the surface of his mind were nightmares planted by the Shadowlands. One he was gray again he would be healed.

Meryn drank without looking at his face or the color of the water. It tasted worse than it looked and left a residue on his tongue like he'd licked the digestive tract of a half-rotted deer. His stomach clenched but held onto the liquid. Hunger and thirst were human traits that had no place in the Shadowlands. He had no place here.

He shouldn't be so thirsty he was forced to drink from the slippery river. He fondled the gold in the pouch on his belt. It was cold and heavy and reassuring. Gold he knew, even if he didn't want its comfort or find satisfaction in its shine.

He spat the taste of the water out of his mouth and wiped his lips on his sleeve.

He had to gain an audience with the king of all goblin kings. The spire castle of the Goblin King rose up out of the ground as a jagged warning. Smart goblins avoided it. Those who went near it were never seen again. Did the Goblin King kill them and eat them? Did he let them join him? No one knew, and it added to the mystery of the most powerful goblin to ever walk the dust of the Shadowlands.

And he was almost there.

And when he got there?

How would he convince the king to remove this pink humanity and give him back his gray skin before he was killed and eaten?

Maybe it would be better if he was killed and eaten. His nose wrinkled at the thought. He didn't want to die. He wanted to stop the unnatural pain that had invaded his body when he'd turned human. He closed his eyes for a moment and tried to find the emptiness that had filled him.

Being goblin was easy. Gold and battle, was there anything grander?

There should be. But he didn't know what, and the memories that held the answer were too raw to explore. He didn't want to know what had caused the wound, only that it had something to do with the endless screaming.

He had to stop the screaming.

Dai's apartment was suffocating him. He needed sleep and for that he needed daylight. Crossing the globe would test how far he could travel, but he knew exactly where he wanted to go. In a step he was on his way to the Andes. Nestled into the side of an east-facing cliff was a ruined temple. No one had been here for centuries, except him. It was his place when he needed to think in fresh air without interruption. He wrapped the blanket around himself and sat in a corner out of the wind. The sun shone on his face but offered no heat. He didn't care; he just wanted the light. He was so tired. Tired of running. Tired of fighting.

He couldn't win, but he refused to be defeated and he wouldn't surrender.

His eyes closed. What other options were there?

Claudius's cape billowed out and stained the gray sky like a crimson dawn. Again they faced each other in the Shadowlands. Would there ever be a night free of his dream?

Fight. Kill him. End it. Dai swung his sword, ready to fight. But Claudius was dead. He was fighting a nightmare kept alive by the Shadowlands. At the edges of his vision a goblin crept through the blackened, skeletal trees. He risked a glance. Like last time, the goblin wasn't right. It was…it was more like a man, but he was too swathed in clothing and dust for Dai to be sure.

He frowned. His dream wasn't right. There were supposed to be goblins, heaps of them. Where were they? This dream was more like a reminder of what it had been like during the first few decades of survival. Hungry and covered in dust, hoping to blend in to the bleak landscape.

Claudius advanced, laughing. "Like old times. A boy in a man's body. You know how I like it when you fight back."

He let himself be distracted as he tried to figure out what was wrong with the dream. He stepped back several paces, keeping the distance between them constant. Dai needed to attack, stab his sword through his heart, through his neck...hell, he wasn't fussy; any killing cut would do.

He kept one eye on the not-quite-a-goblin and one on Claudius. He shifted his weight and drew out a knife for his other hand. It was cold in his palm. He glanced down. Goblin bone. When he looked up Claudius held Mave in a vicious grip.

Dai clenched his jaw but kept the hold on his weapons loose. He would not make that choice again. He circled slowly, inching closer while Claudius grinned like he'd already won. He always won no matter what Dai did.

"Stop." A hand landed on his arm, coving the Sanskrit. "Amanda?"

She smiled, and golden light burned his skin and traveled up his sword until it was ablaze. He dropped the blade then realized it wasn't hot in his hand. He glanced back at Claudius, who stalked closer, dragging Mave with him. Dai raised the knife, ready to throw and kill. He wouldn't be defenseless. Never again. He wasn't a slave to be commanded anymore. He would kill Claudius and save Mave.

"Dai." Amanda held out her hand to him. "Come with me."

She lit up the Shadowlands with her perfect light. On her body he could see her scars had healed. That didn't mean they didn't hurt, but the wounds no longer ruled her body.

"I can't." And she shouldn't be here. "I have to finish this." His voice echoed oddly across the plane.

"None of this is real."

"It is…it was." It still felt real. The fear resurfaced every time he saw Claudius, but he cloaked it in anger and used it to make himself strong.

"You can't change the past. No one has that much power."

His eyes narrowed; did he have that much power? Could he unravel the Roman invasion of his lands and save himself? What of Roan and Eliza? They'd never meet. Changing the past would unravel the present and re-create it. Even subtle changes could destroy a thousand lives and re-write history and wipe out cultures.

He couldn't go back and undo the damage without causing more.

"Get on your knees," Claudius barked in Latin. Wine soured his breath. It was always worse when he'd been drinking. For a heartbeat, Dai wanted to obey just to get it over with. Gods help him, he was weak.

He should have run the bastard through, but he'd been warned. If he did, his sister and brother would pay the price. So he'd kept his silence and fed the rebellion in retaliation.

"Trust me." Amanda's lips curved and promised sweet refuge. Behind her, the sky lightened to blue, and grass pushed through the dust as she brought the perfect beauty of Summerland and turned his nightmare to a dream.

"Obey me, boy, or I'll have you whipped."

Dai flinched. Better the leather than the blade. Claudius kept Mave in front of him as a shield.

"Dai?" Amanda's hand closed over his fist. "Don't you want me anymore?"

He stared at her. Of course he did, who wouldn't? She was beautiful, smart, and too kind to be wasting her time on the likes of him. He turned back to the man who made four years of his life worse than two thousand years in the Shadowlands. Amanda's touch warmed his skin, tempting him. He had to choose where he wanted to spend his nights.

The Shadowlands or the Summerland?

The past or the future?

Battling Claudius or with Amanda?

He lowered the bone-handled knife, not in defeat. He couldn't fight nightmares of his own creation and win. He saw that now.

But he could banish them. "You don't own me anymore."

"I will always own you," Claudius yelled as he lifted his sword to Mave's throat.

Dai sucked in a breath but refused to give into the nightmare. He shook his head. "No. I don't give you that power." He sheathed the knife and took Amanda's hand. "I am free."

The general's armor tarnished. His body caved in, crumbling from the inside as if the rot and corruption finally succeeded in eating him. The short Roman sword in his hand became dust as the body of the man who'd been in charge of slaughtering the Decangli toppled over and broke apart.

Mave stepped away from the dust and vanished.

Dai faced Amanda expecting to experience the per-fect dreams the Summerland brought. Around them the sky darkened to black, but nothing hid in the darkness seeking his blood. He opened his mouth to speak and ask why he didn't get a dream.

She kissed him gently, her lips on his for a moment. He ran his fingers ran through her golden hair and held her close, not wanting to let her go. Not ever.

"Sleep," she whispered in his ear.

And he obeyed her command.

Dai's muscles were stiff and cold. His body was scream-ing for motion. But he didn't move. Sleep clung to the edges of his consciousness. Real sleep. The restful kind that he almost forgot existed. He opened his eyes. Above him, the moon hung close to the top of the Andes. He eased his legs out into a stretch after being crossed for too long.

Pins and needles filled his limbs as his blood began to move. He raked his teeth over his lip. The effects of Amanda's kiss hadn't worn off. But he didn't fight the erection pressing against his jeans. He eased the denim and ran his palm over the hardened flesh. The lust didn't hurt, and it didn't try to tear him apart. So he let the heat in his blood remain as memories of Seiran, and everything they never got the chance to do mingled with everything he wanted to do with Amanda. He tipped his head back against the rock and let himself sink into the warmth of desire.

The talons in his chest squirmed and adjusted their hold. He clasped a hand over his heart and glanced down. He saw what he already knew—they were still there, trying to squeeze the life out of him. Claudius was gone. What did he have to do to be free?

He remembered Amanda holding out her hand to him in the dream. All he had to do was have the courage to accept what she was offering.

—◠◠◠—

Amanda thumbed the pages of Flynn's psych file, looking for a clue. He'd never appeared suicidal. What had she missed? Nothing. As Dai had said, she'd done everything she could. Sometimes people couldn't be saved; they had to save themselves. Her thoughts remained on Dai. He hadn't called her yet and she wasn't going to make the next move—it was his turn.

It was the first time she'd tried seeing anyone since Matt; maybe she was reading him wrong and he wasn't that keen. But in her heart she refused to believe that. She saw desire shimmer to the surface in Dai's dark eyes. That wasn't a trick of the light or the desperate fantasy of a woman who hadn't kissed a man since before the birth of her daughter.

If he was attracted, why was he so hesitant?

The easy answer was she was too much work, she came with an instant family with high demands. But that wasn't the logical answer. The silence was something she saw in her office every day. Each new teen who walked through her door went through a period where they tested the bonds of trust before opening up and revealing their wounds. Was that what was happening?

She pulled out more files that needed attention. If she kept busy, she wouldn't think about him. Life was much simpler without wondering if he was ever going to kiss her again—outside of her dreams. Dreams that had been disturbed by Brigit's nightmares. Eliza's stories of goblins and the Shadowlands had freaked the child out. She would have to talk to Eliza about her choice of bedtime story.

Her cell phone rang. Without looking she picked it up and answered, "Hello."

"Meet me for coffee."

Her heart jolted at the sound of Dai's voice, but she forced herself to remain calm. She wasn't fourteen. She was an adult. "I'm at work. I can't just leave."

But she wanted to. She couldn't sleep without dreaming of him. There was a moment's pause and for a second she thought he was going to retract the offer.

"When are you free?"

She might be an adult, but she was too old to play games and make him wait a few days. "I have a couple of hours free this afternoon before I pick up Brigit from school."

There went her errands and food shopping time, but there was food in the freezer. She could shop tomorrow. She could take Brigit out after seeing the healer and make it a treat with takeout dinner. Amanda closed her eyes as bubbles of excitement began forming in her belly. It was only coffee. She'd drunk coffee thousands of times before…but not with Dai. And he made everything different.

"At the tea house?"

"That would be lovely." A smile formed on her lips. "I'll see you in a couple of hours."

Amanda put her phone into her bag. It would be

the first time they were going out without Brigit. She wouldn't have to watch what she said because her daughter might be listening. And Dai wouldn't be worrying about watching the girl who looked like his dead sister.

When she got to the tea house on Cottesloe beach, Dai was already there. He was sitting at a sunny table, his hands cradling a cup. His gaze focused on the waves rolling in against the sand. His mask was down. There were no lines of tension scratching his face. She waited a moment, willing him to turn so she could catch his eyes and see how deep the water ran beneath the surface, but he was lost in his own world. He seemed different—like he'd lost substance, yet was more at ease as if just living no longer cost him.

Her lips curved as she slid onto the seat opposite him. "Hi."

Dai flinched as if she'd woken him, but he managed a smile. For the first time his gaze wasn't gridlocked with pain and secrets. They were still there, slithering among the shadows, and darting below the surface, but they didn't have control. Whatever demons troubled him were sleeping at the moment.

"I'm glad you came." His voice was warm.

A waiter came over and she ordered coffee. Dai asked for another tea, chamomile, and paid for them both. She would've argued, but he didn't seem to expect her to chip in. It was she who wasn't used to having anyone else pay. She was used to doing everything on her own.

"You don't like coffee?" she asked instead of dwelling on the reasons why he'd asked her out and what the etiquette should be.

"It doesn't help my insomnia." As he spoke she could see his guard going up as if admitting he didn't sleep was a defect.

He was telling her the things he thought she needed to know before anything else happened. The idea that the strange dance they were doing was drawing them closer was scary and exhilarating, and she had no idea how to do it without Brigit asking what was going on. Brigit was part of her life, a big part, but she needed to carve out something for herself. A few hours of being more than Mom.

She smiled and leaned forward a little. "How much don't you sleep?"

He took a sip of tea. "A lot. I find it easier to sleep during the day, but it's not the same." He turned the cup a full rotation on the saucer.

She waited to give him the chance to continue. He did.

"Last night I slept all night. I can't remember the last time I got more than a few hours."

"You must be exhausted all the time." She had a fuzzy recollection of being up half the night with a new baby, but that lasted only months, not years.

Dai just nodded.

She accepted her coffee from the waiter. The rich honey scent of real coffee perfumed the air. It was so much better than the freeze-dried supermarket stuff she had at home. The smell alone was worth the price.

"Do you know why you can't sleep?"

He glanced out the window. The fine lines at the edge of his eyes bunched. Amanda wanted to reach out and smooth them away.

"Nightmares mostly. Things I can't change."

His sister's death still kept him awake. She'd been on the beach when Matt had disappeared, but watching someone be murdered must be another level of hell. "Post-traumatic stress?"

He frowned like he'd never heard the term.

"People who've experienced a shocking event or trauma often suffer flashback, panic attacks, and nightmares." How did he not know this? "You never had counseling after your sister's death?"

He shook his head and his dark hair skimmed his shoulders. In that moment, he looked younger than thirty-three. How had he never been counseled when he was a witness?

Was he just a witness? Roan never talked about their sister. Was there a family secret Dai wasn't sharing? Did Eliza know everything about her new husband that she should?

"What about Roan?"

"He wasn't there at the time."

"Did you know her killer?"

He looked her in eye. For a heartbeat she thought she'd pressed too hard and he was about to bolt. "Yeah. I knew him well."

The coffee wasn't hot enough to remove the chill from the air around them. He was there and knew the killer. She asked even though she was sure she knew the answer. "Did he hurt you?"

"What do you think?" Then he shrugged. "He's dead now; it doesn't matter."

It was no wonder he had nightmares. But if his sister was eleven, it must have been years before. "Can I ask how old you were?"

"Nineteen." He poured himself another cup of tea with his long-fingered hands, careful and precise.

"It must have been hard on all of your family to lose her."

"My mother died soon after Mave's birth. My father…died when I was sixteen. They weren't there."

It was just the three of them, and then Dai was responsible for cutting them to two.

"I'm sorry." Her hand clasped his and he returned her grip.

The room disintegrated around her until it was just the two of them locked together. She held her breath, not wanting to damage the moment. Would he share the rest and tell her what had happened? The tips of his fingers stroked her skin so gently she had to concentrate to feel his touch. The pulse of her blood became the only sound.

His eyes darkened like light night was stealing the day. "I can't change the past, but I'm trying to move forward."

Then he was next to her, on his knees. He traced her cheek. "I want to kiss you again. I've been thinking of nothing else." His finger touched her lip, sending shivers down her spine.

The room spun back in a storm of noise and color. She couldn't breathe as longing burst through her carefully placed walls, and all the reasons why she should say no were washed away as one word left her lips.

"Yes."

Chapter 15

AMANDA LEANED DOWN. HIS FINGERS PUSHED INTO HER hair, drawing her closer. Their lips met. A touch. A taste. A tentative caress. Her eyes closed as she wished he'd continue. Her hand moved over his chest, his neck, his jaw. Stubble grazed her fingers, burning nerves as only a man could do. His tongue traced the shape of her lower lip. She tilted her head and opened her mouth anticipating more, needing more.

When the welcome invasion of his tongue didn't happen, she went after what she wanted. She sought him out, his mouth warm from the tea. Their tongues connected and the moment shattered like crystal.

Dai pulled back, smile gone, guard up.

People around them catcalled.

Her breath returned, adding oxygen to the fire that was consuming her insides and creeping up her cheeks. So many saw such a private moment.

Dai looked over his shoulder at the grinning onlookers. He got to his feet as the color drained from his face. He was going to flee. She wasn't going to let him; she wasn't going to lose him to a past she didn't understand. She grabbed her bag and his hand.

He pulled her out the door, dragging her in his attempt to escape, but not trying to escape her. Around the corner he stopped and spun her against the wall. The bricks were cold against her back, but he was warm as his body melded to hers. Every inhalation pressed them closer. Their hands still locked together against the limestone wall.

"What happened?"

"I didn't want an audience."

She caught the edge of the lie but let it pass. "Then kiss me again."

Like they were the only two people in the world. She couldn't escape her past any more than Dai could. But she had to move forward.

She relinquished control of the kiss and let him draw her into something slow that stole her breath. Her eyes closed as she sank deeper under his spell. His tongue darted over her lip and she let him in, moaning softly as his hips pressed against hers with a promise that couldn't be fulfilled.

She wanted him. It felt like she'd been waiting for him to wake her up and make her feel alive again. She forced herself to breathe. All the air smelled like him. Male, and heady. Body to body she couldn't escape and didn't want to. He placed a final kiss on her lips and drew back a fraction.

His eyes were dark but not with shadows. And his lips curved in a way that suggested he knew exactly what she was thinking.

Yet they were in the open where nothing more could happen.

"You could've invited me to your place." Her words were more breathy than she'd expected.

"I could've. Would you have come?"

She glanced away. "No."

Because she didn't trust herself to behave around him. Maybe that was the point. She shouldn't have to worry about behaving, only giving in and enjoying herself. And when it ended and she got hurt? What then? She pushed aside the voice of doubt she'd listened to for far too long. Life was too short to be afraid. Love was too precious to turn her back on it.

"Then I'm glad I didn't." And yet every part of him indicated otherwise. If they were alone there would be less clothing, and much less talking.

She watched him from beneath her lashes. "Are you going to let me go?"

"Do you want me to?"

She shook her head. But she couldn't spend the day making out with him. She had other responsibilities. "I can't stay. I have to pick Brigit up from school."

"I know." He swallowed and his fingers slid away from hers. "You're taking her to the healer today?"

"Yes." She smoothed her hair. Her lips were sensitized from being crushed for the first time in too long and her skin ached from the loss of contact.

He frowned.

"What? I thought you believed in this stuff?"

"Oh, I do. But that doesn't mean she's legitimate. Just be careful."

Amanda paused. "I always am." Like she'd do anything to put Brigit at risk. The shadows on the side of the building crept into her blood and made her shiver. "She was recommended to me."

He stepped back. "Okay. I'm sorry."

"No. I asked for your opinion. And I am cautious. If it doesn't feel right, we'll leave." She smiled at him, but the mood of the afternoon had shifted to something more serious. "You're actually worried."

He grimaced and looked out over the beach. "My understanding of healing is limited but I know it's complex. Plus magic isn't always predictable."

Amanda nodded. Her hope that it would be the cure diminished as he voiced every fear she had tried not to acknowledge.

"How dangerous is it?"

"I wish I could tell you, but my focus was curses and other magical rites."

She laughed. "Do you know how silly this conversation sounds?"

He raised one eyebrow. "Just listen to Brigit; if she doesn't like the way the magic feels to her—"

"I know." She ran her hand up his chest. She hadn't imagined the hard planes of muscle the other night. What did he do in his spare time? She kissed his cheek, skin to skin for a moment longer than needed. His hand slid over her waist, but what she wanted was his hands against her flesh. He turned his head to catch her lips in another slow kiss. Her insides were molten with a need that would have to keep for another time. "Thank you for the coffee…and the warning."

Dai walked past the nondescript building three times in his search for Birch. The only reason he kept coming back was because the building was *too* perfect. The magic was so tight there was barely a ripple of energy in the fabric. And that was the only clue. No other building had so few disturbances. Just existing caused connection and webs to form. Birch's building appeared in his sight as if it had been scrubbed clean. He shook his head with amazement. That was powerful magic, but with one flaw. It lacked camouflage. But then the average human wasn't able to see magic…or the lack of magic.

As he approached the double glass doors, the hairs along his arms spiked. A strong urge to turn away followed. He ignored it and his stomach curled up and lodged in the back of his throat. The wards were getting harder to ignore with each step. He put his hand out and pushed through air that thickened like concrete. The concentric circles on his back spun up ready to deflect any magical strike. Then the door opened with a hiss of air and the resistance vanished.

He let out the breath he hadn't noticed holding. While he was tempted to look behind him and see what he'd passed through he didn't. He kept his eyes in front like he had every right to be there and hadn't forced his way past the locks designed to keep humans away. All that and he was only five minutes late.

A security guard with all the charm of a pit bull and the grace of a Rottweiler stopped him two paces inside the door by planting one giant hand on his chest.

"I was watching you." The guard's nostrils flared and twitched. His eyes narrowed. "You think you're something special, getting in here?"

Dai tensed. The guard was the type of man who liked to abuse the little power he had. He knew the type. He maintained eye contact and didn't move, even though he wanted to rip the creature's hand off. The guard had no right to touch him. "Do you always treat clients like chew toys?"

Claws pricked through his shirt. He wanted to glance down but didn't. That would be a sign of weakness and he'd end up flat on his back with a dog on his chest. The guard curled his lip and bared a lengthening fang. At the edge of his hearing there was a growl so faint it could be mistaken for traffic.

"Who are you?"

"Dai King." His name was catching less in his throat.

The guard removed his paw and wiped it on his pants like being cursed was as contagious as the common cold.

"The boss is expecting you. You're late."

No kidding.

"Took me a while to find the place." Dai smiled and hoped it looked cold and threatening, as if he could turn the oversized humanoid guard dog into a pet rock if he wished. How much did they know about him?

The guard stepped back. "Up the stairs, second door on the left. Don't get lost," he said with a toothy grin that was anything but friendly.

Dai walked past and resisted the urge to glance over his shoulder. The guard wasn't as human as he looked, but what did he expect from a bank that dealt only in special cases? Not everyone on the globe was as human as the humans thought, and not every fairy tale monster was pretend. There was a grain of truth in many of the stories people told, no matter how hard they tried to forget it.

He shook off the prickling sense of unease that was never present when he'd made deposits as a goblin. He felt like he was intruding, like even the air was trying to push him out as he climbed the stairs. His skin pulled tight. The tattoo on his lower back spun without raising any magic. It had protected him from the druid, but not the Shadowlands magic, and not his own nightmares. In here it was useless. He was defenseless.

At the top of the stairs he paused. There were no doors, only a corridor that stretched on as far as he could see. More magic and tests. His lips thinned. Once again the acolyte searching for the truth and the reward of knowledge.

Fine. He could play their game. It wasn't a hard one. The door was where he wanted it to be.

He took several paces down the corridor. This time he did check behind him; as expected the stairs had vanished and he was in a never-ending corridor. Very unimaginative.

He closed his eyes and steadied his heart. He was where he was supposed to be. Then he knocked on the wall three times. When he opened his eyes there was a door and a handle. Before he could turn the knob the door swung open. The man, if it was a man, in the room was five feet tall in his well-heeled boots.

"Mr. King, welcome to Birch." He stuck out his hand for Dai to shake.

Vexion's hand was cold, uncomfortably so, against his flesh. Like gripping ice. His vision slipped and in the weave of Vexion's body he caught a glimpse of a tail that snapped like a whip. Dai blinked and it was gone.

"Come, sit down and we'll talk about your special cassse." This hiss slid down Dai's spine like a handful of snow.

"My books."

"Yesss, yesss, the booksss."

They sat opposite each other at a desk made of wood so dark and polished it shimmered red over black like hot coals. Like coals, it was hot to touch. Was Vexion some kind of reptile that needed the heat? Dai kept his hands away from the wood and folded them in his lap as if he had all the time in the world to wait.

Vexion rested his forearms on the surface of the desk. He shivered and his eyes widened in pleasure. "I'm impressed you found usss."

"You didn't make it easy."

Vexion's lips thinned. "We spent a lot of time debating what to do with you. Be grateful you were allowed to live. Asss for your booksss...we can't return them." Vexion gave a little shrug.

Dai put his hands flat on the table. The skin on his palms began to heat. He forced cold through his hands as if he could will the wood to cool. "I need my books."

Vexion tilted his head as if he were appraising dinner. "We let you live. It wasn't an easy, or unanimousss decision. This world hasn't seen the likesss of you since Merlin. The booksss you collected are best locked away."

While his palms grew hot, they didn't burn. "I'm not doing this for myself. There is information I need." Important information if he was going to be able to save Brigit's life and heal the damage he'd done to his sister so long ago.

Vexion dropped his gaze to the wood and then glanced back at Dai. "The fabric of society isss at risk."

"A child will die." And Amanda would break apart. He didn't want to see her hurt.

"People die. You know that."

"She is dying because of me."

"Not my problem." Vexion curled his lips. "You're chilling my desk."

Dai let thoughts of a bitter Welsh winter flow through his fingers. "Not my problem."

Vexion chuckled like this was a game. "You aren't what I expected, mage."

"Sorry to disappoint. I need access to the scroll on healing—you know the one; it's made of skin and can repair itself."

"Yesss, but do you know why it repairsss itself?" Vexion said with a grin that was anything but friendly.

Dai blinked. He didn't. Damn it. He was about to fail. Did he try for a plausible lie or admit defeat? He hadn't expected to be tested. He eased his hands off the desk and let the heat return.

"Because it embodies the magic it explains." He inclined his head in an acknowledgement that he had no idea and would defer to Vexion's wisdom, if he saw fit to share. Dai waited, not expecting an answer if he was wrong. A test failed was sometimes one that couldn't be repeated.

Vexion leaned forward. "Almossst, mage. Almosssst. The magic is in the wordsss. The wordsss have power and thusss restore the scroll whenever it isss damaged."

That had been his other answer. It was either embodiment or words. There was a third option but that scroll never appeared to be haunted or possessed. The one that bit him had been a nasty, vengeful piece of hex law. That Vexion believed him worthy of knowing the correct answer was a good sign.

"Thisss world isn't ready for magic again. Your booksss will be cared for and catalogued. Your donation to our library isss appreciated." Vexion reached into his jacket. "I'll write you a check for your trouble."

"I don't want money." He had enough; the compound interest on what they'd put away made them wealthy enough to buy a small country.

"Gold?"

Dai shook his head. "I'll give you everything I have to read that scroll."

"You don't want to do that. Trust me when I say your soul is just the start. Doesss this child mean that much to you?"

Amanda flickered in his mind. She would be fine without him, and with Brigit healed she would be happy. He would have righted his past and be free to move on in his next life. "Yes."

Roan was going to kill him if Vexion didn't first.

Vexion cocked his head at an angle too crooked for him to be anything other than not human. "You are no use dead, mage." He stood up. "The decision has been made. I hope you and your brother found our service useful, but our relationship isss at an end."

"Wait." He'd failed Brigit and he didn't even know what he'd done wrong. He'd been willing to give everything to save her and it wasn't enough. "How do I tell this child she will die?"

"You don't. If you heal her, then where will you stop? One, one hundred, one thousand? You could bring down religion." Vexion opened the door. "I wish you well. Next time you come here, you will not be allowed entry."

The idea that he would bring down the world for his own gain was laughable.

"Who is making these decisions?" Who was deciding whether he should live or die, or get his books? He tried to pull together some magic but grabbed nothing. He'd only been allowed to use a little because Vexion had permitted him. It was a charade. The whole damn place. A test to see what he knew and how he'd react.

"Good-bye, Mr. King."

He put his foot in the door. "Her death is on your hands."

"Everyone diesss. Don't pressss your cassse. You may not be able to live with the outcome." Vexion gave him a toothless grin.

A threat coated with honey. They, whoever they were, would kill him for pursuing magic. He stepped back and found himself back on the dusk-cloaked street gazing up at the building. He pressed his teeth together. If his death couldn't buy her life, what the hell could?

What was his purpose in living if he could do nothing?

He thrust his hands into his jacket pockets and started walking. As he did, the cold wind lost its sting. He wasn't walking anywhere in particular. Nothing waited for him at home. His shelves were bare. The knowledge in his head wasn't enough to heal Mave—Brigit.

Did it matter how Brigit got healed as long as she got healed?

No. Maybe there was nothing he could do and that was the point. He had to let the past be the past and move on. Behind him the bones in his back rattled in the breeze, a constant reminder of the past still casting a shadow on his life and blocking out the sun. He'd seen the specter of Claudius disintegrate, so why was he still held by the bonds of Rome? Why didn't they release him? He trudged on waiting for a solution or an idea to appear.

Amanda's words formed in his mind. *Forgiving is about freeing yourself. Until you do he still holds the power.*

He stopped and looked up from the pavement. In

front of him a church loomed, the crucifix black against the darkening winter sky. In a supposedly non-magical time there were traces everywhere. People's faith and hope and fear took shape and form.

Magic was familiar and safe. He'd lost himself in its lure for so many years. Even then he was deaf to the teachings of the wise men who'd warned him about how holding onto the bitterness poisoned his heart.

He could blame Claudius for many things he didn't want to remember, but the one that hurt the most was at his feet. He'd made the choice that now weakened Brigit. It was his hand that held the sword. Claudius gave him a choice and he fell into the trap without touching the sides or stopping to question.

His hate and fear never let him see the other option. He could have let Mave live. That was on him, not Claudius, not the druid's curse. That choice was still creating ripples of anguish and doing damage he couldn't undo.

His feet moved up the path toward the church. Inside it was silent. Whispers left traces on the air like incense. Here was the home of the most powerful God that lived—for the moment. Feeding on people's will He had a life of his own, sustained by prayer. Like all gods He would eventually fade when people's beliefs changed and a new god would rise to power. This God had been a fledgling power when Dai was born. Could He help now?

He sat on the bench seat and rested his forearms on the back of the pew in front of him, then laid his head down. He wanted to shake off the past as easily as Roan did. Roan had washed his hands and the stain of blood

and gray was gone. Dai closed his eyes. He wanted a
future. He wanted everything that had been taken from
him. But his hands had done the snatching. He'd lost
Seiran because they had been careless. Mave because
he was blinded by rage and venom.

He didn't want to make the same mistakes again. His
life was so worthless Birch wouldn't take it in exchange
for Brigit's.

"Are you all right, son?"

Dai raised his head. A man in his fifties, dressed in
the robes of a priest, gazed down at him. But the face
Dai saw was that of his father. His father's sharp blue
eyes had seen everything Dai was trying to keep hidden
to prevent a battle the Decangli couldn't win. Unable to
stand what he saw his youngest son becoming, he led a
rushed rebellion and died pointlessly. His sons were left
wounded and struggling to keep their people together. At
least he didn't have to watch his sons become goblins.

"I haven't been all right in a very long time."

The priest's face remained smooth and neutral. It
lacked the lines and hardness and scars his father's had
developed. This man was no Celtic king, and no longer
his father—even though he still led people and cared for
their well-being. Some habits lasted through many lives.

"The Lord is forgiving. Can I ask what brought you
into his house?"

Dai couldn't answer. The swelling in his throat
prevented the words from forming. His father had
never spoke so softly, not after his mother's death. He
forced the lump down. He would admit his mistake
and hope Amanda was right. That he held the power
to free himself.

"Do you hear confession?"

The priest nodded. "How long since your last confession?'

Would he hear his confession if he'd never been baptized? The priest understood his silence.

"Have you ever confessed before, son?"

"No." This crime had never been spoken aloud.

"But you have faith and a need for God's forgiveness?"

Would God forgive him? None of the gods had cared when they were cursed. Some had acknowledged Roan and Eliza's vows. Not even God had the power to make right what he'd screwed up.

"Yes."

"That is a start." The priest led him down the aisle and around the side to his office. On one side was a bookcase filled with Bibles. He scanned the names, but none of them were the version he'd read. Maybe that got lost beneath the weight of time.

Dai sat and folded his hands in his lap. In here the whispers were louder, like the rustling of leaves as they forgot the green of summer and gave into the red of autumn, waiting to fall from the tree and return to the earth.

The priest made the sign of the cross. "Are you ready?"

Dai nodded. He was silent as he tried to find the right words. The priest waited, his face calm in a way his father's never had been. There was no kind way to say what he'd done. After two thousand years and a thousand languages all he had were four words.

"I killed my sister." The words didn't tear out his throat as he'd expected.

"Murder is a serious crime," the priest said without

judgment. But his eyes assessed Dai again as if looking for a threat.

"I know…I believed the alternative to be worse."

The priest inclined his head, willing to hear the full story before casting him out. "What, son, was the alternative?"

Dai squeezed his eyes shut, fighting the memories that wanted to be viewed again and again like a broken horror film stuck on a loop of violence. He could skip to the end, but it would have no meaning without the start.

"I couldn't let Claudius…" The words locked in his throat. He couldn't say it. Not to the man who looked like a softer version of the man who'd tried to save him and died for his troubles.

"Let Claudius do what, son?"

What would his father say once the truth was out? Suspicion was one thing, truth was another. He shook his head. This man wasn't his father, this man didn't know him. It didn't matter what he knew.

"I let him use me. I kept his hands off her for four years." Took everything like the man he was supposed to be. Old enough to swing a sword, old enough to be a hostage and slave. Young enough to accept the cruelty from a man who'd do anything for a scream. "At the end he gave me a choice. Her life in his hands, or her death by mine."

The priest blinked, but Dai saw the flicker of abhorrence pass in his eyes. The priest understood.

"Did you go to the authorities?"

"He was the authority." Dai clenched his fists to stop the tremor.

The priest was silent for a long moment. "Have you killed since?"

"No, father." Not in the way the priest meant. He hadn't murdered. Those that died in battle expected to.

"Do you believe you did the right thing by taking your sister's life?"

Dai looked at his hands. What kind of a question was that? There was no one answer, no right answer—that didn't mean there wasn't a wrong answer. "I thought it was at the time. But after..." The red of her blood on the sword and the way her body had fallen to the floor as if she were a worthless piece of rag. "I don't think so. I don't know. I didn't want her to suffer."

Yet she had, through too many lives because of one cut made out of fear.

"Yet you killed her."

"She was eleven. He would have destroyed her."

The priest rested his elbows on the table and brought his hands together. "I must pray for guidance. You must pray for forgiveness."

With that, the priest closed his eyes. Dai watched him for a few seconds. The magic of faith swelled around the man as he prayed. Its wave of calm broke over Dai and he closed his eyes. The bones in his back moved and their weight eased with each beat of his heart.

Had he made the right choice?

If he'd done nothing, she would've carried different scars though different lives.

As he sat contemplating the choice, a new question appeared. What would Mave have wanted? What decision would she have made?

The answer had always been with him. She'd never flinched or begged for her life because she'd made her choice. She'd chosen death at her brother's hand. Quick and sure.

The guilt he'd held for too many years heaved out, and with it the bony eagle wings growing through his chest slipped free and clattered to the floor. For the first time in centuries he was able to take a breath without the tightening in his back. He rolled his shoulders, but the weight was gone. His heart beat without pain. He was free. In his ears he heard Mave's last words. Words he'd never believed himself to be worthy of:

I forgive you.

Dai opened his eyes. The priest was watching him.

"You are ready to hear the Lord's words?"

He'd lived in fear of anyone ever finding out what he'd done. But once told the secret had lost its power. "Yes."

"I can give you no penance greater than the price you have already paid in body and mind. Your sister is in the loving arms of the Lord. You aren't to blame for her death. I absolve you from your sins in the name of the Father, and of the Son, and of the Holy Spirit. Forgive yourself and go in peace, son."

Chapter 16

AMANDA FINGERED HER WEDDING RING. THE POLICE had found it and returned the plain gold band, but she couldn't bring herself to wear it. Carefully she placed it back in her wallet, then slipped her wallet into her handbag. Would Matt understand? Her stomach tightened with nerves. Was that what having an affair felt like? She shook off the feeling. She couldn't cheat on a ghost, and she couldn't be married to one. And yet that was exactly how she'd been living.

She'd been alone for longer than she'd been with Matt. She smoothed down her shirt. Was she ready? She'd put on makeup, but only a little. A touch of lipstick. Had Brigit noticed? Eliza had, but she'd raised one eyebrow and let it pass without comment.

Did it matter?

She was entitled to an adult relationship, so why did she feel like the worst parent in the world by dropping Brigit off with Eliza so she could go out? Maybe she should've rung Dai first, but that felt too formal. She just needed to see him. To talk to someone about what had happened with the healer. Brigit had refused to cooperate and Amanda had ended up taking her home. But Brigit didn't relax until Amanda promised not to take her again. The promise of takeout dinner and a sleepover at Eliza's—by herself—had made up for the disastrous afternoon.

For Brigit anyway. She was left with a gnawing fear for her daughter's life and more questions about magic than she'd ever thought possible. While she told herself she was going to see Dai for answers, it was a partial lie.

She wanted him to kiss her again. The kiss revealed more about him than she could ever learn in words. Tender, spine-shaking with a lingering heat full of potential…but it was missing something. Some of his responses weren't what she'd expect. What he didn't say was telling. And it wasn't a pretty story if she was reading him right. She wanted to be wrong.

But she needed to know; her heart was already on the line and she needed to understand who she was risking it for. A bent fork, some dead languages, and a mysterious murder didn't match the man with shadowed eyes and a half-smile that would melt ice.

She knew she couldn't put her life on hold until Brigit was grown up. Yet she didn't know what type of life she wanted anymore. She got out of the car and looked up at the fancy apartment block. Baby steps. Nothing had to happen except conversation. But no one had ever kissed her like he had. Soft and hard. Asking first, then not taking everything offered. But he wouldn't, not if her guesses were on target—Claudius had hurt him a lot.

The tension of her stomach didn't ease as she paced the lobby waiting for him to answer his cell phone. It was such a mistake. She'd ditched Brigit so she could chase after a man who wore his broken heart on his sleeve.

The call went through to voicemail and she hung up without leaving a message. She sighed as disappointment flooded through her, draining away the nerves that had bound her since deciding to come and see him. Now what?

Her phone lit up and sang as she walked out of the lobby. She glanced at the name and answered without waiting to seem casual.

"Sorry, I couldn't find my phone." His voice sent a shiver through her body.

"Can you buzz me up?"

"You're here?" His shock was almost hidden.

Was he sheltering the same doubts she was? No, his were bigger and took up more space. "I can go."

"No. Come up."

"Thanks."

They hung up. The elevator ride was too fast for her to settle her stomach. Was she only interested because he was unreachable and safe?

The elevator doors opened and Dai was waiting for her. He looked like hell had run him over and reversed for good measure, yet he seemed happier. The smile on his lips rested easier on his face. Just seeing him made her feel alive, and she couldn't ignore the lure no matter the risk.

"I should've called first." She eased her grip on her handbag.

"You surprised me. I wasn't expecting a guest."

That made two of them. She was surprised she'd actually gotten there instead of getting halfway and then turning around and driving home. The only reason she didn't freak out was because he was the only person she could talk to about Brigit without being thought of as a crazy person.

"Come in." He held the door open for her.

His luxury apartment was sparsely and inexpensively furnished. His bookcase was empty except for the books Roan and she had bought him.

"Still with customs?" She inclined her head at the shelves.

His shoulders stiffened. "Stolen."

"What?" Who stole books? Books on magic?

"No books." He walked into the kitchen. "Can I get you a drink? Beer, tea, coffee?"

"Coffee, thanks."

"I've only got instant."

"That's what I'm used to." She leaned her hip against the marble counter. "Any chance of you getting your books back? Are the police investigating?"

"They're gone. Very hard to trace unless they go on sale. They're probably in someone's private collection." He reached into the pantry and pulled out a jar of coffee, still sealed.

"What about insurance? I know that won't replace them…"

He paused, his back to her. "What price do I put on a lifetime's collection? On works that I hadn't translated yet?" He half turned. "I'm sorry. I shouldn't be taking it out on you." He flicked on the kettle. "You take two sugars?"

"Yes. And milk." She hid a smile. He remembered, after meeting for coffee once.

The kettle boiled, and he made her coffee, opening a new bag of sugar and a carton of milk in the process. Was she his first visitor? He handed her an eggshell blue cup, then made himself a cup of herbal tea.

"Thank you." She wrapped her hands around the cup

and let the warmth seep through. "Brigit wouldn't let the healer help."

His eyebrows knitted for a moment as if he didn't understand the problem. "Do you want to tell me why?"

Amanda nodded. "I'm hoping you can make sense of it for me." Around Dai magic made sense even if nothing else did.

"I'll try."

With the marble island between them she told him what had happened. The way Brigit had refused to even lie down and let the healer anywhere near her. Usually when they went to see someone, hoping for a miracle, Brigit at least went along with it. Amanda was always careful to never raise Brigit's hopes. It was only hers that soared and crashed every time something else failed to help Brigit. Dai listened without asking any questions, only nodding at parts, as if he understood everything that had happened.

She took a drink of her cooling coffee and waited.

He watched her carefully. "There's a web that makes people and things and connects everything." He paused. "The theory is that if there is damage to the web, then the body is also damaged. So heal the web and the body is healed. But like any healing, it's a specialized art."

"I'm not even sure I believe it."

"You must or you wouldn't have taken Brigit."

"Maybe, or maybe I'm just desperate for a cure so she doesn't die."

"Healing is possible." He flicked her a smile that held the reassurance that she could tell him anything and he wouldn't be surprised.

Amanda raised her eyebrows. "How? What do I need to do to help Brigit?"

"Magic is like science. There are actions and reactions." He turned his cup of tea on the counter, a frown forming. "The recipient has to be willing."

"What are you saying? That Brigit wants to be ill?"

"No." He shook his head. "But maybe she doesn't know how to let the damage go."

"If," and it was a giant if, "that is the case, then what can I do to convince her to let the healer help her?"

"Nothing."

Amanda stared at him. "Would you have done nothing for your sister?"

He looked away. "As much as you'd like to, you can't force her to get better and that is what you're asking."

"Brigit has to want to get better." Amanda whispered the words. Her daughter was killing herself. "Why wouldn't she want that?"

"I don't know. Maybe it was the healer, maybe another one would have more luck." He concentrated on his tea.

Amanda stared at her coffee. Just because he could bend a fork didn't mean he knew anything about magic; he'd admitted he didn't know anything about healing. "You could be wrong."

"I could be. So could the hundreds of cultures I've studied."

Meaning he wasn't...if she believed in that kind of stuff. "Can you see this web?"

"Yeah."

"What do you see? Are we walking through it?"

He blinked slowly. His eyes darkened and seemed

to shimmer like iridescent gems. "Objects like this," he tapped the counter, "have a dense weave. You can't go through them. Strung across the apartment are lines, from you to the book you gave me. Between us."

She glanced at the space between them but saw nothing. "We're connected?"

"A little. There are ribbons that join you to Brigit. Blood ties, plus love."

"You can see all of this, about everyone?"

He blinked and his eyes went back to blue. "Yes, but it doesn't mean I can make sense of it all the time. A lot of it is a jumble that gives me a headache."

Did she imagine the change in his eyes? She looked at her hand as if expecting to be able to see something other than her skin. She glanced back at him as understanding made the hairs on her arms prickle to attention. That was how he'd bent the fork; he'd manipulated the threads that made things. He could do *real* magic.

She let out a slow breath. "How did you learn?"

"My travels."

"What else can you do?"

"Not a lot. I'm a researcher, not a practitioner."

Dai drained his cup and placed it in the sink. He wanted to tell Amanda the truth, but he wasn't ready to lose that look in her eyes. There was a heat and light that was subtle like a candle flame yet brighter than the sun at the same time.

She ran her teeth over her lip as if considering him anew. If she knew how long he'd been studying magic and how he knew about Brigit's past life connection that was now threatening her future, she wouldn't be looking

at him like that. He sighed. He had to help Brigit, so
Amanda would learn something of the truth anyway.

"If you'd like, we can talk to Brigit about letting go of
the asthma and accepting healing." Even though Mave
had chosen death, that didn't mean the shock hadn't
stayed with her…and after a while she'd forgotten to
move on and let go of the damage he'd caused.

"It's worth a try?" Hope lit her face. She was desperate for a solution.

"It might work." And it might not. He hadn't had any
luck talking to Fane, but he had to do something.

She held out her hand and forced a smile. "Enough
talk of magic. Would you like to give me the guided tour
of your place?"

He took her offered hand, the contact sparking the
familiar heat in his blood, and he basked in the warmth
instead of running from it. For a moment he didn't know
where to start. There wasn't much to show. She'd seen
the living area, so he showed her the empty bedroom
first. Then he realized he'd stumbled into a little trap.
She was waiting to see his room.

He hesitated, not sure if he wanted someone else in
his space, then he gave in. What harm was there in letting her see? He could've fixed it up with magic as he
opened the door, but he didn't. He had to start trusting
someone with something, and Amanda was that person.
He couldn't kiss her with his fingers crossed behind his
back. Since she already knew he had trouble sleeping,
this was just an extension of that problem.

There were no sheets on the bed. The blankets were
folded at one end with the pillow. Everything was neat,
but not normal. He waited for her judgment.

"Where do you sleep?" They stood in the doorway, close enough he could smell the sweet blossom of her shampoo.

"Sofa."

Amanda turned and leaned her back against the doorframe. She tilted her chin to look up at him. Her fingers reached up and traced his jaw. As much as he'd like to lay her on his unused bed, the idea filled him with equal parts of desire and terror that he'd be too rough. Given her tentative touch, he suspected she was testing her boundaries too. He let himself relax a little. For the moment they were both safe.

She cupped his cheek. "You're not going to invite me in?"

"No." He took her hand away, then saw the curl of her lips. She was teasing him, as if not being able to sleep in his own bed was perfectly acceptable.

Her lips parted to speak. He leaned down and sealed them with a kiss. Somehow kissing her was easier than figuring out how to respond to her gentle taunt. Their bodies met. Her breasts pressed against his chest in a delicious promise that made his body respond and his blood pressure rise. Her arms slipped around his neck and into his hair. He didn't pull away from her touch. His hands caressed her hips and dragged her closer. She moaned against his lips.

He pulled back, but it was too late to hide his lack of control. Around her, all he could think of was having her.

Amanda's eyes glittered like emeralds. "I won't rush you."

Those words knocked him flat. His chest hollowed. No amount of air could fill his lungs. Every secret he'd tried to hide was exposed. He should've known she'd work out how unsure he was about every touch. She was a counselor. She'd added up the tiny bits he'd told her.

"How much do you know?" He raked his fingers through his hair.

"I don't know exactly what happened to you, but I see the result."

He looked away. "The result? The result is I don't trust myself when I'm around you."

"Why?" She didn't move.

"I might hurt you." Silence swelled between them and crackled with tension. The unspoken truths and unspent longing added fuel to the storm ready to break. "If you want to leave, I understand. I'm pretty fucked up."

"Everyone is. Those who deny it are the ones to worry about." She laced her fingers with his. "Did you want to talk about it?"

The truth burned on his tongue. "I want to tell you, but..." But he didn't want to see pity in her eyes. He much preferred the simmering heat.

Amanda pressed her lips together, her green eyes assessing him as if she was weighing up how many more questions she could ask. She gave a slow nod. "You speak hundreds of languages."

Dai held her gaze. She was opening the door. He wanted to tell her everything, and he could. He could tell her his life story from the Roman invasion to being cursed and finding the cure. And she didn't have to understand a word, only listen.

"Do you really want to hear a story you can't understand?"

"Will you tell it to me in one of those *almost* dead languages you speak?" she said with a half-grin.

"I can do that." He brought her hand to his lips and kissed the tips of her fingers. If he was going to tell her a story that began in ancient history they were going to have to sit down. "Would you like another coffee?"

"Have you got cookies to go with it?"

No, but he could. "What type?"

Her tongue touched her lower lips while she thought. "Something chocolate."

"I think I have something suitable." He'd have to leave a twenty dollar bill by the supermarket register to make up for all the stuff he was stealing every time he opened the pantry door.

"Do you want some help?" She released his hand with a lingering touch that left his skin burning for more.

"I'm fine." Even though she knew about magic, he didn't want to be explaining what amounted to theft.

While he made another round of herbal tea and coffee, she sat on the sofa and watched. She wasn't rushing him, she was just opening up every fence he'd put up and waiting for him to walk out. And he was. One step at a time. And it was so easy he was expecting a trap…or punishment.

He sat down next to her, close enough their legs could touch. He picked up a chocolate-coated cookie and broke it in half so he could dip it in his tea. It was a habit he'd picked up in England and continued with because in the Shadowlands there was no one to complain about bad habits. He paused, cookie just above the tea—he wasn't in the Shadowlands anymore—and glanced at Amanda.

"Like this." She bit off diagonally opposite corners and placed one end in her coffee and then sucked. Before the cookie could cave in she put it in her mouth. In an effort to make it polite she covered her mouth with her hand.

He opened his mouth but didn't know what to say. He was about to tell her everything and she was mutilating a cookie. He wanted to be that cookie.

"Sorry. I can't resist. I've taught Brigit how to do it with hot chocolate."

"That was the most disgusting thing I've ever seen anyone do to a cookie." He smiled. He'd never be able to look at a chocolate cookie without thinking of Amanda. Which wasn't a bad thing.

She grinned and reached for another one.

He ate his cookie and licked chocolate off his thumb while he considered where to start his life story and in what language to tell it. Her perfume wrapped around him like cobweb, brushed against his skin until it tingled for her touch.

There was no point in stalling. With the taste of chocolate still on his tongue he started at the beginning in the language he'd grown up speaking, Decangli. "When I was born the world was a different place. As second son of the king I had responsibilities."

Amanda turned to face him, her knee on the sofa, her head tilted a fraction like she was listening for a familiar word. The coffee and cookies were forgotten on the table.

He stumbled over sentences he hadn't used but had wanted to say and gradually his past unfolded like an old blanket coming out of storage. Exposing it to light took away some of the stains, and the colors were revealed beneath old bruises. He talked of memories he'd thought forgotten, his sister and parents, his cousins and their childhood before the Romans came.

She flinched when he spoke of Claudius, Dai's fingers curling against his leg. But the hate that had once accompanied the memory was gone. He'd outlived the general, had survived the curse. He had a chance to have a future he'd never dreamed of. The loss was there when he told of Meryn fading after that first summons. Then Brac's failed attempt to take out the druid. Fane's suicide. And Anfri's death. All of them gone.

Amanda hung on every ancient word. She didn't ask questions. She just let him talk as no one else had ever done. Her lips curved at the mention of Roan and Eliza's names. He stopped when the curse broke, and he was a man again. She knew the rest.

"The language is beautiful." She leaned over and put her arms around him. "Thank you for sharing."

He returned her embrace. His hand skimmed down the vertebrae of her spine, and the fabric of his reality shifted in her hands. In baring his soul, he'd bared his heart, and freed it had found someone he wanted to love.

Dai drew Amanda to him. Her leg slid over so she could sit in his lap facing him. As close as he'd ever been to her, and yet not close enough. He needed to feel her touch on his skin. He cupped her face and kissed her, his tongue sweeping past her lips. Her mouth was sweet from the chocolate and coffee, a taste that would keep him awake all night. Her fingers trailed over his chest and she moved a little closer. Hip to hip.

He let his hand trace down her throat, along her

collarbone, his fingers barely touching her skin. He'd known how to be gentle once. Held Mave as a baby. Been close with Seiran. He could be kind again. Amanda's hips moved against him as her teeth raked his lip and send heat spiraling through his blood, hardening his flesh. There could be no doubt about his intention. She moved against him sensing the shift in his hunger. His hand slid over her shirt to cup her breast. A little moan escaped her lips as her eyelids fluttered down.

Her hands smoothed over his shirt, gripping the fabric as if she couldn't let him go.

"I'm not staying the night." Her words were light and breathless, as if she were convincing herself. She leaned forward and placed her mouth on his. "I want to stay the night."

She gave her hips a wiggle as if trying to get even closer, but there were too many clothes between them. He wanted her in his arms, skin to skin.

"I'd like you to stay," he murmured against her lips. He'd like to wake up in bed next to her.

He felt her lips pull back into a smile. "I don't think I'm ready for that."

Even as she spoke her hand slid beneath his shirt. The muscles of his stomach tightened, but she didn't pull her hand back. Her fingers continued their slow exploration, tracing circles on his skin. Her touch spread out, fingers running over his ribs, brushing the lines of old scars, and showing tenderness where there had only been pain. He swallowed, hard. How was he going to explain them? Truthfully.

But she didn't ask. The knowledge the scars existed was enough.

Amanda flicked the top button of his shirt open. She kissed his collarbone and opened the next button, then she drew back. Her eyebrows went up as her gaze remained on his chest. "Another tattoo?"

"I have many others."

She nodded and shifted the fabric, her fingers tracing the web but not touching the spider in the center. "It's not a gang thing?"

He laughed. "It's a magic thing." He caught her hand to stop her exploration. As much as he wanted to feel her hands on his skin, he wasn't ready to explain all of the marks on his body, no matter how much his body thought otherwise.

"Ahh." She nodded. "Is there anything else I should know?"

"Not tonight." His hands settled on her hips, knowing he couldn't keep her there without telling her everything.

"I should go before it gets too late." For a moment she didn't move. Then she leaned in and kissed him again. Slow and deep. Her tongue glided over his in a caress that left him wanting a little more than what either of them was willing to give.

She pulled back with a sigh like leaving was the last thing she wanted to do. "I'm going to guess that you don't have any protection handy anyway."

"Protection?" From what?

"Condoms?"

"No." But he would acquire some.

"Then it is definitely time I go before we accidently go any further." Her hands covered his. "Another time." She slid off him and stood.

Her green eyes were dark. And he knew if he'd

said yes, she may not have stayed the night but she'd have stayed.

Chapter 17

ABOVE MERYN, THE GOBLIN KING'S ROCK SPIRE PIERCED the gray, timeless sky. He watched and waited until he was sure no one was watching him and waiting to attack. Then he crossed the distance with an arrow notched and ready to use, hoping to find an entrance into the fortress.

Rubble was strewn across an opening as if the goblins had hacked their way into the rock. Meryn glanced around and listened, but he heard nothing over his pulse. He put away the bow and arrow and moved toward the mouth of the cave. His hand rested lightly on the pommel of his sword. A bow was useless in close quarters—and he wasn't expecting to get in without being challenged.

He drew in slow breaths. This was it. He would die or become goblin; either way he would be free of the screams that tore at the inside of his skull, scratching to get out. He hesitated at the entrance, but no one came out to question his presence. Could he go straight in?

"Sire?" His voice rolled over the rock smoothly, not the voice he was used to hearing when he gave orders.

He kept his hand on his sword ready for an attack. None came. Neither did the king. He drew his sword with a whisper of metal and took another step forward over the rubble.

"Sire, I beg for your help." Again the strange voice fell from his lips.

He waited until the echo faded without response—
then he went inside.

The cave was dim. His eyes didn't adjust to the dark
the way they should have. He blinked a few times to
make sure, but his eyes were human, not goblin, and the
shadows didn't disperse.

He crept down the hallway, careful not to trip on the
rocks that were scattered on the floor. Ahead a faint
green glow illuminated a tunnel. Because he couldn't
see in the dark, he went toward the light. Where was the
king? Was he in the Fixed Realm of men? Where was
his troop? His queen?

He stopped when he reached the lit cavern. Candles
burned without melting, casting a green glow on the
polished wood table in the center. Around the table
were the remains of chairs. They'd been smashed
apart. He'd never seen furniture like that before, yet
he knew what it was and he knew people would sit
around and eat at a table. Meryn ran his hand over the
edge and frowned.

Where was everyone?

Meryn took a taper out of a candelabrum and began
exploring the castle, hoping he would find the king, or a
sign of where he was or when he'd be back.

He walked down hallways that lead nowhere or that
looped back on themselves. He found a room made of
shiny white tiles, a room full of empty shelves, and
bedrooms. Every room he found was empty except for
shards of broken furniture.

One huge cavern glimmered with gold dust. But there
was no gold, only shattered amber panels like the sun
had fallen and been claimed by the darkness. Had the

king taken his gold and gone somewhere else or had he left the Shadowlands forever?

"Where are you?" The rock swallowed his shout. "Why won't you help me? I'm one of you!"

The accusation settled and revealed the truth he hadn't wanted to see. The rubble, the broken furniture, the missing gold. The king hadn't left. The goblins had invaded.

The king was dead.

He slumped down against the wall, taper in one hand, sword in the other. The hands that held them were now familiar as if he had used them in another life he couldn't remember but flitted at the edges when he slept and dreamed of blood and tears.

"No!" Meryn shook his head unable to believe he was alone and human in a land full of goblins. There had to be someone. He couldn't live as a human in the Shadowlands. Being human hurt; every heartbeat cut deeper into his chest. "Somebody help me!"

Dai woke up under a starless sky with cool dust beneath his feet. He didn't need to turn to know where he was.

The Shadowlands.

He frowned. He'd beaten the dream. Defeated the nightmare. His past had no power. The chill crept up his legs even though the scent of Amanda's skin clung to him. He'd fallen asleep on the sofa after she'd left, while thinking of what he would've done with her if she'd stayed. He could only imagine...and dream. But this was not the dream he hoped for. So why was he here?

Dai searched the sky, but the twilight remained empty.

"Somebody help me." The words in Decangli echoed over the flat landscape around him.

Dai reached for his sword but found none. It was a very long time since he'd been weaponless in the Shadowlands, not since that first night. But it was his dream and he could control it. At his thought, a throwing knife appeared in his hand. Bone-handled. Why these knives? He'd had many over the years, yet here, in this dream, it was these blades made from goblin bone.

No goblins appeared out of the gray, and Claudius didn't reform out of the dust. This wasn't his nightmare. Why was he here? He hadn't been summoned. There was none of the compulsion that usually accompanied the transition between realms…he hadn't thought to try traveling between realms. Could he? But then why would he want to come back to the Shadowlands?

Because someone had called him; and while he should wake up and leave, he was curious. Who would call him in his own language? He turned slowly and scanned his surroundings.

"Show yourself," Dai called out in Decangli. His voiced dropped and sunk into the dust like it always had.

The dream was close enough to the real thing that he almost believed he was back in the Shadowlands. The cold bone handle in his hand was the only reminder he was asleep and in control of this dream—to a degree. It depended on who wanted the meeting.

In the rubble by the rock spire a figure moved, like a goblin, but something else. The almost-man he'd glimpsed before while fending off Claudius. He blinked hoping to see the weave of the Shadowlands, but nothing changed. He was powerless here, as he'd always been. His was a magic based in life, not death. But he wasn't defenseless.

The bone-handle was like polished ice against his palm. The handles never got hot. They were always as cold as the Shadowlands and the goblins they were made from. Desperation makes men do desperate things. He'd needed weapons and had made them from whatever he could. These knives had always flown true whenever he used them, as if they carried a little of the death magic of the Shadowlands. Maybe that was why they came to him easily in the dream. Part of them existed in the realm of nightmares.

"You asked for help? Here I am. What do you want of me?" he called out.

From the rocks the man broke free. A goblin battle cry tore out of his very human throat. His bow was raised and arrow notched, aiming at Dai. Dai raised his hand ready to throw the knife and froze. His blood shattered in his veins. He knew that face.

The face of a warrior he'd never thought to see again after watching him fade to goblin the night the Decangli died.

Meryn.

Meryn changed his aim at the last moment and the arrow flew wild, hitting the man's arm. *A man. Not a goblin. There were no humans here. Did I really call the man here? I wanted help, but what could a man do?* He needed the king.

His brow furrowed as their eyes met. The man wrapped a hand around his arm, cursed in a language Meryn hadn't heard for a long time, then vanished.

He was there, and then he was gone without a fight.

Meryn walked around the spot where the man had stood. Not even his footprints remained. Meryn shook his head. A trick of his mind and nothing more. A nightmare from a past he didn't want to remember. He retrieved his arrow but color caught his gaze.

Blood.

Red blood stained the point. He sniffed it and ran his tongue over it, tasting the coppery sweetness. Human blood. Meryn wiped the arrow clean on his trousers.

The man's face lingered in his mind like a memory of another life. He couldn't dislodge the scraping inside his skull that he should know the man who left no trace.

Dai fell off the sofa, crouched and ready for battle, but with no weapon in his hand. His palms were cold like they remembered the bone-handle. He glanced around his apartment, but he was alone. His heart returned to a slow and steady beat.

The dream was so vivid, as if he was actually there. The cold, the peculiar echo. He hadn't been. He was sure of that. He'd been traveling between realms for long enough to know what that felt like. A new nightmare then. One he could never fix. Meryn had faded and they'd all watched helpless to the unfolding horror.

In the quiet of his lounge room water dripped. He looked down. Not water, blood. His blood splashed onto the floor. It dripped from the soaked sleeve of his ripped shirt. Cautiously he examined the tear in the black material and the flesh beneath.

He was rewarded with a sharp rasp of pain escaping his lips. Damn it. He hadn't been shot in decades. He glanced at the floor, and then the wound. He'd been shot in a dream.

He'd been shot by Meryn.

Meryn was human.

His blood plopped and burst into tiny suns on the floor as his world collapsed and got sucked into the endless gray of the Shadowlands.

Roan and he had never thought of what would happen to Meryn when the curse broke. Dai pulled his hand away; brilliant scarlet blood stained his fingers. Now he knew.

Meryn was alive and human and trapped.

Dai picked up his cell phone and found Roan's number. His thumb hovered over the green call button. It was four o'clock in the morning. His brother had a wife. Dai released his phone. He couldn't ask his brother to leave everything he'd ever wished for to chase after Meryn in the Shadowlands.

He was going to have to get Meryn on his own.

The room spun. Dai tried to focus. Blood on his hand, blood on the floor. He had to stop the bleeding. He dripped his way to the kitchen and wrapped a hand towel around his upper arm. Red soaked through the white. It would be too awkward to stitch himself as it was too high on his right bicep. He pulled the tea towel away and twisted for another look. If he was left-handed, he would've given it a go.

He leaned against the pantry door. He couldn't go to the hospital. They'd want to know how and why—so did he. How had Meryn pulled him into the Shadowlands and why had Meryn shot him? Dai blinked and examined the threads linking him to Meryn. The gray fiber was there. Thin and sticky, but without enough substance to follow to the Shadowlands. But maybe that bond was enough for Meryn to reach him in his sleep and give the dream enough life for it to have repercussions. He gritted his teeth against the long forgotten burn of injury.

The other option was worse, that when he slept he did return to the Shadowlands where his nightmares could kill him. He shook his head. He'd always survived his dreams, and he'd never once felt the spiraling sense of dislocation that came with crossing realms.

Dai peeled away the tea towel. With the sight he could see the ragged fibers of the wound that let the flood of life out. His body cut as if it were multilayered cloth, now weakened from the severed threads. He had to do something or he was going to lose too much blood. He studied the deep slash in his arm. He couldn't stitch it with a needle, but maybe he could sew it up with magic. It would be like darning clothes. If he could just pull the edges together and keep them together, the wound should hold. He concentrated on a handful of threads, pulling them toward their counterparts. Then he knotted them, tying each thread off. Not as good as new, but close enough that the bleeding stopped. He tossed the towel in the sink and stripped off his shirt to inspect his handiwork. His first magically healed wound.

Who needed books when he could experiment on himself?

The wound was closed. But it didn't look like any healing injury he'd ever seen. Bridges of skin joined the sides; between them the wound was raw. He'd closed the wound as if he'd been sewing, probably not the best way to approach magical surgery, yet he couldn't help but grin. He'd healed himself.

And while he was a long way off from the delicate work that would be required to help Brigit, it was a start. He could learn. He glanced around his living room half expecting someone from Birch to appear and re-open the wound. No one came. But his celebration was short-lived. He still had to go back to the Shadowlands and retrieve Meryn before the goblins ate him. His soul gave a shudder of fear. He had no idea how to get to the Shadowlands, and once there he had no idea how to get back. He could get stuck.

And he'd just discovered someone worth living for. Amanda.

Chapter 18

Sleep didn't return when Dai tried forcing it. Meditating on the Shadowlands had provided plenty of wide open nothing, but no connection back to the Shadowlands. No object he owned was connected to the Shadowlands with a thread strong enough for him to follow. All the things he owned, even those he'd brought from the Shadowlands, had been made in the Fixed Realm. He raked his fingers through his hair and paced his living room floor. Who'd have thought he'd ever need to go back?

He was running out of ways to get to the Shadowlands, really get to the Shadowlands—not the reflection he experienced in his nightmares. Crossing realms wasn't as easy as crossing the globe. He couldn't just will himself there. He needed something that was made of the Shadowlands.

The nightmare provided the answer. He needed one of his goblin bone knives. His palm chilled as if the skin still felt their cold touch and death magic. Did they even exist anymore? How would he even find one?

His steps faltered as he remembered the confusion and terror of those first years, before they settled into the monotony of hunger and fighting. Gods, just existing, had taken everything they had.

Even if he got back to the Shadowlands, how would he get Meryn out? Would he even be able to get out again himself? As a goblin, he could pass through realms easily. As a human, everything was different. And everything that he'd been denied would again be lost if he became stuck in the Shadowlands. He wanted more time with Amanda; he wasn't ready to leave. And yet he had to. Time moved differently in the Shadowlands. One more day could be the difference between life and death for Meryn.

Meryn deserved another chance. The man had lost everything to the curse; his wife, his children, and his humanity. While Dai couldn't bring back his wife and kids, he could give him a chance to rebuild.

What if Dai couldn't bring them both back to the Fixed Realm where they belonged? He pushed away the thought, refusing to give power to anything that would steal his hope.

He pulled on a shirt, grabbed his phone and keys, and headed out of his apartment. As he walked down the street, he let his vision slide so the world became a mass of threads weaving around each other. Occasionally a sticky gray thread would appear. He followed one by sight; it ended with a woman who caught him staring and scowled, her weave becoming tight like she was trying to hide from him. He looked away. A false lead, she had no connection to the Shadowlands, but her fears tied her thoughts there. That wasn't what he was looking for. He wanted something hard. A tangible object. Magic worked best with an item, something on which energies could focus and bind. In his quest to break the curse, that item had been his body, a vessel of the curse.

Around him, the city moved like a river, constantly in motion, never stopping for breath. His head started to ache as he searched a thousand threads with each heart-beat. If he couldn't find something there, he'd go to a bigger city. He would keep looking. In the back of his mind he heard the ticking of a clock. Meryn didn't have forever to wait for Dai to find a way back.

He blinked and cleared his vision. He was doing it the wrong way. If one of the six bone-handled knives still existed, he should be able to find it no matter where it was in the world. Jumping into someone's private collection or a buried tomb was a whole lot less appealing now that he had a life worth risking. Stepping into a trapped stronghold hadn't really bothered him as a goblin—okay, the flooded tomb had given him more than a moment of panic before he'd gotten out. But he'd gone back better prepared.

He had to be smart. He couldn't go jumping through reality and into a brick wall. He leaned against a building and closed his eyes. An image of the knife built quickly in his mind, along with the ever-present chill. They'd come to him easily in his dream, so he expected no trouble if they still existed in the Fixed Realm. Sure enough a fragile thread extended from him to somewhere. Then another, and another.

Three blades.

Two were far away, over the sea, and the gods knew where. At least he had a second and third option. He let them go and focused on the close one, looking for any clue about where it was. He got none, only a resonance of age that made no sense. The knife was old, and he had no idea how old the goblin had been.

He opened his eyes and took a step, careful not to close the full distance between him and the knife. He stood in front of a large building. Well, it was more like two old buildings joined together by a large glass structure. A museum. He turned around and faced the museum again. He knew where he was. To his left was the library, glittering as the knowledge inside created a world of its own. The museum by contrast was swathed in the threads of history.

A strong gray rope spun around the brickwork, but it wasn't part of the building and there was no tail end to follow. It grew around the building the way a vine might. He frowned and walked closer to examine the thread. Thick and gray and cold. It was definitely a part of the Shadowlands' death magic that had been allowed to take hold. And it was growing from something inside the building. His knife.

His lips curved. He glanced over his shoulder but no one was looking at him. If anyone knew what he was planning, they would've thought him mad.

He let out a breath. He was mad. There were so many what-ifs. What if he couldn't find Meryn? What if he was too late? What of he got pinned down by a troop of goblins? If Roan came with him, at least he'd have someone he trusted at his back. And if it all went bad, everything would be lost.

In his pocket his cell phone rang. He cleared his vision of the tangled threads and the tension in his forehead eased. He glanced at the screen, and his heart lurched.

Amanda.

He shouldn't have been surprised. She was the only person who rang him. What was he going to tell her? She'd already lost a husband. He didn't want her waiting for him if he got stuck. No matter how hard he tried to quash the fear, it kept sticking out its ugly head. He wasn't even in the Shadowlands yet and the desperation and despair were already giving life to fears he shouldn't acknowledge.

He smiled as he answered, even though the magic from last night was buried in the gray dust of the Shadowlands. "Hello."

"Hi, how'd you sleep?"

Great until he was shot. Still, he'd been lucky. It was unlike Meryn to miss a target. "Not too bad."

"Good." The warmth in her voice traveled down the line.

But it didn't warm him. Instead he felt the razor edge of loss against his skin, cutting deep. He wanted to see her again, just in case he couldn't make it back. He needed to see her and let her go. He rubbed his hand over his eyes as if he could wipe away the headache. Two thousand years to have a chance at what most men took for granted. But she would be there when he got back. It was a temporary break. He'd tell her he was going away for work. Then he'd leave a letter for Roan in the apartment. That way they'd know what had happened. He didn't let the thought grow.

If he planned to come back, it was more likely to happen.

He glanced up at the sign on the building. "Did you want to do something today?"

"Sure." Her voice raised and he could taste her excitement. "What did you have in mind?"

"What about a trip to the museum?"

"Okay…but Brigit will be with me."

"I kinda expected that." He'd take any time he could steal with Amanda.

When Amanda arrived, Dai greeted her with a smile and a kiss on her cheek as if he was aware he was being supervised by Brigit. She would've turned her head and offered her lips, but she didn't want her daughter asking more questions that she wasn't sure how to answer.

She was falling for Dai. Not in the sudden flash of knowing that it was with Matt—one look was all it took. But she was younger then and less wary. Now her heart was more guarded, and while she recognized the spark of attraction, there had to be more.

She slipped her hand into his, needing to touch him, as they went into the museum. Her skin craved the contact the way a plant stretches toward the sun. The night before seemed so long ago, she'd been so tempted to stay, to respond to the heat burning in his eyes. Would she have regretted it? Probably not. Would he?

She didn't know.

Watching him speak yet not understanding a word except a few names—Mave, Roan, Claudius, and at the end Eliza—had still revealed a lot. She heard the emotion in his voice and saw the tension in his face and hands. Felt the scars on his skin beneath her fingertips. He must've had a hell of a time growing up. But the damage didn't seem as great as she expected. And for all his concern about knowing how to be gentle, his touch was soft and sure.

Desire tightened her stomach for a moment. His fingers tightened around hers as if he was also remembering. He gave her a look, and his eyes shimmered as if he was using magic.

"I enjoyed last night," she whispered.

"So did I." The shadows in his eyes were gone,

replaced by a new danger, something she didn't recognize. And there was a silent *but*. They were walking side by side, yet they might as well be in different states. Something changed.

Amanda couldn't help but watch him as he talked and laughed at Brigit's badly constructed jokes. The weight was gone, he seemed happier, but he wasn't really with them. Was he having doubts about telling her everything and nothing? But that didn't fit. He asked her to come out; he was the one to lean in and offer her a kiss.

Brigit darted from display to display until she came face to face with the skeleton of a Tyrannosaurus Rex. She gazed up, her mouth open, as if she was able to see the fearsome creature in flesh and blood.

"Dai, you're old, do you remember dinosaurs?" She walked around, not taking her eyes off the bones, like watching it could keep it still.

"Brigit!" Dai was only a few years older than she was. Did her daughter think she was old enough to remember dinosaurs too?

"I'm not quite that old," he said with mock seriousness. "But I did meet a dragon once."

"A real dragon?"

Dai nodded. "Of course, she wasn't as big as the dinosaur…"

Amanda stared at him. Was he playing, or had he really met a dragon? He could do magic, he'd made her believe in magic. How did she know if he was telling the truth or making up stories?

"And where was this dragon?" Amanda raised an eyebrow.

"Africa," he said as if dragons prowled the savanna.

His eyes glimmered for a second as he scanned the room. To anyone else they would think it a trick of the light, but she knew better. And she knew him. Dai was looking for something. A chill slid down Amanda's spine. What would he be looking for in a museum…and more to the point why? Was it something to do with healing? Her breath caught in her throat. Had he found a cure?

"Mom, can we go to Africa so I can see the dragon?"

Dai looked at Brigit. "The dragon died."

"But there's more?" Brigit tore her eyes off the bones and stared at Dai.

"No. She was the last." His smile was gone as if he were talking about losing an old friend.

"Well, there are no dragons here, but there are plenty of other animals to look at." Amanda steered Brigit onto the next display.

"What were you looking for?" she said as they walked on.

He opened his mouth, paused, and then spoke. "How did you know?"

"Your eyes, there's a reflection or something. Besides, you scanned the room like you were looking for something, not at something. Is it for…" Amanda nodded her head in Brigit's direction.

"I'm working on that. But this is for something else."

They moved onto the displays of objects from daily life over the centuries. Brigit pulled open drawers and pointed at things that were protected by a sheet of glass. Dai answered all her questions. He seemed to know a bit about everything. Was it truth or tales though? Where did the occult law of one culture end and another begin, or reality start? Was he even sure anymore?

Maybe she was rushing things? But when she was with him she wanted to hear about the places he'd been and the things he'd seen as if she could live vicariously through his travels, yet she never felt like he resented her asking. It was like he enjoyed talking about the things he'd learned.

But she wasn't sure she wanted to know what he was looking for or what he was going to do with it. "Nothing illegal?"

"No." But it was what he didn't say that made her concerned.

Not illegal, but almost.

She tugged on his hand. "What's going on?"

"I'm looking for a magical item, that's all."

"And then?"

They stopped in front of a display on Iron Age people. Their weapons were held up for the world to see. Arrows and axe heads. Life must have been so hard back then. How would they feel knowing the things were being gawked at by a bunch of people with the free time to stop and stare?

Brigit pulled open the drawers to see more artifacts. Dai paled and stepped back. Amanda leaned over Brigit to have a look, but all she saw was a collection of knives, one with a bone-handle. She glanced at Dai and raised her eyebrow. His hand slipped from hers and he moved onto the next display by himself. Was it the knives? Was one of them magical? Ice settled in her stomach. What was he going to do with a magical knife?

Brigit bounced after him, oblivious to his need for space, and Amanda followed.

"Ohh, look at that spider." Brigit placed her hands on the glass display cabinet.

"It's a bird-eating spider," Dai answered without the snap of exasperation of a tired parent who'd responded a thousand times before. He looked over his shoulder at Amanda. Instead of the shadows that had roamed his eyes there was sadness of a thousand things he couldn't explain to her in any language.

In that breath, she knew he was going to leave. He was going to walk away before they even had a chance to see what could happen. Just as she was getting used to the idea that maybe she could risk being in love again. She took his hand and laced her fingers with his, knowing it wouldn't be enough to keep him. He'd made up his mind.

Amanda drew him back a few paces from Brigit. "What's happened?" Last night she'd thought there'd been hope, more than a chance of something.

He looked away. "I have to go away for a few days."

"And take one of those knives?"

He didn't answer.

"Will you be coming back?" she asked. He was pulling away and shutting her off.

He paused. "I don't know. I want to."

"Then what is stopping you?"

Dai looked at the other patrons, at Brigit only a few steps away staring at bees from around the world. "Let's just enjoy today. I'll tell you tonight."

She shook her head. She wasn't leaving Brigit with a baby-sitter every night for him. For any man. "Tell me now."

He turned and faced her, held both her hands as if he could make her understand. "A friend is in trouble."

"What kind of trouble?" She searched his face for

answers but saw nothing she was able to read. "Trouble with magic?"

None of this was making sense. He had her believing in love and magic and was now tearing it away.

"Serious trouble. It doesn't matter what. I have to help him."

"It matters to me..." She lowered her voice. "Are you running? Is this because of last night?"

"No." His eyes hardened, cold like hail. "I don't run."

"Then what is going on? The truth, in English." His secrets were too much for her to handle.

There was a pop, like a change in pressure. Her chest was constricted for a moment and then she could breathe. She glanced at Brigit, only steps away still fascinated by the pinned bugs. The other couple in the room was just as focused on the display in front of them. Motionless.

"It's not as pretty when you can understand the words." Dai's eyes glimmered like the darkest ocean in moonlight.

"Try me." She'd heard plenty of ugly over the years.

Dai's face seemed to change, like he was preparing for judgment. He held himself tall, but he was already defeated. As if he knew what her reaction would be, and was ready for the killing blow.

"From the time I was fifteen I was tortured by Claudius. I stopped fighting back when I realized he enjoyed the struggle even more. But using me kept his hands off my sister, Mave." He stepped closer to her. "When I was sixteen, my father found out. He rallied the tribe. There was a battle and he was killed. Roan almost died. He became the new king of the Decangli. I got a beating and then some. At nineteen I helped Roan organize a rebellion, one that wouldn't fail, but our cousin betrayed us to the Roman invaders." His lips twisted as if the acid words still burned his tongue.

Amanda's mouth opened, but she had no words. What had happened to him was awful but clouded in things that couldn't be true. Had he created a delusion for himself to cope? What of the magic? The things he'd learned while overseas? Last night she'd thought she understood, if not the details then the emotion. Today how could she believe him when he spoke of things that had happened hundreds of years ago?

"The Roman Empire has been gone for centuries."

"I know that. You asked for the truth and this is it. That fairy tale Eliza told Brigit is real, but Roan and I were the ones cursed. Damned to the Shadowlands to live as goblins."

"Goblins don't exist." She stepped back and tried to pull her hands free. She didn't know him at all. Beneath the surface of a scholar was a man who had lost touch with reality. "It's not possible."

He mimicked her step. "I've just had my twentieth human birthday. I've never even been with a woman because I don't trust my hands not to repeat what I've learned." He let go of her hand as if it burned. "Adapting to this changed world might be hard. But I'm not running. I like you, more than I should. More than is safe. But a friend is trapped in the Shadowlands and I have to help him before the goblins eat him."

Amanda blinked. What could she say? He believed in this world he'd created so he could escape reality. But Eliza had told Brigit a story about goblins and the Shadowlands. About a king who'd been cursed and saved by love.

"Dai, you need help, counseling." She touched his arm, but he jerked away.

"Ask Eliza how she met Roan."

She had, and she'd gotten a vague response about running into each other. She should have asked more about Dai…Eliza had never warned her, nor had Roan. Did they both think he was stable?

"Ask Roan about the scar that slashes across his chest. Ask him about Meryn, Brac, Anfri, and Fane. You knew Fane, the albino kid who loved gold. Ask Roan how Fane died."

She stepped closer to Brigit, determined to put as much distance as she could between the man she'd thought she knew. She'd been so close to making a mistake. But it was hard to move, like walking through syrup. While they talked, no one had moved. She looked at Dai; his eyes were still unnaturally lit. Magic. Was it real or an illusion?

"What are you doing to me?"

He blinked, startled. Then her ears popped and movement and noise returned. She hadn't realized how quiet it was. She grasped Brigit's hand and pulled her away without explanation. A wave of loss threatened to drag her to the floor. How stupid was she? She glanced over her shoulder to make sure he didn't follow, but he was already gone taking a piece of her heart with him.

Amanda's throat ached. She'd trusted him even though she knew he was damaged. She didn't realize he was rusted to the core. Her left hand covered her heart. The ring that protected her for so long was absent, and she wanted it back. She wasn't ready. It was easier to be numb than have her heart sliced open for inspection.

Brigit stopped, refusing to be dragged any farther. "Where's Dai?"

"He had to go." Damn him. He'd made a friend out of Brigit and would hurt her too.

"Why?"

"Because he did," Amanda snapped.

"You made him go." Brigit tugged her hand free.

"He wanted to leave."

"What did you say?" Brigit crossed her arms and pressed her lips together looking as cross as a seven-year-old could.

Amanda gritted her teeth. "Nothing."

"Daddy sent him. You were supposed to help him. Dai was supposed to stay."

Matt was gone, yet Brigit held onto the belief he was watching over her. It was a lie Amanda started, but one she thought they'd both grow out of. She sniffed, trying to lock up her turbulent emotions that didn't know whether she was angry or upset, or both. Even if Matt was watching them, he certainly wouldn't have brought Dai into their lives.

Brigit sucked in a breath. "I hate you. You never listen to me."

"I've done everything for you."

Brigit's lips moved, but no words came out. Her lips faded from pink to blue. She leaned over and put her hands on her knees as if she were trying to catch her breath. Amanda dropped to the floor and pulled the inhaler out of Brigit's bag. Her daughter's eyes were wide as she sucked the medication down. It made no difference.

She pulled Brigit into her lap, waited, and gave her

another dose. Brigit couldn't breathe. Amanda fumbled for her cell phone and called for an ambulance.

"It's okay, Brigit." She smoothed her daughter's hair and gave her another dose, willing her to breathe again. Brigit couldn't afford another major attack. These were the ones that did the most damage to her fragile lungs.

Brigit gripped her hand, crushing her fingers as she began to panic. Tears burned Amanda's eyes, but she wouldn't let them fall. Wouldn't let Brigit see how scared she was. She had to be strong for both of them, even when her world was being torn in all directions.

She lifted her head, looking for help, but there was no one there. She was alone. Always alone.

Chapter 19

DAI STEPPED INTO HIS APARTMENT. TIME HAD STOPPED in the museum. Localized around him and Amanda—she'd walked away and he'd let her take the threads that linked them together. They'd trailed after her, shortening with each step. That way would hurt less. She wouldn't feel the sting if he died.

But he felt the loss of each one. The tear as it left his body and the raw, gaping hole that remained in him once she was gone. Even if he made it back, he'd lost her. And he had no one to blame but himself. His shoulders hunched as he battled the agony crushing him. The talons of his past had never cut so cruelly and made breathing seem like such hard work.

He fisted his hand. He'd kept one golden ribbon, the first one that had moved through his hand when she'd touched him, as a reminder of her light. He'd need it in the Shadowlands. He always knew she wouldn't believe him, even though he'd wanted her to with every cell in his body.

Was that what love was? Wanting to protect her from his past while at the same time wanting her to know him the way no one else did?

He cursed Claudius for ruining him so much that he couldn't recognize love when it was right in front of him. And then the druid for cursing them all. And finally Meryn for being alive and needing rescuing. After

everything he'd been through, after getting everything
that had been taken back he was being asked to give it
up. But he couldn't leave Meryn in the Shadowlands. If
he did, his nightmares would never end, and he would
know he'd bought his new life with the blood of the
man who'd been closer to him than his own father
and brother.

It would have been easier to lie to Amanda and act
like nothing had changed, but he couldn't. After her
husband's death he couldn't leave her shipwrecked and
waiting for him when he might not be able to get back.

Damn it.

He didn't want to leave. He might not have ever
planned on having a human life again, but now he had
one, he wanted to keep it. He wanted it more than anything else. He'd trade all the magic in the world to have
one more night with Amanda. One more kiss. One more
smile. But he'd been denied the first time, so what made
him think he'd be allowed a second chance?

Dai sighed and looked at his blood-stained floor. He
hadn't cleaned up after Meryn shot him. Maybe some
people just weren't entitled to a life. Maybe this was
what he deserved. With a thought he gathered up the
dried blood and it vanished. The blood-soaked towel
followed. At least it wouldn't look like he'd been murdered if anyone came looking for him. The only person
who would notice his absence was Roan. His apartment
echoed around him. He'd never been so alone and yet no
one had ever demanded so much of him.

He wanted to hate Meryn but couldn't. If it had been
him in the Shadowlands, Meryn would have done the
same. And Roan would've been after him in a heartbeat.

The people who gave a damn were the same ones who'd damned him. Cursed because of Roan, now lost because of Meryn.

With a snarl he pushed aside all thoughts of living and focused on the Shadowlands and what he'd need to survive. That was something he knew how to do. He tossed items on the bed.

Water, flak jacket—in case Meryn tried to shoot him again and didn't miss—food, and throwing knives. The shop down the road must be wondering why there was always extra cash in the register. When he came back the first thing he was going to do would be to buy food. Lots of it. All from the little supermarket. Then he put all but the weapons into a backpack. He unpacked and repacked, anything to stall inevitable theft from the museum. He scanned the items again. It was a lot to take for a quick rescue visit. He tried not to examine the darkness in his heart. Or listen to the quiet voice that whispered *you'll never make it back*.

But he wasn't ready to go yet either.

He stripped out of the civilian clothing he was just getting used to wearing. The ink on his skin was dark and stark against hard muscle and pale skin etched in ancient scars. He checked the wound on his arm, running his fingers over the cut. The knotted threads made lumps of skin; between them the wound was still raw. With the sight he checked how it was healing. Not well. The other threads weren't joining as he'd expected; instead they seemed to be wilting like plants that were denied water. He frowned and as he concentrated on the wound, and willed it to heal. The strands thickened and pulsed. Why the change?

He'd put energy into the wound…the same way Amanda was pouring life into Brigit without even realizing. That was what he'd been missing. Healing wasn't just about tying off wounds and untangling threads; it was about energy.

The tree's rapid growth made perfect sense. Once unknotted, the energy from the earth flowed freely. Humans, generally, weren't that well connected and healing energy had to come from somewhere.

He looked at the wound. There was only one way to find out if he was right or if it was just another theory. This time he pulled the strands together and let some energy slide into the area, and as they drew close they joined without the need for a knot. The familiar pressure built in his skull, but he hadn't yet reached the point of pain, so he kept going until the wound was sealed. He ran his hand over the muscle, but only a dozen clumps of knotted skin remained. Another decoration on his highly marked body. He allowed himself a grim smile.

Pity his magic had never worked in the Shadowlands.

Dai dressed in the gray-and-black, military style clothing he'd worn in the Shadowlands. While he had no sword to belt on, he slid his knives into the vest. Was he arming himself against Meryn or goblins? He didn't know. He didn't care. He wasn't going anywhere without being armed.

There was nothing left but to get the knife.

With a wrench of will he reached out, found the sticky gray rope, and pulled the knife out of the museum. The knife wasn't as old as the display had claimed, or maybe it was. Maybe the goblin bone did date back to the Iron

Age. Who knew how long goblins lived, or who they were before?

The knife's handle hit his palm. Cold as ice and coated in the gray threads that bound it to the Shadowlands. He tossed the knife from hand to hand to get the feel of it again, to test the weight. The knives had always flown true, as if they were attracted to their own kind.

The knife had found him.

Like all things from the Shadowlands, it closed in on his dreams and turned them to nightmares. He turned it over in his hand. To hell with the museum. The ugly blade would remain in the Shadowlands where it belonged.

Dai rolled his shoulders. All he had to do was follow the knife's threads back to the Shadowlands. He forced out a breath and found the calm he needed to make the step between realms.

When he closed his eyes, he could still smell Amanda. The last remains of her perfume clung to his skin. How long would the delicate scent last in the Shadowlands? He already knew the answer. Not long. Her perfume would fade before his memory of her did. The thread through his palm linking them vibrated with pain. He could follow the golden trail to her, but she didn't want to see him. He was the cause of her hurt. Sometimes it was easier to live with a sweet lie than taste the bitter truth. He closed his fist around her light. She would guide him home. Maybe once he was back he could put things right…that was the dream he could hold onto, one the Shadowlands couldn't take.

With the gray strand in one hand and the gold in the other he was ready to go. Cold crept up his arm, crawled down his veins, and pooled in his stomach like he'd been eating snow. He checked to see if the fine thread linking him to Meryn was still intact. It was. His cousin was alive. If Meryn died while he dawdled, he'd never forgive himself.

Before he could stall any longer he grasped the solid gray threads that joined the knife to the Shadowlands and pushed through the layers of realities, different worlds, and possibilities to the nightmare where he'd spent most of his life. The familiar jolt of dislocation was coupled with a crushing of his temples that lasted only a couple of heartbeats before fading. Around him was the Shadowlands in all its dullness. The cold sucked away his breath and left raw ice crystals in its place. Had it always been so cold and desolate?

Land met sky in a never-ending continuum of gray. The oiled snaking river slithered to his right. He turned slowly, scanning his surroundings. Where in this hell was Meryn? He stopped when he saw the rock spire thrusting out of the ground and into the sky like a bridge between hell and heaven. An eternal monument to the time they'd spent in the Shadowlands and Roan's ability to control the dark magic.

"Home sweet home." He words fell flat into the dust.

Chapter 20

BRIGIT RESTED, TUCKED INTO THE HOSPITAL BED WITH a mask over her face. It wasn't the first time Amanda had seen her daughter like that, but she wished it would be the last. While she hadn't seen Matt die, she'd imagined his fight to breathe would've been like Brigit's. Lungs burning for air, but not being able to find any. She hated it. It never got any easier or any less terrifying. The doctor had yet to examine Brigit and confirm her worst fears—that there was more damage.

If there was, she was going back to the healer; she didn't care what Brigit said. She blinked, refusing to shed any tears. There was nothing else she could do but put her faith in a cure she only half believed in. Dai made it so easy to believe in magic and her heart cracked a little more…damn him. This was his fault. His leaving upset Brigit. Damn him for being such a beautiful liar. So smooth at deception no one knew how deep the damage ran. He lived in a world of make-believe and she lived in reality, and she'd been sucked at first glance because she was lonely and desperate. Never again.

Amanda stroked Brigit's forehead and Brigit's eyelids flickered open. She glared at Amanda, the fight that had caused the attack not forgotten. She picked up her daughter's hand. She wasn't cross with Brigit. She was angry with herself for holding onto her daughter so tightly she was suffocating her. Her baby was growing up.

"It doesn't matter how mad you get with me, or how old you get; you will always be my baby." Amanda gave Brigit a small smile.

The resentment drained from Brigit's face. "I don't hate you really." Her words were muffled. "Will you stay?"

"I haven't left." Amanda kissed her cheek and Brigit moved over to make room for her on the narrow hospital bed. They lay next to each other, the way she did when Brigit was just a toddler and afraid of the doctors. Soon there wouldn't be room on the bed for her. When had Brigit gotten so big? Where had the time gone? How much of their lives were spent in and out of doctor's offices and hospitals? Or trying alternative therapies hoping for a cure?

What if there wasn't one and all they had was now? She didn't want to waste what time she had with Brigit arguing over things that didn't matter and chasing all over for magic that didn't work. She had to make the most of now. Amanda hugged her close, not wanting to think of the future so shrouded in shadows no amount of light could break through.

~~~

Dai barely had time to take in the harsh landscape before he heard the snap of a bowstring and the whistle of an arrow cutting the air. Then his leg went out from under him and he dropped to his knee. Pain scored through the muscle where the shaft protruded. Black crow feathers had guided it true. The arrow had Meryn's fine touch all over it. Shot again by his cousin. The pain coalesced in his gut. Didn't his cousin recognize him? How much of the man remained after being a goblin so long?

"Meryn, stop trying to kill me and we can talk."

Nothing moved in the endless gray.

He glanced down at the shaft. His first reaction was to rip out the arrow, but it was better to leave it in his leg. Pulling it out would do more damage and would release any vessel that wanted to bleed out. He couldn't heal himself. He dropped a knife, clenched his teeth, and snapped the shaft. A new wave of pain rolled through his nerves and hit his stomach like a fist.

Bloody Meryn. Still, if he'd meant to kill him, he'd already be dead. He tossed the broken shaft into the dust and picked up his knife, keeping one eye on the horizon, searching for his shooter. He was somewhere near the old spire. Dai squinted, trying to pick shapes out of the gray on gray. An impossible feat. Everything blended as it always had. And he was a sitting target.

A wild man charged at him, yelling the coarse battle cries of a goblin. It was enough to turn Dai's blood to ice water. He couldn't run, even if he wanted to. He held his ground, because it was Meryn, or what Meryn had become.

Meryn notched another arrow.

Dai pulled out the goblin knife just in case. In Decangli he called out: "Meryn. It's Dai. Remember?"

The goblin-man slowed and stopped.

How many memories had Meryn lost? Was there even a man to save or was his mind gone?

Dai seized the delicate opening. "I'm your cousin. We grew up together. We were cursed to be goblin, but the curse broke and we're men again." He didn't lower the blade pointed at the man who taught him how to swing a sword. But the knife was heavy in his hand. He

didn't want to kill Meryn. He was past living for the
fight. He just wanted to live.

Meryn circled with the arrow pointed at Dai's heart.
"You speak lies. Men are not goblins. Goblins aren't men."

"When the curse broke, you were freed." And he had
failed to consider the impact. He should've known, or
guessed, what would happen to Meryn. He was lucky
they shared a blood connection and Meryn was able to
infiltrate his nightmares. The alternative, that he may
have never noticed and Meryn would've died there, was
too awful to acknowledge.

Confusion blanked Meryn's face. "No. I'll find the
Goblin King. He'll take me back. Make me goblin again."

"I can take you to the Goblin King. He now lives in
the world of men."

Dai swallowed; it was uncomfortable kneeling on the
cold dust while his blood pooled beneath him, but he
didn't shift his weight. He could show no weakness or
Meryn would cut him down. The weakest goblins were
killed for fun when there was little else to do. And he
was the weakest. He had no magic and the biggest injury.

Meryn edged to the side, and Dai watched, willing
himself to still. He knew how Meryn fought. In their old
life it was only for practice, never to the death. In one
move Meryn dropped the bow and pounced. He pinned
Dai in the dust. But Dai kept hold of the knife. They
grappled. A knee connected with the broken arrow
shaft, driving it deeper into the muscle and grinding
against the bone. He clenched his teeth as the pain exploded up his leg. In that second Meryn slammed the
back of Dai's hand into the dirt to try and break his hold
on the weapon.

Practice kept his fingers locked around the handle. "I came here to help you. To take you home," he pleaded through gritted teeth.

"This is my home."

Dai pressed the tip of his goblin blade against the soft piece of skin beneath Meryn's beard.

Meryn stilled, then grabbed a spare knife out of Dai's vest and brought the cold metal to rest against the base of Dai's throat. A killing position.

A fight wasn't fair when only one person was willing to kill. Dai swallowed and the blade bit deeper. Above him, Meryn stared down with eyes as gray as the Shadowlands. But his irises were free of the yellow that marked a man fading to goblin. He had a chance to recover if they got back to the Fixed Realm. With his next breath, Dai arched and pushed, throwing Meryn to the side. He scrambled upright, ignoring the shaking in his leg and the tightening of the muscle that didn't want to support him. He hadn't returned to the Shadowlands to die at his cousin's hand.

"You don't remember Roan? What about Brac, Anfri, and Fane?" He held the knife out, keeping Meryn away. He couldn't kill him and he couldn't leave him. The goblins would have him eventually. "Your wife? And babies?"

Meryn went for his legs. Dai brought the hilt of the knife down between Meryn's shoulder blades. Meryn grunted, but his hands were on the arrow, and he twisted as they fell. Dai's back hit the dust.

Stars exploded in the Shadowlands, and Dai struggled to find a breath as burning agony swept through his blood. Screw this. He grabbed a fistful of Meryn's

clothes. They could fight in the Fixed Realm and sort it
out there.

Even though he couldn't see it in the Shadowlands
he knew the bright golden light of Amanda was still
threaded through his hand. He pictured it as he'd last
seen it and felt along it. The pull of the Fixed Realm was
there. Then the thread stretched tight and snapped like
a whip that cut him to the bone and shocked his heart.
For a moment he couldn't think or move. He'd never experienced pain so severe. The smarting brought tears to
his eyes. He'd lost her. Really lost her. The connection
was gone. Severed. Amanda didn't want anything to do
with him; she'd cut him free to die in the Shadowlands.
Letting Meryn kill him would hurt less. He sucked in the
cold, tasteless air that froze his lungs. Each breath got
easier even if the pain didn't lessen.

Meryn's hand pressed against his throat, his nails
biting into flesh. In the darkness of his mind he groped
around, searching for a thread strong enough to draw
them back to the Fixed Realm. The sky got darker and
his lungs burned like he'd swallowed hot coals. He felt a
connection and let himself be dragged back to the Fixed
Realm, Meryn held tight in his other fist.

Dai stumbled as his feet his solid ground. The room
was dim and smelled like antiseptic. Something wasn't
right. He'd expected to arrive in Eliza's house, after
being pulled back by his brother. Roan wasn't there
and yet the thread ended. He'd been dragged here for
a reason. He glanced around the room and realized he
was in a hospital. He stomach sank as his gaze landed
on the bed. Brigit.

She had pulled him back. The girl who'd once been

his sister had saved him. The wound that bound them together was strong enough to bring him back from the Shadowlands…and the last piece of the puzzle fell into place. Mave knew her brother would need to be rescued from the Shadowlands after seeing him as a goblin. But she wouldn't have remembered why she was holding on to him in her next life—only that she couldn't go. Her love for a brother she couldn't remember had saved him from a slow death in the Shadowlands.

Meryn snarled and shoved him as if to continue the fight. Dai struggled to keep his balance and grip on Meryn. Brigit stirred. Dai glanced at her and saw the extent of damage in her little body. In that second of distraction Meryn slammed his knee into the wound. Dai grunted as pain spiraled through his body and burst in the pit of his stomach. He couldn't do this here in front of Brigit. But he couldn't leave her either. With every breath her body was unraveling. He had to do something to save her.

Meryn's fingers dug into his arm. He couldn't split his focus between the two of them. Meryn would have to wait—he might be damaged, but he wasn't dying. Dai released his grip on Meryn's tattered clothing and thrust him through the fabric of reality to his apartment.

Dai's muscles shook as he dropped to his knees next to Brigit's bed. Her tiny form was swathed in blankets, a mask over her face. She was falling apart as he watched.

Without a second thought he sent out delicate fibers loaded with his life energy. They brought the damaged pieces of Brigit together and sealed the rips. Once helped, her body began fixing itself. As he watched, the weave of her body strengthened and thickened, healing damage that he'd done too many lifetimes before. The connection they had wouldn't be broken, but next time she would be free. His debt to her was settled. And her need to help her brother was completed.

He leaned heavily against the bed, struggling to stay upright as the tension that had been building became a full-fledged headache. Too much magic. Too much energy expended. He needed to lie down, but he couldn't stop there. He had to get himself home…and then face Meryn. What was he going to do with his goblin cousin?

Brigit touched his hair and Dai lifted his head.

She looked at him, her eyes clear. Then she tugged off the mask. "I was dreaming of you. I knew you'd come back."

"You brought me back. Thank you." The floor beneath his knees was slick. He glanced down. His blood stained the floor. He was losing too much blood. He went to heal the wound but the gray threads of the Shadowlands embedded in his leg with the arrow made that impossible. He'd have to cut out the arrow before he could he heal the injury. He had to leave before he passed out. He tried to stand.

She sat up. "Don't go."

"I have to." He couldn't stay any longer.

"Mommy needs you. Daddy says you have to stay so he can go."

He couldn't let Amanda find him there. He wasn't ready to face her, he didn't know what to tell her or how to explain how he'd healed Brigit. Yet he knew he'd have to. The same way he'd have to tell Roan about Meryn. Just not tonight.

"I'll see you soon."

Dai drew up all the energy he could manage and prayed he got it right. With a whoosh, he fell back into his apartment. For a moment he did nothing but lay on the wood floor, breathing hard, a cold sweat on his skin and the pounding of his heart in his ears. He'd poured too much magic into healing Brigit. He closed his eyes and let the dizziness pass.

After a moment he realized something was wrong. Meryn didn't try to attack him and there was cold wind blowing through the apartment. He cracked open his eyes. Had he come to the right place?

He saw his empty bookshelves. Yes. It was his house. He went to sit up, but a polished black boot stepped onto his chest and forced him back down.

Mr. Vexion leaned over. "Welcome back to the Fixed Realm, Mr. King. You have been busy."

Dai couldn't shift beneath the weight and he couldn't grab onto any magic. He was exhausted and enjoying his last few breaths—he sighed and let his bruised and tired muscles relax—they may as well be peaceful.

Vexion pulled off his gloves and placed them in the mouth of his fur stole. The stole blinked at Dai and snarled.

"Manipulation to acquire property." Vexion raised one finger. "Theft." Two fingers. "Time distortion and inter-realm transportation." Four fingers. "Healing of an unaware minor." Five fingers. "Have I left anything off?"

"Breathing?"

Vexion's lips twitched but didn't make it into a smile. "You didn't listen very closely, did you?"

"I listened. I ignored."

"Come on, sorcerer, you've got to do better than

thisss—bleeding out on the floor of your trashed apartment." He put more pressure on Dai's chest. For a little man he was heavy.

Dai grunted. "I've made amends for killing my sister. I've rescued my cousin from the Shadowlands and lost the only woman I've ever loved. So if you're going to kill me, just do it so I can be reborn and start again in my next life."

Vexion laughed like sheets of sandpaper being rubbed together. "You won't be reborn with your knowledge; you're human."

"I don't care."

"I do. I've been watching you. Waiting to see what you'd do without your preciousss booksss. To see how you'd apply the knowledge you'd learned. I needed to see beyond your mind and into your heart." He lifted his boot off Dai's chest. "Men like you don't come along very often. It's even rarer that they will risk their own life for another." Vexion pulled a book out of his pocket. "Rules for magic in the Fixed Realm." He dropped it on the floor next to Dai's head. "Learn them. You'll need them."

Dai forced himself to sit up. This had all been a test to see if he was worthy of getting his books back? He should've known. No lore was gained without a trial of some kind. "What's the catch?"

"Your transgressionsss will disappear." Vexion patted the head of his stole and the tail twitched, wrapping itself around his other arm.

"What do you want from me?"

"Your servicesss occasionally."

"I'm not for sale."

Vexion squatted down. His coat raised its head and

growled around the gloves. "You're on retainer. Birch might need your services. Artifacts are discovered that would be better left hidden. People put what magic they can use to ill purpose. Occasionally there are bigger threats. We'd much prefer you on our side."

"Do I have a choice?"

"Of course. I cannot force you to do anything. However…I believe time distortion is still a mandatory memory wipe."

"You're blackmailing me?"

"Blackmail is an ugly word. I prefer coercion and a good outcome for everyone."

A good outcome for everyone? Dai took the opportunity to ask for what he'd wanted all along. "I want full access to my library."

"I'll go one better. You'll have access to the full Birch library. It makes Alexandria look like a private collection."

In exchange for his services they were giving him the opportunity to become more powerful. Access to their library was an offer he couldn't turn down. But he didn't want Vexion knowing that.

"And if I refuse?"

"I have time to wait." Vexion looked at the spreading blood. "Do you?"

Dai laughed. Whether he lived or died, Birch still solved their problem. But if he lived, he still had a chance to solve the one thing he cared about. Putting things right with Amanda.

"You must have other mages in your service. Why me?"

"We have no one human on staff. We haven't for a long time. Maybe it is time to fix that. The world is changing again."

Dai nodded. He'd seen many shifts over the years.
The old ways were coming back. People were trying
to be more in tune with the world and to look beyond
themselves...or some were. At the moment there was a
balance. Which way would the scales tip? Not even he
could predict that. "Okay."

Vexion smiled, but the toothless grin didn't fool Dai.
Vexion could still bite. "Got some clear skin?"

Dai tapped his left bicep. It was that or his upper
thigh and he didn't want Vexion's hands that far down
his body. His nails looked a little less human and a little
too sharp.

Vexion placed his hand over Dai's arm. Dai turned
his head away; he didn't want to watch. He gritted
his teeth expecting the pain that usually accompanied
a mark. Beneath Vexion's hand his skin bubbled as if
it was burning and blistering, then as it cooled and re-
settled it tingled. He looked back when Vexion pulled
his hand away.

"You won't have a problem finding or gaining access to Birch again." Vexion stood up, pulled on his
gloves, and walked toward the open apartment door.
Then he turned. "You should find your cousin before
I have to."

"Wait." Dai couldn't stop himself from asking
when he should be letting Vexion walk away. "What
are you?"

Vexion glanced over his shoulder, and his stole turned
as well. "When you discover that we'll talk again." He
shuddered. "Fix that door once you fix your leg. It's
freezing in here."

Dai glanced at what had been the glass door leading

to the balcony. The curtains around his door billowed in the breeze, catching on the jagged teeth of glass. Meryn had used a chair and broken the glass instead of unlocking the door. In that moment Dai realized the world was not the same one Meryn knew—Meryn was two millennia behind.

Why had Vexion let Meryn go? Surely he could've stopped him? Dai turned back but Vexion was gone, leaving only a lingering warmth on his bicep. Birch was once again refusing to intervene—unless Meryn started breaking their rules.

For a moment, Dai just sat, trying to gather up the energy to fix his leg and then get up and go after his cousin. He looked at his leg with the sight. The Shadowlands hadn't taken hold, yet. But the arrow had to come out. That meant either cutting it out or ripping it out. He didn't have the stomach to cut himself.

With his teeth pressed together hard he gripped the arrow shaft. On his next exhale he yanked it free of the muscle. He bit back the yell and kept it locked in his throat; he was used to biting back on pain and giving nothing away, then he tossed the broken arrow. It skittered across the floor, taking the Shadowlands strings with it.

He gathered the severed threads of his leg and started drawing them together, not with the same finesse as he'd used on Brigit. He didn't have the energy to make a nice scar. He just needed the blood to stop. And it did; the flow between his fingers slowed and stopped but was replaced with a chill that had come straight from the Shadowlands. Shock from the magic use and blood loss, combined with the new ventilation courtesy of Meryn.

Dai got up, cautiously testing his leg as he stepped over the chair and broken glass, then peered over the balcony and into the night. His fingers were tight on the railing as the world dropped beneath him. Had Meryn scaled the wall? Or fallen to his death? He checked the fragile thread that stretched between himself and Meryn. It hadn't snapped. Meryn was alive—but there were many places for a goblin to hide in the city, and Meryn was a goblin in a man's body.

What had he brought into the world? He couldn't have done it any other way. And if he had, Birch wouldn't have let him live.

He tried to use the fragile bond to go to Meryn. He couldn't leave him out there alone. But aside from increasing the pain in his temples, and turning his vision black at the edges, nothing happened. He was out of magic. Too tired and too wounded to do anything to help his cousin. He hung his head and closed his eyes.

Exhaustion clawed through his muscles and scattered his thoughts; only his grip on the railing kept him upright. He'd worked enough magic and spilled enough blood for one night. He wasn't even sure what night it was. Was it the night after the museum or had more time passed? He felt himself sway. He needed to sleep and to recover before he went after Meryn. If he went like this, he would lose the fight and it was one he couldn't afford to lose. He would have to search for Meryn in the morning…and tell Roan what had happened.

Roan would be less than impressed that he'd gone alone, and less than thrilled Meryn was now wandering the streets. Dai walked stiffly back inside, using the wall for support, feeling the bruises that had yet to form.

His blood was streaked across the floor, but he didn't have the energy to clean it up, magically or manually. So he left it. He paused at the book Vexion had dropped on the floor. His arm throbbed from the new mark, but Birch's mysteries could wait. He'd never wanted to sleep so badly in his whole life. The sofa had never looked so comfortable. Then he looked at his hands, his arms and legs. He was covered in blood and the dust of the Shadowlands. He couldn't sleep coated in the stuff nightmares were made off. He had to wash.

As he walked to the shower he stripped off his clothes, leaving them in a gray and scarlet mess. Tomorrow he would clean up and fix what he could. He ran the shower and checked his arm. A birch tree in full leaf was burned onto his skin. As the muscle flexed, the tree swayed as if in the breeze; its roots seemed to tap into his skin. If he looked closer, he would see them weaving into him. A mark that couldn't be cut out, like most of the other ones, it went soul deep.

He ran his hand over the knitting wound on his leg. It was healing, faster than it should. Maybe that was why he was so tired; healing took more energy than he was used to expending. He'd have to look in the library and find out. The water swept away all traces of the Shadowlands, and when he was unable to stand up anymore, even leaning against the tiles, Dai got out and dried off. His never-used bed was where he fell.

And he slept.

Chapter 21

AMANDA BIT HER LIP AS SHE WAITED FOR THE DOCTOR to finish checking Brigit over. She couldn't push aside her dream of falling. Of trying to grab a rope that was too slippery for her to hold, but never hitting the ground. It had jerked her awake and left her with a sense of loss she couldn't explain. She waited for the doctor to give her the bad news—that Brigit was getting worse. That next time the attack could be fatal.

Brigit glanced at her with a smile on her face like she was hiding a secret. She forced her lips to move in response but didn't feel any joy.

"Well. I think you can take her home, Ms. Coulter." The doctor wrote a note on Brigit's chart. He shrugged and kept writing.

"She's okay?"

"Perfectly healthy even though it says here she is a chronic asthmatic." He looked at Amanda like she was an over-protective parent who was making her daughter's condition out to be much worse than it was.

"She *is* a chronic asthmatic and has been for years."

"Well, I can't hear anything. She has the lungs of an average seven-year-old."

Brigit beamed as if she were a cat that had just caught and swallowed a mouse. "Can we go now, Mom?"

Amanda looked at the doctor. "Any further tests?" Usually they wanted a follow-up, or a review of her medication.

"No." The doctor hung up the chart. "Have a good day."

She blinked at the doctor not quite understanding. Had the doctor just given Brigit the all clear? "Do you mean she doesn't have asthma?"

"Maybe it was a misdiagnosis or an allergic reaction, because there's nothing wrong with her." He gave Brigit a high-five.

Brigit jumped off the bed. "Let's go, Mom."

She glanced from Brigit to the doctor as if they were in cahoots. It wasn't possible. She shivered as if someone ran their nails down her back. Not possible, but exactly what she hoped for. A cure.

Brigit skipped down the hallway at her side. "I don't need my bag anymore, do I?"

Did she? Did she believe a junior doctor who knew nothing about Brigit?

"Did the doctor take away your asthma?"

"No. He's just a doctor."

Of course. "Well what happened?"

"Magic," Brigit said easily, like people were magically cured every day of the week.

"Magic?" There was only one person she knew who could use magic that shouldn't exist. "I thought you didn't want anyone doing magic on you."

"This was different magic. It was Dai's magic."

Amanda's stomach contracted like she'd been hit. "What did Dai do to you?"

"Fixed me."

When did he fix her? How had he convinced Brigit

and the doctor there was nothing wrong with her? "What did he do?"

"Magic. He just wanted you to believe him…you do, don't you?"

Amanda hugged Brigit close.

Dai had no right to help Brigit and heal her. Her stomach twisted. She should be grateful; her daughter was well. Yet she felt betrayed. He hadn't asked. And if he had, what would she have said? No, you can't use magic, let my daughter suffer? She wasn't sure she believed in real magic. It was one thing to knot a fork, but another to heal a child. She sniffed and blinked back tears.

"How about we go and see your usual doctor? We'll double-check with him." She tried to sound like she was happy.

"Why?"

Because Dai was a mystery, and nothing added up the way it should. And even though he'd told her the questions she needed to ask Roan she hadn't listened. She'd been too angry and upset and scared for Brigit to do anything other than hate him for causing the attack. What he'd told her wasn't possible. What had happened to her daughter shouldn't be possible yet Brigit was bouncing with life, and for the first time in years she wasn't tired with worry.

Maybe everything Dai told her was true. Every awful bit and the only way he'd been able to prove it to her was to heal Brigit.

"Because I'm a grown-up."

~m~

In his dream Dai leaned back against the ruined temple in the Andes. He tipped his face to the sky, but it was dark. He wanted the sun. He crossed the globe to Wales but it was night. The Sahara was blanketed in darkness. Antarctica cloaked in black. Everywhere he went it was night when all he wanted was the sun. He ran, punching through reality, searching for daylight. But the sun was hiding as if she could no longer bear to shine on him.

Dai jolted awake and blinked in the sunlight streaming through his bedroom window. The sense of loss moved through him with each breath. It wasn't the sun he'd lost; it was Amanda. He didn't remember falling asleep. For a moment he just lay there and let the pain radiate. It was easier to be searching in a dream than acknowledging the reality—he didn't know how to win her back, or even if it was possible. Magic or not.

He pushed back the blanket that he must have pulled over himself during the night and sat up. His body ached like he'd been thrown to the ground too many times. The arrow wound on his leg was a shiny pink scar. Soon it would fade and match the rest like a permanent souvenir he would carry with him to the end. He traced his finger over the fresh skin. Maybe he didn't have to keep the scars. It was possible he could erase them all. The tattoos would remain; he couldn't remove them. But the scars?

What would getting rid of them change?

It wouldn't change what happened. He'd earned every mark one way or another, and while there were many he'd rather forget, they were part of him. Just because he could didn't mean he should. He hauled himself off the bed and tugged on jeans. He couldn't lie in bed when Meryn was out there alone and thinking gods knew what. The world was very different than the one he'd last lived in.

Dai got to the bedroom doorway then stood there, stunned at the wreckage of his house. Blood, glass, a shattered door, and a broken dining chair lay across the floor and out onto the balcony. His place had been trashed by a fight that had never happened. He sighed and he reached to the shards of glass; with a turn of his wrist he pushed them back into the broken mesh that made up the door. With the glass gone he padded through the living room. As he went he gathered the blood and clothes, destroying the evidence and letting the remains of the items join the fabric of reality to be reused and recycled elsewhere. He put the flak jacket and all but one knife away in his room.

With the knife in his hand he squatted down near the book Vexion left. He couldn't leave it where anyone could find it, but touching the gift might have its own consequences. He put the fingers of his other hand out, not game enough to touch its dark green cover, but interested to see what impressions he'd get off the little book. Deep magic rippled off the surface. The book seemed to have its own power source. And while it was certainly old enough and powerful enough to be considered alive, and it wouldn't be the first sentient item he'd handled—the faint crescent of a bite mark was still visible on his palm in the right light—it wasn't, nor was it possessed. He used the knife to flick open the front cover, half expecting to get a zap just from touching the thing.

The book didn't bite. It was blank. He ruffled a few

pages with the tip of the knife. Every page was empty. Another one of Vexion's tests. His lips curved; he was on familiar ground. He had a place at Birch and access to their library. He could spend centuries trolling through their texts…except he no longer had centuries. He was human, with a human lifespan. Spending the days he had left in a library wasn't as appealing as it had once been. He wanted someone to share the discoveries with.

Dai frowned and gingerly picked up the book and placed it on the coffee table. He scooped up the arrow he'd pulled out of his leg and put it next to the book and a now empty package of cookies. He hadn't eaten all of them. Meryn must have finished them off.

Would he ever have Amanda over for coffee again? He closed his eyes as the crushing loss bound him tighter so he couldn't breathe. It was better the cookies were gone. She didn't want to see him, and he didn't know what he could do to make her believe. He crunched up the package and it vanished.

A dusty handprint lingered on the surface of the table. Dai placed his hand over it and Meryn's gray smeared face formed in his mind. The arrow turned of its own accord. Dai spun it, but it spun back. He smiled. A magical lodestone that would always point to Meryn. It made sense; Meryn had crafted the arrow.

Using the arrow for guidance, he freed his mind and stepped through the fabric of reality. He opened his eyes to find he was in a hospital room. But it wasn't Brigit sleeping in the bed. It was Meryn. Dai glanced around but the other occupant was sleeping. He took a couple of paces toward his cousin, then stopped. He didn't have a plan beyond taking Meryn home…and then? Supervise him to make sure he didn't escape or do something that would draw Birch's attention? He wasn't his cousin's jailer.

He looked at Meryn again and saw the bandage on his head. What had happened? He should've taken better care of him. The world was very different than the one he'd last walked as a man. But he couldn't have fought Meryn and healed Brigit at the same time; he'd been too weakened from blood loss and magic use. And he couldn't have left Brigit when he saw how close to death she was. Whatever choice he made, he failed someone.

Dai sighed. Meryn didn't even recognize him in the Shadowlands. He was more goblin than man. Yet Dai struggled to believe his cousin was totally lost. He looked the same as before the curse. His dark hair and skin free of the gray dust. Dai reached out his hand to heal the wound and wake Meryn, but stopped.

The wound was little more than an abrasion. If Meryn didn't remember him he would do more harm than good. Dragging him home to see Roan would serve no purpose but to soothe Dai's conscience. He couldn't force Meryn to remember any more than he'd been able to force Fane to fight what was happening.

His fingers curled. He had to give Meryn space and time. All he could do was keep an eye on him. He hoped Meryn wouldn't give in like he did in the Shadowlands. That first summons had broken a man who lived only for his wife and kids. The knowledge he'd never see them again was too much for his heart to take. Dai had an inkling of how bad that could feel after Amanda had left him to die in the Shadowlands. Losing a lifetime's worth of loving ties would be devastating. Dai closed his eyes.

Is that was Meryn was feeling, the remembered pain? Did he remember anything of being human?

He glanced at his cousin again, and while the sticky, gray thread that connected them was changing, there was other damage in Meryn's body. He was full of holes, like all the connections he'd ever made had been ripped free. With a jolt that hit the pit of his stomach Dai knew that was exactly what had happened and why Meryn had turned goblin. They were wounds he couldn't fix with any amount of magic. With all the loss, did Meryn even remember who he was?

"I'll be back, Meryn," he whispered, not wanting to wake his damaged cousin. With clothes and a plan. Until then Meryn was safe—unless he tried to flee again. After years of running with the goblins maybe rest was what his mind and body needed to start healing.

How was he going to explain any of it to Roan?

Footsteps came down the hallway. Dai glanced at the door, then stepped back into his apartment. He turned a full circle not sure what to do next. Roan wasn't going to like it at all. Dai closed his eyes. But it wasn't about Roan. He had to do what was best for Meryn. For the moment that might be nothing…he'd go back and check on him. Once he was awake maybe they could talk. And if Meryn tried to kill him again?

He pushed the thought aside. Meryn would recover. He would not let him give up and become goblin—because the next time it would be permanent. He considered going back, but made himself be still. He couldn't force Meryn to do anything.

However, he did need to tell his brother.

Dai glanced at Vexion's book. He'd have a quick

look at it, then go and see Roan, but he knew he was stalling because he didn't know what to say. He flicked the pages of the book without touching them, controlling their movement with magic. Every single page was blank. Not even numbers marked the soft, cream-colored paper. He ran the edge of his thumb over a page. No, that wasn't right. There was information there. The book was brimming with knowledge, waiting to spill out. A smile formed, turning his lips into a grin of understanding…he wasn't thinking the right question.

For the first time in his life he didn't know what to ask.

How could he restore Meryn's humanity was the obvious one. So he tried. The page shimmered and text appeared. Letters morphing and switching before settling into English. He read the page and the next one, a dialogue on the state of a man's soul that could be boiled down to one line he was well versed in: It was his own to enrich or destroy and shall not be meddled with.

That was a rule he learned long before. He suspected most of the rules he already knew about the use of magic were in there.

Healing Brigit, while allowed by the laws of magic, obviously wasn't allowed anymore. He thought about healing and the little book filled with examples of allowable and banned practices. It wasn't healing her that had upset Birch. Brigit was under eighteen, and uninitiated—which meant that even if he had asked Amanda's permission it wouldn't have counted because Amanda wasn't part of the magical community. Double damned.

He could've wasted some more time by looking up the other rules he'd broken but he actually didn't care. He hadn't broken any of the oaths he'd taken when

KISS OF THE GOBLIN PRINCE

getting marked so a few rules about when, where, and how magic should be applied in the Fixed Realm didn't mean a lot. He closed the book. None of his problems could be solved by magic.

He put the rule book on the bookshelf and ran his fingers along the empty space until he reached the book Amanda had given him. She'd taken every connection they'd made. Maybe he should let her go…but he wanted a chance to tell her he'd healed Brigit, at least, and hear from her lips that she didn't want to see him again.

Facing his brother would be easier than seeing Amanda. So with a sigh he turned and in a step was on Eliza's front porch. He knocked on the door and waited. He was sure Roan was there. But every moment made him doubt he was doing the right thing. Maybe he could wait until Meryn was more human…and if that never happened, he would be carrying another secret around for the rest of his life. He had too many of them already. He forced out a breath and went to knock again.

Eliza swung open the door before he could. Paint smudged her cheek "Hi, come in. Roan is upstairs painting." She looked at him and her brows drew together. "Are you okay?"

"I'm fine." He brushed off her concern. What would she have thought of him last night as he lay bleeding on the floor?

She nodded, but the look on her face said she didn't believe him. "I was just on my way to the kitchen. Did you want anything?"

"No, thank you, I won't be here long."

He watched her walk away, giving him time alone with his brother. Eliza was the reason Roan was moving forward so easily, she was leading him, directing him. He didn't have that help and he didn't want to be leaning on Eliza and Roan. He'd do it himself or die trying. Living couldn't be harder than surviving in the Shadowlands, or existing under the boot of Rome. Dai shut the front door and followed the fine string that joined him to his brother up the stairs. He could've just followed it to Roan, but arriving unannounced and magically wouldn't have been the best start to an already awkward conversation.

Roan was happily rolling cream paint onto the bedroom walls. Was this the same man who only weeks before had been ready to die so he didn't become goblin? It was hard to see him as a warrior when he looked like any other modern man. What did other people see when they looked at him?

"Hello." Roan slipped back into Decangli. If they didn't speak it, no one would and it was hard to let their language die. "Come to practice?"

Dai sat on the stepladder. "Language or swords?"

"We buried the swords." Roan turned to face him, his face set in the familiar fierce scowl. The king lurked not far beneath the exterior.

"I know. Maybe we shouldn't have." Dai looked out the window hoping to find the right words written in the sky, but there was no easy way to say it. His gaze settled on the tree and the cubbyhouse. At the bottom was the memorial to the other men who'd been cursed. "You're going to have to change the plaque."

Roan blinked in surprise. "What do you mean?"

"Meryn is human again."

Roan put down the roller in the paint tray, immediately

ready to go on the rescue mission. "We can't leave him in the Shadowlands."

"I've brought him back." Dai kept his answers short. Even though he wanted to give Roan all the details, it wasn't the time. That would come later once Roan got over the shock.

"You went alone?" Roan crossed his arms; without armor and sword the stance lacked some of the menace Dai was used to.

"You just said we couldn't leave him there."

"Meryn was my second and my cousin too. You should have told me what you planned."

"It doesn't matter now. He's back and I'm alive."

Roan ran his hand over his close-cropped hair. "Where is he?"

Dai studied the paint-splattered drop sheet not sure how to break the news that he'd found Meryn and had lost him—well, not entirely lost him, but he was lost for the moment until he decided to be human and not goblin. "There was a complication. His mind is damaged." Along with his heart, and probably his soul.

"But he's here, in the Fixed Realm?"

"Yes."

Roan uncrossed his arms and his shoulder relaxed. "You should bring him here. He should be with us."

"He doesn't know us. He didn't remember me."

"All the more reason—"

"Forcing him to remember will do more harm than good." Dai stood facing off with his brother. For too long they'd shied away from an argument in case it brought the curse closer to claiming them. Now it didn't matter.

"So you're a medic as well as a magician?"

Downstairs the doorbell chimed. Both men looked up.

"This isn't over," Roan snapped.

"I will bring Meryn back to us. Have some faith." He glared at Roan, daring him to admit he didn't trust his brother.

"Fine. But I want to be kept informed this time."

"I don't answer to you. You aren't king."

"No, I'm family."

Footsteps ran up the stairs and Eliza appeared in the doorway with a plate of sandwiches in her hand and worry on her face. She glanced between the men as if sensing the thick layer of tension blanketing the room. "Amanda is here for you."

Dai sucked in a breath, then realized she wasn't here to see him. She didn't know he was here. She'd come to see Roan. His heart swelled with hope until he glanced at his brother and saw the hard line of his mouth. Would Roan lie to Amanda or answer truthfully?

Eliza handed him the plate but spoke to Roan. "You need to go down. She has questions."

"I should leave." Dai found a thread ready to disappear back to his home.

"Wait here," Roan ordered as he stalked out of the bedroom, leaving Eliza to make sure Dai stayed put.

Dai sat back down on the stepladder and picked up one of the sandwiches that Eliza had made for Roan. He hoped Amanda was there to ask the questions he'd told her to ask. No doubt she'd realized that Brigit was healed. Was she happy or angry? Surely happy. Her daughter was mended and would never have trouble breathing again—in any life.

And when she knew he hadn't lied and had lived

ancient history? That should go about as well as the conversation he'd just had with Roan.

Eliza watched him as if she were waiting for an opening so she could ask her own questions. "The sandwiches okay?"

"Great, thanks." He took another couple of bites then put her out of her misery. "What do you want to know?"

"Roan said you can do magic, real magic, not just knotting up my silverware kind."

"I can unknot it." But he knew that wasn't what Eliza wanted.

She shook her head. "You'll have to pry it out of Brigit's hands first."

Then she pulled up her sleeves. The pink new skin of fresh scars ran up her arms as if a large cat...or crow had attacked her. These were the marks left when the druid had tried to force Roan's hand in the Shadowlands and make the curse take what was left of his soul. While Roan stopped the bleeding and saved her life, he hadn't healed her properly and gotten rid of the scarring. Had he been that close to the edge?

"I know it's vain, but can you make them go away? I don't want to see them, and Roan blames himself."

Dai finished the sandwich. He could've eaten another two. "I can. Are you sure you want them gone?"

She nodded.

"Is that all of them?"

"No, they're on my back too." She went to lift her shirt.

Dai waved his hand. "I don't need to see." Not like that anyway and he didn't want his brother walking back in while Eliza had her shirt up.

He blinked and his vision became a mass of lines.

The wounds showed up as tears that were almost healed, but where they had rejoined the surface was uneven. He began smoothing them out; fixing the rough surface required very little energy. Then he stopped.

In Eliza's belly was a tiny bundle of new threads weaving together to make a new life. It drew on her and Roan. Lodged in her arm was a sliver of poison, leaching into her system, stretching toward the life trying to take hold. He knew which one would win. There wasn't enough of the little one to put up a fight.

"What's in your arm?"

"Birth control."

That hadn't worked so well. "You need to have it removed."

"Why?" Eliza's hand covered her stomach instinctively.

"Because it failed." As an afterthought he added, "Congratulations."

"Congratulations?" Her eyebrows lifted. "I'm pregnant?"

"With the first Decangli to be born in nineteen centuries."

She threw her arms around him. "Are you sure?"

Dai removed her arms and stepped back. "Positive. And your scars are gone."

"Thank you." She smoothed her hand over her skin. "Can you take out the birth control?"

"Yeah." With a pinch it was in his hand. He handed the thin tube to Eliza.

She stared at it for a moment as if not believing. "I didn't know. How did you?"

"I saw it."

"You saw the baby?"

"No. I saw a web made up of you and Roan. Give it a week to take hold, another to take shape…"

The smile slipped from her mouth. "It's too soon to tell him. Too many things can go wrong."

He sighed and closed his eyes. Eliza was asking him to keep a secret. "For how long?"

"A few weeks."

"Okay, but you have to go and find out if Amanda hates me."

"She doesn't hate you. She doesn't understand you. Roan made me promise not to tell her anything about the Shadowlands." Eliza smiled. "He didn't make me promise not to tell Brigit stories about a group of cursed men banished to the Shadowlands."

Dai gave a low laugh. Eliza had his brother all figured out.

"Amanda knows now. I told her everything." Another thing Roan wasn't going to be happy about. Too bad, he'd get over it.

Eliza grinned at him with her hand on her stomach as if she still didn't believe. "I'll go see what's happening."

Chapter 22

AMANDA RANG THE DOORBELL HALF EXPECTING ELIZA to be out, or not answering because she was busy with her mysterious new husband. It was a waste of time. What was she expecting Eliza to say? What did she want Eliza to say? That everything Dai had told her was true? It was so farfetched and yet when she thought of him it fit. He didn't just know about history—he'd lived it. He didn't just understand magic—he could use it. He'd saved Brigit even after she'd argued with him. She needed to at least thank him when…when he got back from the Shadowlands. Wherever that was, assuming it was real.

"Can we stay for dinner?" Brigit peered through the glass panel.

That depended on what kind of answer she got from Roan and Eliza. If it were all true, they had lied to her, and if Dai had lied, would they want to hear the truth? "Maybe."

"Someone is coming."

The door opened and Eliza stood there in a paint-covered T-shirt. "Come in." She gave them both a hug.

"Can I see if the veggies have grown yet?" Brigit danced from one foot to the other.

"Yes," said Amanda, eager for Brigit to be out of earshot. She watched as she ran through the house. In Amanda's hand was Brigit's bag. She opened her mouth to call out but then bit her tongue. The doctor said she didn't need it. Even if she didn't believe in magic, she had to believe the doctor.

"Eliza, I…" Her mouth felt like sand. She couldn't pretend this was a social call. She wanted to learn the truth, even if she wasn't sure that was what she wanted to hear. What if Dai was delusional, or what if she'd walked away from the only man since Matt who'd made her heart beat for more than survival? "I need to know how you met Roan."

"We ran into each other…fate." Eliza shrugged and smiled as she evaded the question.

Amanda shook her head. "The truth, Eliza."

Eliza bit her lip and looked away. "Let me get Roan." Then she turned and went up the stairs.

There was definitely something going on. She could almost taste it. Amanda walked out to the back patio so she could watch Brigit inspect Roan's veggie patch for sprouting seeds. Brigit leaned over and carefully checked each section before moving on to the next. Her lips moved as she sounded out the names of each plant from the tag.

Amanda turned at the sound of heavy footsteps.

Roan stopped a few paces away and crossed his arms. His lips were pressed into a thin line. He didn't look thrilled to be answering her questions. "I met Eliza when she summoned me from the Shadowlands. If you know of the Shadowlands, you know about goblins. Which means Dai has said more than he should have."

"What has he said?" Had Dai mentioned her to Roan?

"My brother says little about his life to me. We rub along because we are blood, but he is cast from a different metal."

An alloy no one had ever seen. If Roan didn't like Dai talking about being goblin, she couldn't mention Eliza's bedtime story without creating trouble. So she focused on the things Dai had told her to ask. She had to ask all the questions, even if the answers didn't make sense because she may not get another chance.

"Who's Claudius?"

"He was the Roman general. He held Dai as a hostage for good behavior." Roan sighed. "My good behavior."

"Who were you?" But she already knew. Roan was the king from the fairy tale, saved by Eliza's love.

"King of the Decangli."

She looked at him blankly.

"We were Celtic."

Which made Dai a Celtic prince. A royal hostage. She swallowed around the lump in her throat. Her history was good enough to know how cruel the Romans were to their slaves. Dai had paid dearly for his brother's obedience and the safety of his people. Even as she understood, her mind rebelled at the sheer scope of time.

"You know how this sounds?"

"That's why I told Dai not to talk about it. This is ancient history best left in the past."

"Can I play in the cubbyhouse?" Brigit called.

"I've cleared out the spiders, it's fine," Roan called back.

Brigit ran over to the tree and paused at the base. She squatted down to read something. "Who are Brac, Fane, Anfri, and Meryn?" She looked over her shoulder back at the adults.

Amanda's blood cooled. She knew those names, but she waited for Roan's answer, dreading his words.

"They were friends," he said, looking at Amanda. Then he lowered his voice. "They wore the curse with Dai and me."

Dai had told her the truth and she'd run. She threw away a chance she'd never dreamed of with a man who shouldn't exist.

"How did Fane die?" But Amanda already knew. He died the same way Flynn did. They were the same person. Her skin prickled into gooseflesh. Flynn was still fighting the curse; his love of gold was because he'd lived as a goblin.

"He cut his own throat," Roan said without meeting her gaze.

In ending his life, Fane had locked himself into a pattern he couldn't break. She should've tried harder, done more to save him instead of letting him hoard gold and slide into becoming goblin.

"Hello, Mommy." Brigit waved out of the tree house window.

Amanda waved back. Dai said Brigit looked like his sister Mave, but that hadn't been the whole truth. Brigit was Mave, reborn but still with the same problem. She couldn't breathe after her throat had been cut. If Dai hadn't healed her, how many lives would she have lived dying too young from a disease that reflected a past she couldn't remember?

Amanda shivered and turned back to Roan. "Dai went to help one of the men on the plaque, didn't he?" He was so much like Matt, thinking of others and not the danger to himself. He'd been trying to say good-bye at the museum in case he didn't make it back. He'd been thinking of her, trying to protect her heart.

Roan nodded. "Meryn is alive. Dai rescued him."

If Meryn was alive and safe, that meant…"Dai's back? He's alive?"

Eliza appeared in the doorway with a silly grin on her face. She hooked her arm through Roan's. "Dai's alive."

Amanda rummaged in her bag for her cell phone. Her hand shook as she searched for his number.

Roan put his hand over hers, stilling the movements. "Be sure."

How could she be sure of anything, when everything Roan and Dai had told her was more like a fairy tale than reality?

"I'm not sure of anything anymore, but I need to see him." And then it would be up to Dai. Would he be able to trust her again?

She dialed with her heart on her tongue. Time was counted in rings and beats. Behind her a cell phone rang. She turned away from the garden and lowered her cell phone. Her heart stopped for a moment before remembering what to do. Dai stood in the doorway, unsmiling, a twenty-year-old warrior from another age. The magic in his blood laid claim to her heart and she had no words.

He held out his hand to her.

"Brigit?" Amanda couldn't just leave.

"Will be fine for a few hours," said Eliza as she took Brigit's handbag full of unneeded medicine from Amanda. And Amanda no longer had an excuse to say no.

"Where are we going?"

"Not far." Dai's gaze hadn't left her, but his stance was rigid, as if he was contained in invisible armor. Protection from what she might say.

It was a test. Pass or fail. Either she trusted him or she didn't. If she didn't trust him, it made liars out of Roan and Eliza. It made every sensation that Dai had awakened false and every smile he had cautiously thrown her way worthless. She wanted to believe in the fairy tale—that magic and handsome princes existed.

Amanda took his hand not sure what to expect from a man who'd healed her daughter and rescued a friend from a land of nightmares. His warm fingers closed around hers. Then his eyes glimmered like water in sunlight and her body was pressed through a sieve. She gasped and held tight to the hand gripping hers. She took a step, but she wasn't at Eliza's house anymore. She was at Dai's.

"Oh my God." Her free hand flew to her chest. That was what it must feel like to skydive—and forget the parachute.

"The first time is the worst." He let go of her hand as if the contact burned.

It wasn't the sensation that bothered her. "You moved us with magic."

Beneath her feet the floor felt solid. This was real, not some kind of dream. "You used real magic on Brigit." She rounded on him as the protective mother surfaced fast. "You should have asked first. We talked about possible cures and you never said anything."

"I didn't know I could. I didn't want to risk it. But she was the one who pulled me back from the Shadowlands. When I saw her in the hospital I knew she was dying and I had to take the chance. Would you've said no?"

After the fight in the museum, probably. "Who were you saving? Mave or Brigit?"

"Both. Myself. You." As he gazed at her his dark

blue eyes were clear like an ocean with no bottom. She could drown forever and never need air.

"Brigit is Mave, isn't she?"

He nodded. "I wanted to tell you."

"That didn't work out so well." She glanced away. She'd almost thrown away everything, but he was giving her another chance. "I'm sorry I didn't believe you."

He sighed. "I wouldn't have either."

For a moment they were silent. He saw the world differently. Saw people differently. "What do you see when you look at me?" Amanda asked.

Dai's lips moved in one of his rare unguarded smiles. "Golden light, like the sun shining on a dewy spider web. Everything you touch is made beautiful. I wanted to feel that."

"You are beautiful." Inside and out. From the way he moved, to the calmness that surrounded him. She couldn't remember ever having that peace. Her life was a series of rapids to be overcome, when all she wanted to do was glide and enjoy the view.

"You might want to reserve that opinion." He unbuttoned the cuffs of his shirt, and then the buttons down the front.

Her eyebrows rose in expectation, but this was no seduction. The movements were too sharp.

"I have a collection of scars." He held the edges of the shirt closed. "And tattoos." Then he shrugged out of the shirt.

Beneath his clothes was the lean body of a fighter, not an academic. The black ink of mystical markings was bold against his pale skin, but under the tattoos, his skin was lined with fine white scars. Together they formed a tapestry of his life. The spider on his chest looked like it was ready to scuttle away on the fine web that stretched over his skin. Other symbols seemed to shimmer or pulse like they had life of their own. They belonged in a world she didn't know or understand.

She couldn't read the text that scored his ribs, or the cluster of wedge shapes that started above his hip and disappeared into the waistband of jeans. He seemed to be wearing many of the dead languages he spoke. She knew he'd understand each tattoo and be able to tell her when and how and why each mark was made.

Dai stood still as she walked around him looking. His back was crisscrossed with old scars. She swallowed, not wanting to think about how he'd received them, but willing to bet on who'd marked him. On his lower back an intricate pattern of rings seemed to spin with each breath. It had to be an illusion.

Amanda reached out her hand, but stopped before her fingers connected with his skin. Now that she knew the details of his past she was more cautious. "Can I touch you?"

She waited two breaths for his carefully considered response.

"Yes."

What had it cost him to grant her permission, or was he testing his own boundaries? She traced the circles with her fingers; they were warm to touch, hotter than the unmarked skin. She brushed aside his hair and let her hand wander over his muscles to trace one of the scars that marred the skin on his back.

"These are whip marks?"

"Some are from a knife." He said it as if they were discussing the color of leaves.

"If you healed Brigit, you could get rid of them."

He turned to face her. "Would you erase your past?"

She glanced down. "No." Not even the bits she thought would kill her. "Will you tell me the stories behind the tattoos one day?"

"Some of them I can't. You're not initiated." He took her hands. "This is all new to me."

"Slow is good." She didn't want to squeeze a lifetime of love into a few short years. She wanted it to last.

He cupped her cheek and leaned in to kiss her. His lips were soft against hers. Tentative at first. Her tongue flicked against his lips. He responded, learning the taste of her mouth as his hand slid around her waist. His fingers brushed skin that hadn't been touched in years. She slipped her arms around his neck, her hands in his hair, not wanting to push but not wanting him to stop.

She held her breath as his fingers skimmed the side of her breasts. His touch was soft and sure, but the clothing between their skin was too much. She arched her back pressing into his hand. Her hips were hard against his. The length of his shaft teasing.

He paused so they were nose to nose. "Is this where I invite you into my bedroom?"

"That might be a good idea." Her words were made breathy with desire. The heat in her belly spun and spread through her blood. They would finish what they'd started as if everything hadn't changed in the days between.

Dai picked her up, his hand on her bottom. Her legs wrapped around his hips automatically. She gasped at the close contact as he carried her into his room, the bed making itself with magic before he sat her down on the edge.

She smiled and unbuttoned her shirt while he watched, drinking her in. Excitement simmered in her blood. His fingers traced the curve of her breast, pushed the shirt off her shoulders as his lips claimed hers again. She drowned in the kiss. They fell back on the bed, side by side. He ran his hand over her stomach to the button of her jeans. He flicked it open, then slowly drew down the zipper. His fingers skimmed over her underwear. She helped him shuck her jeans, wriggling like she couldn't get out of them fast enough.

Today of all days she was in un-matching plain under-wear, but from the look in his eyes he didn't care. His fingers traced tracks on her skin leaving shivers in their wake. Her nipples peaked, pushing against the soft pink cotton of her bra. His fingers circled, slowly as if learning her reactions.

Her hand glided over his skin to the cuneiform text that started above his hip and disappeared into his jeans. "Can I see the rest?"

His lips curved in the smile she was used to seeing. "I'm not wearing any underwear."

"Lucky me." She touched the first button. Then lifted her gaze to meet his eyes. "Are you sure about this?"

"I've wanted you since the day I saw you in the church."

"There was magic in the air."

He nodded. "But not mine."

She flicked open the button on his fly. Her fingers brushed against his shaft and her stomach tightened. It was so long since she'd done this. While she was sure she hadn't forgotten how, the nerves of being with someone new mixed with the heat and need pooling in her belly.

He lifted his hips as she pulled off the jeans. Then she let her gaze track up his body. Tattoos were wrapped around both calves. Text ran down his thigh in several lines. His left thigh was unmarked except for what looked like a recently healed wound. She touched the smooth line of pink skin, but didn't want to know how it had been made.

Her fingers trailed slowly up his thigh, not sure if she was testing herself or Dai. "You've really never been with a woman?"

"I never got the chance. She was stolen from me and sold."

"How old were you really at your party?" Her fingers caressed his hard flesh.

He drew in a breath. "One thousand nine hundred and seventy."

She let out a sigh. "And you never…"

"I didn't want to. I didn't trust myself. You reminded me what a gentle touch was like, and that I could be gentle." He brushed a strand of hair off her face and tasted her lips then her throat, kissing down her neck. He flicked open her bra and took her nipple in his mouth. Her fingers pushed into his hair as a moan slipped from her lips. He glanced up.

"That was good." Her hand closed lightly over his shaft, stroking, an idea forming in her mind.

He sucked in a breath as her thumb smoothed over the slit. But she knew how to take his breath away. She pushed him onto his back and he watched as she moved down his body. His eyes widened but he didn't stop her. Amanda lowered her mouth to his hot, hard flesh to give him a kiss she knew he'd never had as a slave. Her tongue glided over his skin and made his hips move.

His groan spiked through her. She needed more. She was beyond ready; she was aching.

As if knowing he pulled her up. "I want you."

Amanda cursed silently. "I've got no birth control." No sex for her. "You can enjoy."

Why couldn't she be like other single women and keep condoms in her bag...not that that would have helped. Her bag wasn't there; it was still at Eliza's. His shaft rubbed temptingly against her panties. He rocked her hips enjoying the tease as much as she hated it. She wanted him. Could she tempt fate? She did a rapid calculation and decided that fate wasn't on her side and the risk was too great.

His eyes shone with the inner light that meant magic, and a box materialized on the bed.

"Ohhh." She was still getting used to the magic thing. "That's a neat trick."

"Impressed?"

"You have no idea how much." She ripped open the packaging.

His hands pushed her panties down and she rolled onto her back so he could remove them. His hands brushed her inner thigh and eased her legs apart, using teasing touches as his finger slid against her sex. She couldn't wait. She thought she'd be okay going slowly, but all she wanted was to feel him inside her.

"Yeah, I do," he said against her mouth.

She tore open the foil. Her fingers found his shaft and rolled on the rubber as he kissed her until she couldn't breathe for the lust riding in her blood. He eased over her. She'd forgotten what it felt like to have a man's weight above her, but her body knew what to do. And so did his. They moved together creating the magic only lovers can make, the ancient rhythm merging with the new as a spell of their own wove around them. Love.

Chapter 23

ROAN HELD THE PLAQUE IN HIS HAND AS IF WEIGHING it, then he handed it to Dai. "You can make it right."

Dai nodded. The metal was cold and heavy in his hand. He placed his hand over the four names. The metal warmed as he altered the engraving. Then he lifted his hand. This time there were only three names engraved on the plaque: Fane, Anfri, and Brac.

He'd told Roan about seeing Fane, and how he was still repeating the curse and his death. Unable to break free because he wouldn't face the consequences. He glanced at Eliza and the new life taking hold. She hadn't told Roan yet. Would they know the baby when it was born? Would they want to know? He still hadn't told Roan about Mave, but there wasn't any point. Everything was as it should be.

Except one person was missing.

Meryn.

All of them hoped he would find his way back. His family was waiting. He'd make daily visits to Meryn, and he was sure Meryn would talk to him eventually. The alternative was too awful to think about. He had to make Meryn see life was worth fighting for no matter how different it was from the life they'd led before.

He turned his head and smiled at Amanda. It had been worth waiting nearly two thousand years for her to come into his life. Her touch banished so many dark memories and replaced them with light and love. Her lips curved as if she knew what he was thinking.

They would be sneaking around for a little bit. She wasn't ready to tell Brigit, and he wasn't ready to be Dad. He turned his attention back to the tree. With a little magic, he fixed the amended plaque into position.

No one gasped. They all just stood there looking at the names of those who didn't survive the curse. The cool night air wrapped around them, summer still too far away to warm the nights.

Amanda pulled the gold wedding band out of her pocket. Brigit handed her a drawing folded into a tiny square. Together they put them in a small hole under the rose bush planted on top of the swords and torques and patted down the soil. No one spoke. There were no words to say in any language that could ease the loss of those who were no longer around.

She dusted off her hands and joined him, her hand slipping into his. Between them, the strands thickened with each look, each touch, each kiss that brought them closer together. He wasn't afraid of where the future would lead because Amanda walked with him, holding back the shadows.

Read on for an excerpt from the next book
in the Shadowlands series

FOR THE LOVE OF A
GOBLIN WARRIOR

by Shona Husk

Chapter 1

NADINE SURVEYED THE EMERGENCY WARD OF THE hospital. What was it about the full moon that turned this place into an overflow of hell? Crowded would've been great. This was just madness.

She checked the stats of a man who would need stitches on the side of his face, and she let out a sigh. Two more hours to go. Gina owed her for this shift swap.

A nurse tapped her on the arm. "Nadine, you're wanted at triage."

Nadine frowned. She didn't work the front counter.

When she saw the cop, her stomach tightened. Police never brought good news. What had her father done now? He'd barely been out of prison for two weeks.

She gave the officer a tight smile and forced herself to be professional. "How can I help you?"

"I've got a guy with a head injury who doesn't seem to speak English."

Nadine looked past the cop to the man sitting in the waiting room. Blood ran down the side of his face and stuck in his shaggy hair. His eyes looked red and irritated. But it was the clothes that struck her most. He looked like he'd crawled out of a third-world jail. His loose fitting tunic was worn with age, as were his pants and boots. None of it seemed quite right, as if he was wearing castoffs from another age. His gaze was firmly fixed on the floor and his shoulders slumped in defeat.

"He's having some kind of episode. Freaked out when we brought him in."

"What did he do?" She had no intention of being attacked by a psychiatric patient, yet he didn't seem dangerous…just lost, locked in his own world. She'd seen that look before on a returned soldier who wasn't coping.

"He was being a nuisance." The cop paused then leaned a little closer.

"And?" Nadine prompted, still not sure she wanted to be involved.

"Waving a sword," the officer said quietly.

Right. A sword. Of course. She glanced at the man, but he hadn't moved. Not a third-world jail, a medieval jail. Had he raided a prop department? "How'd he get hurt?"

"No idea. He speaks gibberish. Look, I don't want to take him down to the station. He needs help. Can you get him a psych consult?"

If she said no, the scruffy man would spend the night in lockup with real criminals and be back on the street by morning no better off.

"I'll have a look at the wound, but unless he speaks French, he'll have to wait until we can get a proper translator in." A serious head injury could explain his lack of proper speech.

"Thank you."

Nadine grabbed a pair of gloves, went through the security door and into the waiting room. A second cop pulled the scruffy man up from the hunched over position he'd been in. The man's gray eyes focused on her. Shadows she didn't understand gave him a haunted look, as if he'd seen too much. She couldn't leave him in the care of the police; he was already traumatized.

He spoke, but his words were unintelligible. Fast and fluent. They had the rhythm of language that gibberish lacked. Nadine bent down so she was at eye level, but far back enough to be out of range if he lashed out with his feet. His hands were cuffed behind his back—even though the cops claimed he wasn't a threat. "*Monsieur, parlez-vous français?*" She smiled encouragingly while she held his gaze and studied his eyes. The pupils were even and they weren't dilated.

The man's eyes darted between Nadine and the cops. His forehead furrowed as if he were trying to make sense of her words.

His voice was quiet but strong as he spoke again. This time in a different language.

"Pardon?" Nadine moved closer to listen again.

He inclined his head at a crying baby and repeated the same words more slowly as if she were simple.

She glanced at the baby and then at the man. He was talking about the crying child. *L'enfant.* But what was he saying? Nadine pointed to the shaggy man's bleeding head. "You're bleeding."

That he seemed to understand, but he shook his head, spoke, and looked at the baby, adding extra sentences filled with force. Yet his words were formal and he stumbled over some as though this wasn't his first language. It was no one's language.

"I think he's speaking Latin." As she said it aloud it didn't seem possible. Maybe she was wrong and he was speaking an obscure dialect of…of what? Not Italian. Breton? She glanced at the dust-covered man again. What was he covered in?

"Who the hell speaks Latin?"

"No one." Nadine frowned. "It's a dead language." And the man speaking it looked like he should be dead, but had refused to quit.

His gaze lingered on her, gray and endless. There was something about him…a half-hidden nightmare glided through the back of her mind. The child began wailing in a higher pitch. The man shook as if he couldn't bear the sound, tears pooled in his eyes, and he hung his head as if to hide them, repeating the same line about the baby over and over.

"The baby." She turned to the cop who had come up to the counter. "Take the woman and baby up to triage and get them seen. They shouldn't be waiting."

Nadine touched the man's shoulder to get his attention. He lifted his head as if expecting reproach. She smiled and softened her voice from the orders she'd given the cop.

"Look. The baby is getting help." She pointed at the mother and child, now getting fast tracked through emergency. "Can I take a look at your head?" She pointed to his head, not sure how much he understood, but he didn't seem disorientated or confused. He just didn't comprehend the language.

He watched the woman with the baby be taken behind the doors. He blinked, but his tears had already tracked a line through the gray dust covering his face. Once they were gone, he nodded.

If he spoke no English, it was no wonder he was having an episode when the cops dragged him in. He had no idea what they were saying or where they were taking him. Yet he'd had enough compassion to ask that the baby be seen first. That said more about the man than anything else.

"Uncuff him and I'll bring him through to the ward for a proper examination." The cop gave a visible sigh and freed the man. He looked at her, smiled, and said something that had the tone of gratitude.

He rubbed his wrists and she noted the fresh grazes and cuts, but they didn't bother her as much as the gray coating on his skin and possible damage to his irritated eyes or his lack of regular language. She noticed a gold broach securing his cloak around broad shoulders. It was a beautiful piece, two wolves chasing each other in an endless circle. If he'd been living on the streets, that would've been stolen. And he'd been picked up carrying a sword. Nothing about this man was adding up.

She shook her head. "Who are you?"

The woman in front of Meryn smiled. Her teeth were white against the honey color of her skin and around her neck was a gold necklace. A crucifix. A man was forever dying at her throat. He flinched at the symbol of Roman punishment, and her friendly smile faltered. She spoke, a question in the other language. Not that it mattered. He didn't understand her.

Without the crying of the child he could almost think. He could almost shove the memories that tore at his mind away. Lock them back behind the walls he'd constructed when he'd become goblin.

The woman's soft hands touched his and flexed his fingers, checking the cuts made when he'd fled the tower in the Shadowlands. The things his hands had done. So much blood. So much battle. So many things he hadn't recalled while he'd been goblin. As if a goblin's mind couldn't hold all the horror. Now he remembered.

And he couldn't live with the weight of his past.

He'd failed his wife and his children.

He'd failed his tribe.

He'd failed his king. Finding the traitor had been his responsibility. The pain he'd locked away when he'd surrendered to the goblin curse sucked him under, tore at his heart, and the screams of his family echoed in his head. This was the reason he had given up being human to run with the goblins and devote his life to the endless need for gold.

The play of light on the woman's gold necklace held his gaze for a moment too long. The chain and cross hung just out of reach. It didn't tempt him the way it had when he'd been goblin, but it offered salvation. In taking gold he could once again be goblin and free of the deaths his failure had caused. Gold didn't hurt and cry and scream.

He glanced from the gold necklace to the green-brown eyes of the woman trying to help him. He tried to place the words that made no sense, but his mind was crowded with the memories.

He wanted the silence of being goblin. He wanted the pain crushing his chest to ease.

The crucifix swung in his vision as the bronze-skinned woman probed the wound on his head. Her hands were gentle on his tender skin. He wanted a piece of her calm and kindness.

In the Shadowlands there had been stillness. He'd known a measure of mindless peace. He didn't under-stand the Fixed Realm anymore. It had changed beyond his understanding. He wanted to be goblin again. He understood the rules of the Shadowlands.

Gods, he was weak for wanting to go back.

What had happened to the man who'd raised an army for his king against the Romans? Not once, but twice? What had happened to the man who'd sworn to the rebellion and promised to free the Decangli from the Roman stranglehold?

That man had died the night his wife and children were murdered. The body had kept going because it didn't know how to stop even after his heart was gone. Now he was a husk full of unwanted memories with no reason to go on.

The cross was in reach.

His gaze darted to the humans in blue uniforms, but they weren't watching him. Then back to the woman. Could he steal from her? He needed the screaming in his head to stop. The necklace swung closer and with a flick of his fingers the gold came away in his hand. The woman didn't notice. Her gold burned his palm. He waited for the swell of desire, the pleasure of holding wealth, the rising need for more, but it didn't come.

Instead there was silence. The screaming stopped and for a moment he glimpsed clarity of mind he'd thought lost. Then it was wiped away as a slippery sense of disquiet took hold of his gut. Taking gold had never caused him discomfort before. He tried to push aside the unease and regain the calm, but it slid through his fingers. Goblins didn't have feelings. They had urges. He couldn't allow himself to feel. If he did, he would drown in despair.

He imagined gold, piles of it, the cold metal in his

hands and a hunger that couldn't be sated. But his skin
didn't change, his joints didn't thicken into goblin form.
   He remained stubbornly human.

The Goblin King

by Shona Husk

Once upon a time...

A man was cursed to the Shadowlands, his heart replaced with a cold lump of gold. In legends, he became known as

The Goblin King.

For a favored few he will grant a wish. Yet, desperately clinging to his waning human soul, his one own desire remains unfulfilled:

A willing queen.

But who would consent to move from the modern-day world into the realm of nightmares? No matter how intoxicating his touch, no matter how deep his valor, loving him is dangerous. And the one woman who might dare to try could also

Destroy him forever.

"Shona Husk put together an amazing story
about loss, love, redemption, and discovery..."
—*Night Owl Reviews* Reviewer Top Pick

For more Shona Husk, visit:

www.sourcebooks.com

Enraptured

by Elisabeth Naughton

—w—

ORPHEUS—*To most he's an enigma, a devil-may-care rogue who does whatever he pleases whenever he wants. Now this loose cannon is part of the Eternal Guardians—elite warriors assigned to protect the human realm—whether he likes it or not.*

Orpheus has just one goal: to rescue his brother from the Underworld. He's not expecting a woman to get in the way. Especially not a Siren as gorgeous as Skyla. He has no idea she's an assassin sent by Zeus to seduce, entrap, and ultimately destroy him.

Yet Skyla herself might have the most to lose. There's a reason Orpheus feels so familiar to her, a reason her body seems to crave him. Perhaps he's not the man everyone thinks…The truth could reveal a deadly secret as old as the Eternal Guardians themselves.

—w—

"Filled with sizzling romance, heartbreaking drama, and a cast of multifaceted characters, this powerful and unusual retelling of the Orpheus and Eurydice story is Naughton's best book yet."—*Publishers Weekly*

For more of the Eternal Guardians series, visit:

www.sourcebooks.com

The Danger That Is Damion

by Lisa Renee Jones

Lethally passionate, wickedly dangerous...

Renegade warrior Damion Browne is a soldier of soldiers, an enforcer of the code of honor. With ruthless precision, he calculates risks as deliberately as he does his lover's satisfaction. Now it's up to him to defeat a new generation of female Super Soldiers, including the one woman perfectly programmed to be his downfall.

His enemy...or his soul mate?

Lara Martin has never felt powerful, until she's brainwashed to destroy the one man who can help her find the answers she so desperately seeks. Alone and embroiled in lies, Lara must turn to Damion for the key to the truth...

Deliver Me from Darkness

by Tes Hilaire

Angel to vampire is a long way to fall.

A stranger in the night...

He had once been a warrior of the Light, one of the revered Paladin. A protector. But now he lives in darkness, and the shadows are his sanctuary. Every day is a struggle to overcome the bloodlust. Especially the day Karissa shows up on his doorstep.

Comes knocking on the door

She is light and bright and everything beautiful—despite her scratches and torn clothes. Every creature of the night is after her. So is every male Paladin. Because Karissa is the last female of their kind. But she is *his*. Roland may not have a soul, but he can't deny his heart.

"Dark, sexy, and intense! Hilaire blazes a
new path in paranormal romance."
—Sophie Jordan, *New York Times* bestselling author

For more Tes Hilaire, visit:

www.sourcebooks.com

Assassins in Love

by Kris DeLake

To kiss him? Or to kill him?

Misha's mission is to get Rikki, a rogue assassin who hates organizations and always does it *her* way, to join the Guild or give up her guns. He completely underestimated the effect she would have on him…and what heat and chaos they could bring to each other…

"A fast, edgy, and passionate story."—Mary Jo Putney, *New York Times* bestselling author

For more Kris DeLake books, visit:

www.sourcebooks.com

Chase Me

by Tamara Hogan

The secrets she's uncovering will be his to keep...

Centuries ago, when their ship crashed to Earth, paranormals of all types settled secretly into our world, quietly going about their business with humans none the wiser. Self-ruling and careful to stay below the radar, all is threatened when Valkyrie archaeologist Lorin Schlessinger and her werewolf geologist partner Gabe Lupinsky inadvertently draw evil attention to Earth and its treasured natural resources.

As the threat intensifies, Lorin and Gabe struggle to contain the chaos they've unleashed, and to resist their explosive mutual attraction...

Praise for **Taste Me:**

"Chemistry and girl power."—*RT Book Reviews*

"This hip, sensual tale...sizzles with forbidden heat and danger."—Carolyn Crane, author of *Mind Games* and *Double Cross*

For more Tamara Hogan, visit:

www.sourcebooks.com

King of Darkness

by Elisabeth Staab

———

Eternal commitment is not on her agenda...

Scorned by the vampire community for her lack of power, Isabel Anthony lives a carefree existence masquerading as human—although, drifting through the debauched human nightlife, she prefers the patrons' blood to other indulgences. But when she meets the sexy, arrogant king of the vampires, this party-girl's life turns dark and dangerous.

But time's running out for the King of Vampires

Dead-set on finding the prophesied mate who will unlock his fiery powers, Thad Morgan must find his queen before their race is destroyed. Their enemies are gaining ground, and Thad needs his powers to unite his subjects. But when his search leads him to the defiant Isabel, he wonders if fate has gotten it seriously wrong...

———

For more Elisabeth Staab books, visit:

www.sourcebooks.com

Acknowledgments

I couldn't have written this book without the ongoing support of my husband. He's gotten used to my random questions and odd tangents. Brigit's treatments developed from conversations with my sister who has an interest in reiki and alternative therapies. The Winkgirls read and commented on the very first draft of the story. My editor, Leah, pointed me in the right direction when I'd wandered off the path. Thanks to Danielle and the Sourcebooks team. And to the readers who thought goblins could be heroes. Thank you for making my dream possible.

About the Author

A civil designer by day and an author by night, Shona Husk lives in Western Australia at the edge of the Indian Ocean. Blessed with a lively imagination, she spent most of her childhood making up stories. As an adult, she discovered romance novels and hasn't looked back. Drawing on history and myth, she writes about heroes who are armed and dangerous but have a heart of gold—sometimes literally.